Death of an Ordinary Man

Death of an Ordinary Man

Glen Duncan

BLACK CAT
New York
a paperback original imprint of Grove/Atlantic, Inc.

First published in Great Britain in 2004 by Scribner, an imprint of Simon & Schuster UK Ltd., London, England

Printed in the United States of America
Published simultaneously in Canada

Library of Congress Cataloging-in-Publication Data
Duncan, Glen, 1965–
    Death of an ordinary man / Glen Duncan.
        p. cm.
    ISBN 0-8021-7004-8
    1. Death—Fiction. 2. Secrecy—Fiction. 3. Funeral rites and ceremonies—Fiction. I. Title.
PR6104.U535D43 2005
823'.914—dc22   2004056727

Black Cat
a paperback original imprint of Grove/Atlantic, Inc.
841 Broadway
New York, NY 10003

05 06 07 08 09   10 9 8 7 6 5 4 3

For
Andrea Freeman

Acknowledgements

My thanks to: Jonny Geller at Curtis Brown, Ben Ball, Rochelle Venables and all at Scribner, Carol Anderson and Helen Simpson. Special thanks to Kim Teasdale for the psychic, emotional and financial support that made this book possible.

'Courage!' he said, and pointed toward the land,
'This mounting wave will roll us shoreward soon.'

Tennyson, *The Lotos-Eaters*

Nathan

Everything's all right, Nathan thought. Those first mornings in foreign hotels you opened your eyes and knew nothing: where you were, how you'd got there, *who* you were, even. You could be anyone.

Like that, but without the hotel.

It was neither dark nor light but if he lifted his hand in front of his face he wouldn't be able to see it. Whatever was here in potentia – he trawled through his store of waiting rooms, the joyless accrual of plastic chairs and out-of-date magazines – kept promising to become actual, but at the last minute didn't, quite. He thought of all the conversations about dreams he'd had with Cheryl, Adrian, the kids, how difficult this was going to be to describe to them when he got back.

Soon the next thing would happen. He wasn't afraid. Everything was all right because when he summoned it a memory came through of that morning in the kitchen at the old house on Roseberry Road, years ago. Adrian's boiler had croaked and he'd had to come round to theirs for a shower. Summer holidays, the kids all at home. Adrian, hangover notwithstanding, had made everyone a huge cooked breakfast. Cheryl had sat towel-turbanned with her feet up, reading bits out of the paper. How old had Luke been then? Ten? Gina going on eight. Lois four, with the serious face and look of not enough sleep. Bacon, coffee, toast. Afterwards sun-shafts of fagsmoke and the good feeling of surrendering the day. His dad had come round, lonely, looking for shared flesh and blood, poor old bugger, and for once it had been okay, love had stretched itself, brought him into the warmth. Ade made him a bacon sandwich and later Cheryl gave him a haircut, in which spectacle the kids took a peculiar delight, Frank sitting draped in a bedsheet and holding a hand mirror very seriously.

Nathan had this at his disposal, to be produced on demand. Then the next thing would happen. He'd have to find a way of describing all this to Cheryl when he got back.

Loop completed. Realisation: he'd had these thoughts before.

Now he was back at the starting point. The real starting point.

Something was wrong.

You started off knowing something was wrong, but time passed and you started thinking everything was all right. Even now, if you let yourself drift . . .

He could feel himself approaching it again, the untroubled state. Slip into it and the loop would have him. How many times already? Didn't bear thinking about.

No way out. Except – intuition precise and fierce as a paper cut – to remember the thing immediately before this. The last footprint would be the first in the trail leading all the way back. Immediately before this was . . . Immediately before this . . .

But he was close enough to *everything's all right* for a little of it to reach out and pass into him like the first swallow of Scotch in the evening. Warmth, that loosening, things not mattering. Have another. Afore ye go, as the label said.

It almost seduced. He flirted with letting it take him (now it had the feel of Cheryl's arms coming up round him and the kids laughing), held the memory of that morning ready, felt sure he had neither the strength nor the inclination to resist – but at the last moment wrenched himself away, thinking that even if he did there was no knowing what——

He'd seen heads in silhouette, shrieking halogens, three doctors in peppermint green smeared with blood working like insects.

Then something had exploded from his chest and skull, a double birth of pure light followed by total darkness.

Silence in himself. He didn't want anything, only not to have to think. You could make your mind all but blank. You could roll up the incline right to the edge from which your identity, your self, your consciousness, *you*, could sheer off into the void, atomised. But sooner or later you rolled back. To everything you didn't want. He had an image of a black jewel in someone's held out palm. Your birthright. Don't you want it?

Without knowing he'd been holding on to anything, Nathan let go.

And fell.

As a child, Luke had said to him, Dad, if you're in a lift and the cables snap, what about if you manage to jump up in the air just before the lift hits the ground? Wouldn't you be all right?

Light coalesced, below and to the left. Down and to the left. Which way do your eyes go when you're lying? Not a lift shaft but a curved chute. One of Luke's wormholes? A torque of colour. Beautiful. The reason you couldn't travel faster than the speed of light was because you'd . . . Your mass would . . .

Implosion threatened, or some irreversible fragmentation. He tried sheer will as a brake and found to his surprise that it worked. He slowed. Stopped. Chance to think. Whether he really wanted to do this.

The luminescence dilated – pink in there, pale yellow, flecks of amethyst and aquamarine – then contracted, shrank or pulled away from him. Bye.

You go through at its pace or not at all. Of course. If you want the way back.

He wasn't prepared for the new rate of fall, nor the surge of brilliance at the approaching core; but there was no stopping this time.

Last thoughts flickered, distraction from the one thought

that this would annihilate him: This is nowhere. Nothing. Something. Will I remember when I wake——

Then the light engulfed him and sped him on towards darkness.

Janice

When he emerged the people he knew stood below him in negligible rain round a freshly dug grave: Cheryl, Luke, Gina, Adrian. His father. A handful of others. Nearby, a bulbous conifer tilted like a giant microphone awaiting a quote from the sky. Raindrops scurried over the coffin's camber, beaded its edge, dripped into the cavity below.

The body goes back to dust, his father had told him, in the after-Mass-and-three-whiskies voice, but the soul is immortal. As a boy he'd imagined his soul as a wisp of vapour flickering in his chest. At death it would curl from him to slalom up towards Heaven or to be sucked down towards Hell.

Whereas in fact.

Whereas in fact *what*?

Wait. Calm. List the facts. This is St Xavier's. Exeter. Everyone. A grave.

In spite of his injunction consciousness threatened to

petrify, to reach a state from which nothing, surely *nothing* could follow. He started again.

St Xavier's. Exeter. Everyone.

When he was small he'd had a babysitter, Janice. At some point in the evening she'd tell him his parents weren't coming back. Ever. He always started off not believing her. They're at the pub with Aunty Maggie and Uncle Dave. But she'd shake her head. No, that was a lie. They weren't coming back. Ever. The familiarity of the ritual tortured him. The moment he most dreaded was when in his heart he believed her. They're never coming back. Janice wasn't satisfied until she'd brought him to tears. Then she'd tell him no, shshsh, it was just a game. Until the next babysitting, when the whole thing would start again.

He made himself take a moment, while the priest – Murray, whom he hadn't seen since Lois's christening – raised and lowered his arms like a tentatively worked marionette. This rain was the soft rain Cheryl said materialised around you rather than fell from the sky. He couldn't feel it. Knew it, but couldn't feel it.

Taking the moment was to let the obvious in. His funeral.

Best for now to accept what there was, suspend disbelief, assume that what appeared to be the case was in fact the case. Someone had said, the world is everything that is the case. Wittgenstein? One of Cheryl's favourite quotes, back in the days.

There was something close by he didn't want. He didn't know what it was, but panicking would bring it to him. Cheryl always said, if I'm on a machine you switch the fucking thing *off*, okay? No arsing about. He'd said the same, without her conviction. Never been able to lose the image of himself wide awake despite diagnosed brain death, watching in horror as the doctor reached for the switch and his loved ones bowed their heads. *Don't turn it off! I'm still here!*

Did you know, Gina'd said to him one day when she'd reached the age for the laconic delivery of such ideas as fact, if you die in your dream, you actually die in real life, in your sleep? Think about it: you never die in your dreams. Then one day you'll dream it, and that'll be you – snuffed it.

The deep habit of thought dictated that there must be someone, an authority he could consult. He sent out a query (to whom he wasn't sure) vague and giant, just . . . *What . . .?* Then listened as for the sound of a dropped stone hitting the bottom of a well.

Nothing. Or rather not quite nothing. Something was being withheld, he thought. To trip him into a mistake (there was a quick and suspicious way of thinking ready to work for him), to trick him into falling for it, whatever it was. So he wouldn't. He'd wait. Like treading water. You could go on for a long time but not for ever.

With babysitting Janice there was always a period of treating it as a joke they were both in on. He remembered the frailty of his laughter, the way it caught in his chest. Her careful cruelty and how he was childishly in love with her, white shins and that greasy blond bob. I'm going to marry Janice when I grow up. His dad had laughed. They're *never* coming back, Janice used to say, sitting forward, elbows on knees, long-nailed fingers loosely linked. Never *ever*.

Gina was in a black skirt and blouse and carried a bunch of irises by their stems, like a club. Luke still looked too young for a suit, for adulthood, would for years. Nathan imagined them all getting ready this morning, Cheryl dressing in silence. He'd loved the wideness of her stare at herself, applying make-up. He used to lie on the bed, watching. Haven't you got anything better to do? Nothing better than this, no. Then her eyes went sideways to look at him in the mirror, the little acknowledgement that she had this power.

Is there any history of mental illness in your family? Every now and again a form asked something like that and you wondered what it would be like, the psychotic uncle or schizophrenic dad. You ticked NO.

Now this. There'd been that phase of taking acid and mushrooms, two summers in the early Seventies with Adrian, then the mad dabble again in his first year at Goldsmiths, him and Cheryl wandering around Regent's Park looking for the zoo. Flashbacks? The deal was that years later out of nowhere hallucinations assaulted you.

In which case it would pass. In which case he could wait it out.

The classic progression was denial, anger, grief, acceptance. He'd read it somewhere. For the loss of someone, that was. Not for the loss of everyone.

It wasn't panic he was holding off. It was love. All of it with nowhere to go. The horror of this was in him, waiting to be let loose to drive him mad. The thing was to think about something else. Anything.

He'd never said one way or the other, burial or cremation, but there had been a conversation with Cheryl years back, before death had touched either of them. It's not the going into the ground, she'd said, it's the awful contrast, all that satin and silk with your bones and offal slopping around like a stew. He'd agreed: revolting; in the light of which he felt betrayed now, until he realised at the sight of his father standing with head bowed and hands thick that they'd done it for the old man out of sympathy. The Church. Fire whiffed of paganism, the old gods with their genitals and hangovers. Plus the problem of resurrection without a body to raise. Same with his mother's funeral, the insistence on *laying her to rest.* Cheryl had said: It's so he'll have a place he can go to talk to her. She'd said it as much for him, Nathan. At the time, he'd been thinking of his mother's corpse in the coffin, bed-sored elbows and heels reduced to their matters of meat and chemistry fact. The names of body parts – eyeball, liver, heart, tongue – had presented themselves with a new purity, and it had numbed him to think of his father kneeling with nasturtiums or tulips above ground while a few feet below the sluggish divorce of tissue from bone proceeded in sound-proofed indifference.

They'd had Lois cremated. It hadn't needed discussion.

The memory brought closer whatever it was he didn't want. It loomed up and darkened everything like the shadow of a giant wave. He veered, wildly—

Never again, Cheryl, the shape of her. Feel air moving, bare feet on a rucked beach, sun-heat, fingers thawing, stone. All that. If this is—

He hauled himself away. But from 'all that' he'd got a sense, like a glimpse of a terrible army, of the questions, an infinite number, each with its attendant terrible answer. At the moment when in his heart he believed Janice, all the objects in the room, the room itself and the world outside shed an outer layer of disguise and revealed their collusion with her, with all of it, everything they'd told him there was really no need to be afraid of. Then shshsh and him lifted up hot-faced and sobbing onto her lap and her laughing and holding him to her which almost made it worth it to be that close because there suddenly was her white throat and the tiny gold cross-and-chain and the smell of her blouse and Wrigley's Doublemint.

He was a few feet above his mourners' heads, looking down. A couple of dozen people and the priest in white surplice and black stole. 'Hear our prayer O Lord and grant that the soul of your servant may . . .' (That was the thing with Janice: you had to go through the agony, but then there was the bliss.) The shadow had gone but left the promise of its return. He forced himself to focus instead on the novelty of seeing them from this angle. Had he seen them like this before? Cheryl yes, from however many painting and decorating ladders, also a Gaudí spiral staircase in Barcelona. His father? Never. Adrian? Yes. Years ago, teenagers, him, Nathan, up a pear tree looking down between bright leaves and rough-skinned fruit, Adrian arriving below, back from the house with a pilfered and greenly glinting bottle of Gordon's gin. Now for the second time in his life he saw Adrian's double crown, twin points of growth from which the blond and of late grey hair grew in cropped whorls.

Horns, he thought, with affection and an unexpected stab of loss for the friendship. Thirty-five years. But the thought brought something else up, a flavour or smell he didn't want. With an effort he got himself away from it.

Gina's head he'd seen from above countless times, the first more than eighteen years ago, blood-slicked and mango'd by the forceps, the last, a week ago, when, him up on the garage roof in a square of sunlight for a reason he couldn't now remember, she came out to call him for lunch. He'd glanced down, and in the glance mistaken her for her mother; she had Cheryl's gold and brown colouring and as of that morning the same wedge haircut. He'd felt pride, then a pang of sadness, realising his mistake. Her face tilted up, one hand shading her eyes. It's on the table, going cold. He'd thought of her for the first time as having the capacity to have children, and suffered, absurdly, a small pain in his own abdomen. But of course there was the boyfriend. At it, presumably. He didn't know. He was by definition behind his children's times. Dad-lag, they called it, bored.

Shouldn't Lois be here? If this was . . .

He sent out a query: Lo?

Nothing. (Which surely suggested this wasn't, in fact . . .) Or not quite nothing. As before: something withheld. To hoodwink him, he couldn't help feeling. Anything hasty (like what? He didn't know) and he might lose what he had. It had been at the back of him from the beginning, that his purchase here was precarious, a grace that could be withdrawn without warning.

Lois would've been fifteen now, grown out of the knobbly knees and artless hairdo and the smelling of crisps and school, the agony phase of not quite womanhood girls went through. Body Shop perfume, the ubiquitous White Musk. Menstruating, maybe. That time she'd seen a cross-section of the female reproductive organs in Gina's biology textbook and thought it was a sheep's head. His private satisfaction because he'd always seen that, too. He'd had to find some excuse later to wrap her in his arms. Too many times that was all you could do. And Lois didn't always like being scooped up like that, if she was in the middle of something, some girl business.

That whole way gone—

It was no good. Standing still (standing? Hovering, he supposed) these thoughts were going to break through and come at him, bellowing. And if it was that whole way gone then there were questions: How could he see? There were the colours, innocently visible: green, purple, grey. Sounds, Murray's murmur and the rain's exhalation. Smell? There was something, a version so faint he couldn't be sure he wasn't dragging it up from memory, wet Devon afternoon, damp lawns, conifers. Taste? Touch.

He and Janice used to play a game, 'drawing' with the index fingertip on each other's bare belly or back. You had to keep your eyes closed and guess what it was. A house, a car, a flower. The thrill of it knotted his guts. There, after all, was Janice's quivering midriff and deep navel. But also, there was the rich moment just before her finger touched him.

Careful.

Moving was a matter, as formerly, of volition, but with some loss of accuracy, some drift, slightest lapse in concentration and you were way off. Like the bike on the pier at Brighton which when you turned left went right. You fell, every time. He'd wanted Gina, but found himself instead alongside Luke, from whom, suddenly

can't overestimate in the end the power of curiosity he said it'd be all right but obviously not obviously not

before recoil (not from the content but from the bare fact of collision with his son's consciousness, a bearable twinge like the first suck in of air that reveals a tooth cavity) took him out of range or alignment.

Thought-fragments picked up and skirled: telepathy Uri Geller ouija boards ghosts listening those cards with shapes on them circles or crosses and someone trying to think them to someone else mind reading maybe gypsies incredible can't be but you just did it read your son's mind and all of science therefore in the dark.

It wasn't dreamlike, either. Immediate, urgent, and that

distinct little pain. Something like forced intimacy, too, the changing room packed with the male smell that wasn't yours. Spatial location only part of it. Other gravities worked. Feelings, was it? Luke's had leaped like a solar flare, a lash of energy from a furious inner blaze.

It had been a while since he'd had a real conversation with his son. They didn't seem to want it so you let it slide. You did all the things you started off thinking you wouldn't.

A defence he hadn't known he was holding up slipped and there was his own disappointment in himself like a landscape he could get lost in. It halted him, until another flare from Luke

or rather be a billionaire you should ask yourself these questions people say they're stupid they don't want to answer them suppose right now in fact cancel all Third World starvation as long as your dad stays dead

ambushed him, gave him a glimpse of the astronaut's nightmare, the snapped umbilical and slow somersaults away into space. Stays dead. Their certainty that he'd gone was stone-hard and cold. Going near risked getting hurled up against or repelled by it into the nightmare of the broken lifeline and the endless void. He must be careful.

Be careful.

The warning had been inarticulate. Now something articulated it. Or someone.

Lois?

Again the not quite nothing.

Mum?

Ashes to ashes, dust to dust.

Something in Janice's face always convinced him eventually, a way she had of making her eyes go dead. She had all sorts of arguments to bring to bear; all he had was the refusal to believe. You're lying. No I'm not, not this time. This time they're really gone. For *ever.*

He watched Cheryl, who, having tugged finger by finger one black glove off now threw wet earth onto the casket. Then Luke threw, depressed (Nathan knew) by the ashes to ashes, its cheapening evocation of the Bowie song, and by his mother's stripperish glove removal, the image it called up of her on stage to the sound of burlesque brass and wolf-whistles.

Their thoughts go into you. But not yours into them? One way? It was the sort of question he would've asked his father one of those Sundays. Frank, mage-like in his arm-chair, would have taken a sip of Scotch and rolled out some rubbish. The spirit can enter the body, of course, but the body can't enter the spirit. Impossible. Im*poss*ible.

Gina followed and hesitantly threw. Nathan approaching her in careful increments could feel her trying to grow. She was making, whilst throwing, staring down – *how'll he breathe in there? oh god you idiot* – turning away, linking her mother's arm, an intense effort, a neural stretch not to condemn herself for not feeling what convention demanded. As at Lois's cremation. Like Mersault, she told herself, for comfort. Then a horror-bulletin and inner delirious laugh: And look what happened to *him.*

Frank threw next. He paused with the dirt in his hand, jowls quivering. Nathan, negotiating drag and drift – the force like a bad smell around Adrian (something wrong, there), a high-pitched whine around Cheryl that warned him off – moved closer. Touch. Maybe it was the heat from Janice's fingertip he'd been able to feel. He went closer to Frank. (His relationship with space and time wouldn't settle. Bodiless and located. The contradiction threatened diffusion, the loss or dispersal of himself among trees, grass, stones. He had to keep imagining himself, there, however ethereally. If he did he could move, situate himself, rope in the old rules, mangled, but awkwardly workable.) He moved towards the old man's back, felt the chaotic aura, eased through his father's shoulder and side (like ducking his head underwater: local amplification but the loss of the rest of the world) picking up in transit

and now him as well for what for what killed

along with Frank's history there for the rifling: the muscle-memory of the flyweight days; Spitfire innards, the hangar cathedral cold and the peeled moment before the pilots got in, knowing their lives were in your hands; the remnants of half-finished things, education, the plan to emigrate to Canada; the continuous white noise of fear and self-pity, all the ways he'd hurt poor Lil: Nathan saw these, wondered how many, but by then had passed through and re-entered the world with a slight loss of incorporeal balance and sound rushing back in.

Frank didn't feel it. They couldn't. Which meant all these years the dead could have been passing in and out, listening. The little old lady from *Poltergeist* drawling in her tiny Southern voice that sometimes souls couldn't bear to leave the world behind, that they still felt attached, unfinished business among the living . . .

The living. The dead. You are the dead. Thought Police. *Nineteen-Eighty-Four.* That category of memory intact, then. Education. Orwell. Wittgenstein. Princip shoots Ferdinand 28th June 1914. Moon landing, 20th July 1969. That category. And the others? Nathan James Clark born 6th February 1956. Married Cheryl Fenn 12th June 1979. First child, Luke Jacob . . . Gina, January '85, Lois, December

'87 . . . He'd always thought of dates as pins holding down the past, which would otherwise drift and lose its shape; also the constellations as pins holding space's invisible blueprint, at which Cheryl had said Oooh 'ark at 'im, poet laureate. He had the dates, all of them. And the rest? Work was teaching, or had been until he packed it in; years of pupils and their million variations on the theme of not being interested. Home was Roseberry Road – no, they moved, just recently. It was bad with him and Cheryl. She'd gone away, or he had. Was that it? Life was Cheryl and the kids. Loved . . . She'd gone different, hadn't she? Or he had. Everything that wasn't a date had an alternative. Easy to burn himself out that way, trying to choose.

The nearer to now, the more difficult. All historians knew that. What was the last thing he remembered?

Images came willy-nilly: Cheryl's face at nineteen. His mother between morphine shots not recognising him. The Roseberry Road living room. Gina looking up at him and saying, I did *not*, outraged. Lois in the Focus passenger seat after swimming, hair wet and eyes red.

Yes but the *last* thing?

There'd been a profound understanding between him and Janice, manifest at each stage of their game. Her claim, his laughing denial, her increasing earnestness, the terrible moment of conversion, distress, and finally comfort. It was as if he'd known her in a former life. As soon as in his heart he believed her she blazed with new life, became even more beautiful, though he saw her through a film of misery.

Adrian had a bad moment throwing the dirt. Some of it stuck to his palm, necessitating an ugly shake in which there was no disguising revulsion. The flung-off bit hit the coffin in an unseemly splatter. Nathan, feeling sorry for him, moved forward. Send something through him. Ade, for fuck's sake it's me.

No. Something wrong there. That smell like the stink of a cramped zoo.

Gina unlinked from Cheryl and walked away after Luke, who'd gone to stand under the conifer. The priest said something to Cheryl as she passed, but she ignored him. She went a few paces with an obscene hang to her limbs, as if excess or trauma had loosened them, then stood still, feet planted apart. Adrian caught her up and stood in silence next to her. He put his hand round the nape of her neck, gave it a slight shake. The gesture they'd all made to each other, down the years. It meant don't give up. In the face of every reason for breaking don't break because if nothing, absolutely nothing else I'm here with my hand on you. You're not alone.

Nathan turned away (not easy; debilitating false starts, again the threat of absorption by trees and rain and grass, the effort to keep imagining himself, there, turning away) and noticed by the grave two people he didn't immediately recognise. He began the thought that he'd never seen them before, but hesitated. She was a tall woman in her early forties with white skin and yellow-blond hair scraped back and tied with a black ribbon. Small eyes and mouth but long full cheeks and a hint of upturn in the nose – the haughty talking teapot's face in Lois's storybook of years ago. Wealthy. That coat and the emerald and diamond cluster. No wedding ring.

She was accompanied by a plump, prematurely balding young man who had the look of having drunk before coming here.

Her in the black coat and him three inches shorter in a

well-cut dark grey suit. In every way not a couple. They stood at the grave, into which a kagouled and wellingtoned man with excessive earhole hair was now shovelling dirt.

His body in there. The thought brought the belly-emptiness of hunger. He let it go, focused again on the two strangers at the grave's edge. They didn't belong here. Didn't know what to do. Don't go near them.

The young man crossed himself, incorrectly, going to the right shoulder first. The woman stared into the grave.

Nathan had held himself above denial. Denial was the obvious thing so he'd resisted. But as the woman's hands slipped into the coat's slash pockets he found himself weakening into the thought (thought or plea? To whom?) that it couldn't be happening. Any of it. It couldn't be happening because if it was he'd have to bear it and now, realising for the first time his condition *someone did this didn't they* he knew he wouldn't be able to, would rather die, except dying – this straw of irony keeping him from collapse – was no longer, apparently, an option.

Nathan

You are the dead. Robotically repeated at intervals. Bits of the route home detonated unease: a newsagent's window; a redbrick wall under a froth of pink rhododendrons; black-and-white Friesians in a field bordering Prince of Wales Road. Inexplicable surges in the body he didn't have, flashes of hot and cold. Amputees, he'd read, 'felt' things in the missing or phantom limb, ghost sensations, heartless jokes. He was a radical amputee. No body, but a maddening imposture of sensation.

One day when he was about nine or ten two older boys had chased and trapped him in an old air-raid shelter on a demolition site. You entered by going down concrete steps littered with rusty cans and johnnies, through a short piss-stinking tunnel then exited up the concrete steps on the other side. Posted one at each end they'd kept him trapped in the darkness underground. Blood had gone round his head in audible spasms. He'd heard as if at some remove the sound of his own breathing. Kept thinking it couldn't last another second. Another second.

Like this. Hell? Not Heaven. Purgatory, maybe. You did time there, like a Victorian workhouse. Disassembling sins. How much time?

He went along above the cortège, effortlessly now, as in flying dreams, but it wasn't in him to do otherwise. What was will and what seduction he couldn't keep clear. One refrain was: All those things you thought mattered. Another was: They'll feel me. They'll know.

The same deep habit kept him expecting information, a door in the sky to open, a representative with a smile and a clipboard: You'll be wondering what's happened to you. Well, it's my job to help you get used . . .

Immortality meant living for ever. He searched himself for it, potential infinity. Found nothing unusual. Time was more or less what it had been, seconds, minutes. Happening in real time. Just without his body in it. Was that all your soul was? You without your body? He'd imagined something purer, some essence that would surprise him with its clarity when he was reduced to it. This was just *him*, Nathan Clark, partially amnesiac.

Lois?

Killed, his dad said. Someone did this.

There were distractions. The road, flanked by hedgerows, glistened. The funeral cars crawled. Déjà vu worried at him. A part of him he wouldn't grant full admission to consciousness was . . . what? Recognising this? Conceding that he'd known, hadn't he, that this was what it would be like?

Murder is the unlawful killing of

He tried sentences: I've separated from my body. I'm

floating along above them. The words themselves floated, with an inclination to separate. Wet car roofs and boots and bonnets sometimes very near, sometimes remote. It was an effort to keep close. Don't lose them. Their lives inside with pulses and thoughts like full hives.

In the air-raid shelter every second he didn't die from fear was a miracle. The disinterested observer in him stood off to one side, marvelling at his endurance. Eventually the two older boys got bored and wandered off, laughing. He'd crawled out, whimpering, into the daylight. Walked home tender-skinned and humbled by the beauty of pavement and sky, his liberty to notice them.

Killed. A car crash? Hospital negligence, maybe. Adrian had told them not long ago how many millions NHS mistakes cost the government every year. That woman who'd had her breast cut off because they'd mixed up her results. Three doctors smeared in blood.

Thinking was all he had but it clogged and clotted, the feeling after traffic fumes. He'd have to be patient with himself, take it one step at a time. Easy to say.

The wake was at the new house north of the city, a large, white, detached Victorian property with gardens front and back, upgraded-to thanks to Cheryl's profits from what used to be her father's company. (Some facts gave themselves up without fight, without alternative.) Virtually rural here: Stoke Wood and a bend of the Exe to the further north, Exeter proper to the south. They'd only been moved-in a week. I need a bigger house, Cheryl had said. He hadn't argued. She – they; it was still, nominally, they – had the money, and having the money had become the catch-all justification.

Now that he'd thought of it Cheryl's work flagged for his

attention. Fenn Industries. Steam Cleaning. Sandblasting. Textures and Coatings. Not the work, but that she'd chosen to do it. He went near the idea of it for a moment, glanced, then swerved away. Not ready. Did the same with Cheryl herself, went into her broadcast radius, caught

earthworms in and out like tacking stitches when do similes drop it metaphors give up the ghost

then out again as on a self-yanked leash. Further fear was waiting if he went near the sexual Cheryl, which in the black woollen suit and wreath of complex perfume had already pricked half a dozen of the men in the room into fantasies and shame. He'd radared among their denials a lone rationalisation: Terry, a cousin who read, thinking, *Yeah well it's the Richard the Third thing fucking a woman over the husband's dead body to take her in her heart's extremest something something . . .*

Nathan felt nothing much about this; wearily shared masculinity, familiar disappointment. Cheryl, he could tell even at a distance, saw into Terry, didn't care. She saw whatever you thought was hidden. She'd had an earlier phase, Nathan remembered, after Lois's death, in which without doing anything specific she'd dared people to come near her to see if they could stand their own visibility. They never could. Now she was past that into something else. He didn't know what, boredom, maybe. So he went near her

once upon a time there was a stupid cold cunt

but yanked himself away at the last minute. Other people's thoughts and he could get snagged on any of them. *He* had to think. Cogito ergo sum. That first night in his room Cheryl had said, I feel like all my muscles and bones are suddenly in the right place. Her hand on his chest in the dark. All the sweetness, feeling of having become fully human.

But it was hard to think. The things he wanted and couldn't have had set up centres of pain in him. Cheryl was one. Gina, Luke, his dad, the other way of being with them, in the flesh. Each pain would get worse. Already the effort to ignore them was a drain on him. It was – or would be, eventually – hopeless. In hospital his mother had lived under the tyranny of pain, a demonic child she was forced to devote herself to. She couldn't concentrate on anything. Conversation for a few minutes, but her attention off to one side, waiting for it to start up. Sitting by her bed, he'd hoped the afterlife, if there was one, would give her the chance to experience existence without pain; her face in those last days had the look of having forgotten what that was like.

If there was one.

All the years, on and off wondering. The way Lois's body so categorically didn't have Lois in it afterwards. She'd gone, so he hadn't been able to stop himself thinking she'd gone some*where*. (Lois? Still nothing. Or rather something, still withheld.) All the dead who'd gone before (but where were they?); he'd joined the billions. Like losing your virginity, you felt it, that now you knew what all those others knew. Membership of the species. He had an image of long lines of the dead stretching back in time, people in jeans and pin-stripes at first, then gradually Forties hats, bustles, doublets, tunics, loincloths, the shadowy rear ranks getting closer to the ground. Remote languages. Incredible all the faces, inexhaustible uniqueness.

It brought some comfort – until he realised that he was sliding into it, accepting it. Like giving in to sleep.

He snapped back to find the living doubly loud and vivid around him. Mouths talking and hands moving. Relief like the gulp of air after a brain-bending spiral to the surface. He had an image of himself standing with his back to the edge of a sheer drop into blackness, emptiness you could feel, cold gravity, the horror-personality of nothingness. In front of him was this room, these people, the house, the city, green countryside, all of it. You face that way. You keep facing that way. No matter what.

He followed Gina from the kitchen to the dining room. A new instinct told him not to let the aliveness of her loose on himself, but he couldn't help it: strong bones and green eyes, the troubled energy and precarious courage, the way the future came into a room with her; that animal face, porcine to the degree that the man in him knew made it sexually workable, like Cheryl's. The life in her charged her slipstream, gave him what would have been a pre-thunderstorm headache. Once, when she was little, she'd said, in a tone of neutral observation: Dad, your ears are like bacon. The kids delivered jewels like that all the time, reminders, not that he ever needed them, that he had all the wealth he wanted, his wife, his children.

Gina went into the dining room, where there was a cold buffet and emphatically available alcohol. Luke sat in the window seat, drinking red wine. She poured herself a Scotch and water (she'd made it her drink politically, at first, for its unfeminine connotations, but now liked it) and took the space opposite her brother. He wasn't right, she knew, but knew too that you had to pick your moment.

'What're you going to do?' she asked.

'Get shit-faced,' Luke said gently, looking out of the window. The lawn was bordered by curved beds thick with colour. Flowers nodded and dripped in the rain.

'We should be given money,' Gina said. 'Millions.'

Nathan didn't understand. Then picked it up from Luke: so they could invent, manufacture, buy a life which might accommodate their wrong shapes.

'Yeah, well she's working on it,' Luke said, meaning Cheryl. Then after a pause: 'Although maybe this'll do something else to her.'

There were TV shows where they set someone up. The wife pretended she'd had the car sprayed pink or whatever and then the husband came home. Nathan always felt for the person on whom the joke was played, not for having been pranked, but for having been filmed or recorded in secret. It always, no matter how funny, seemed a violation. The innocence of thinking no one was listening. You watched with a kind of compelled dirty glee.

Now he watched feeling naked himself. I never loved him. Mum's better off. He was a lousy father anyway. They might say anything. More than the little moral knot, his own vulnerability demanded attention. He ignored it. Told himself he wasn't afraid.

'I keep wanting to piss myself laughing,' Gina said. 'I know it's inappropriate.'

'I heard Grampy laughing last night. I went to his door and he stopped. Didn't turn round, just stopped, didn't say anything.'

'I couldn't talk to him,' Gina said. 'He'll try and talk to you. I couldn't. It's the way he talks.'

'What, God?'

'All of it.'

'Maybe he won't this time.'

Gina took a sip, swallowed, remembered she used to have to make a face to get the stuff down, suddenly thought of herself as old, knew it was absurd, but people dying compressed time, dog years. Eighteen. What's eighteen sevens?

Nathan wanted to hold her. All that time believing in the future, taking it for granted. The thousands maybe millions of ways he'd tried to make their world safe. Careful, lovey. Hot. Wait. Hold my hand. Wait till it stops. Seatbelt.

'How long are you staying?' she asked Luke.

'Don't know. Had the counsellor on at me before I left saying think about taking a year out.'

They looked at each other, then away, having acknowledged the arrogance of the world's assumptions: time to get over things. In the exchanged look was their history of being more or less in cahoots. Nathan had often thought Luke was at his best with Gina. Now he saw it was more than that: his identity referred to her. The morning after a night with a girl Luke would lie next to her thinking about Gina, wondering what she'd make of the way he'd been. The girl would ask him what he was thinking and he'd have to lie. Nathan had had the sense of this, amorphously; now it had shape.

'What's she been like with you?' Luke asked.

'Minimalist. Very specific requests for help with all this. She's worried about the papers.'

'What, in case it puts people off getting their houses pebbledashed?' Luke said.

Gina laughed with a single snort through her nose. The laugh discharged a jarring shock of life into Nathan. Too much. He gave in. Went closer, felt the margins of her, caught

if you can still laugh unless you laugh in the wrong way unless
it's that kind of laughter maybe whoever he was he laughed

Something warned him not to go nearer but the need was overwhelming—

'Fuck!'

Nathan wrenched himself back.

'What?' Luke said. 'What?'

Gina had started, violently. Half the Scotch had climbed the glass, flown, spotted the carpet. Heads turned. The room's murmur dipped, but took its cue from Cheryl, who looked at Gina, impassively, seeing if anything interesting was coming, then turned back to Terry (who had come closer, having found, Nathan knew, the line he was after *To take her in her heart's extremest hate/With curses in her mouth*); Cheryl was the arbiter and had declared that nothing was required of anyone. The bulk of the room was relieved, Gina's boyfriend, Matt, leaning in the doorway with a glass of Chardonnay, especially. (Nathan had noticed him, earlier, awkward with Gina, afraid of Cheryl, not knowing what to do or say.) Gina, meanwhile, had recovered herself, physically. For a moment her eyes and mouth had opened and all the mental machines had stopped. Now they started again.

'What is it?' Luke said.

'Something weird. Did you feel something funny?'

'Something funny?'

'Something sudden.'

'What are you talking about?'

'Nothing. Forget it.'

'What's the matter with you?'

Gina didn't answer, just got up and walked away.

Nathan shrank back. Sorry sorry sorry. To whoever it was laid the proscriptions. Sorry. Image of himself cringing, expecting punishment. From which followed anger: Find out which things electrocute you by grabbing hold. Fuck you, then, whoever you are, *fuck you.*

He made himself calm down. Can't do that with Gina, that going into. Maybe can with Dad because he's old, the barriers ragged, all holes now, more holes than not. Have to go gently with her. Couples who can't kiss because they give each other shocks. Language of electricity persists. Luke would be pleased. All that stuff will be incorporated, eventually, Luke had said, once, years before, when Gina had been going through a phase of interest in the supernatural. There's nothing out there that won't be . . . (Nathan had been ostensibly reading the newspaper but really listening to every word, which, since Gina and Luke knew, turned the argument into competitive performance in which the right word mattered) . . . subsumed, Luke had said, after a struggle (Nathan had had a job keeping his newspaper and his face straight), within an extended version of the science we've got today. Even Gina had laughed, the sentence having turned into a tightrope walk and all three of them willing to see beyond the argument to the comedy of Luke's having made it without a fall. The memory of that moment was clear and distinct.

'How're you doing, handsome?'

Lynn, Cheryl's sister, had taken Gina's place in the window seat. Nathan felt Luke sag because he'd have to be normal for her. He, Luke, had been thinking he ought to learn a foreign language, several, in fact. (Despite lingering shock Nathan picked this up without effort.) The idea of foreign countries had been growing on him, lately. The more languages you knew or places you lived, the less important your feelings would seem. The two ideas mingled in his mind: white beaches and aquamarine water and himself deeply contented in just the hang of his limbs and one foot in front of the other, leaving prints.

'Okay,' Luke said to Lynn. 'You know. Going quietly mad.'

Gina

Gina's bedroom was big enough for Nathan to keep a distance. She'd closed the door behind her, but he'd passed through it. (Passed through it. All the ghost stories. The younger Gina would've been thrilled.) He remembered walking through the warm mist dispensed by hidden irrigators in a tropical greenhouse.

Killed for what. Frank's thought seared, intermittently, forcing Nathan up to bristling wakefulness, at the peak of which nothing mattered except to find and (somehow) confront the person who'd done this to him. But he fought it, irritatedly – or the distractions did. He felt (it had come from Frank, after all) *nagged*, plaintively. (The countless irrelevant things his dad had dragged his attention to over the years. In the new house they'd given the old man a room on the ground floor and from it he'd exerted the familiar dismal gravity. Look at me. Listen to me. Live for me.) Killed. Frank was flecked with senility. But Nathan had thought it too: Someone did this. He pushed it away, knowing as he had known every time that it would return, or rather that he'd be compelled to return to it, like a dog to its vomit. At the height of wakefulness he'd seen the size of the task: to believe he'd lived the kind of life someone else could want to end.

Gina stood in the middle of the room. Much of her stuff was still boxed from the move. A hi-fi had been unpacked and wired up, a scatter of CDs. There was an original fireplace, blocked off with a black iron plate. The alcoves were shelved, filled with books. The desk showed signs of ongoing work. Luke had teased her for failing to customise her screensaver. Hey, the Packard Bell logo. Cool. She was loved for her obliviousness to certain things

you think you know what a radiator is or a spoon or a chair but you don't. They're all these other ways. It could go on for ever if enough of your people died. Eventually a world only you see your way. Mum must be getting there.

(He went carefully. Different frequencies. Fine tuning.) A lot of her thoughts dead-ended with her mother, at whom she must stop and merely exist, not knowing what could come next. There had in fact been a lone standing stone on holiday in Cornwall, years ago. Gina hadn't liked it. Nathan had enjoyed, with mild paternal sadism, her unease around it, had added to it by telling her that research had found certain standing stones *hummed*, subsonically. Gina had frowned, pretending to not believe. Now the image of the stone was attached to Cheryl in Gina's mind, and along with it the feeling of terminus, of reaching the last outpost before nothingness.

She went to the desk and looked down at the books and papers. Nathan saw loose sheets of narrow feint A4, numbered paragraphs, heraldic doodles, a volume of Victorian poetry open at Browning's 'Childe Roland to the Dark Tower Came', annotated in green biro. It had always thrilled him to see the results of her mind having been at work. Her mere handwriting was a miracle to him, made him remember her as a newborn, lying in a Perspex box that looked like a bread bin next to Cheryl's bed with a plastic name tag around her wrist: GINA ELIZA-BETH CLARK.

When Lois was born Cheryl had been so tired she could barely sit up. The nurse said take it off her she's going to drop it. They used to tell Lois the story. Because you were so tired, Mummy? Yes, because I was so tired. He'd never mentioned it since Lois's death. It would've stuck in Cheryl's mind. She's going to drop it. He'd known, and never said anything. Should've said, that it was nothing, that it didn't mean anything.

It *hadn't* meant anything, not to him. But he'd known it had to Cheryl and yet he'd never reassured her. He'd let her suffer with it

and fuck school and fuck Matt and fuck university and the whole piece of shit idea of the future you might as well take a gun à la Columbine . . .

But that, Gina knew, was just the script. Nathan felt her impatience with herself for letting it reel her in. There was always a script: her dad's funeral so how could she possibly do anything other than exist in a state of grieving rage or deadness? Same as at Lois's funeral: everything people said to her was right and good and comforting and completely at odds with what she was feeling, which was that now she was their only daughter again and what effect would that have and would it make her less their daughter or more? It was what she'd wanted to discuss with everyone – but that wasn't the script. The script was darling and I know it must be but you must be strong for your mum and dad and she's gone to a better place. She'd hardly been able to speak. She'd gone to her room (like this) and lain down on the floor in her funeral dress thinking of the awful Tenniel illustration of Alice with an arm and a leg stuck out of the tiny house, then wondered whether they'd rather it had been her, if they'd had to choose.

In the first years of her teens she'd entered a strange war with her dad. Their wills had set against each other. They argued about insignificant things, were very accurate in their nastiness to each other. Meanwhile he was big chums with Lois, though Lois had by then settled into her own little places – the violin, swimming – and didn't seem particularly to need it. After the arguments Gina felt partly disgusted and partly pleased with herself. He seemed to feel the same. Occasionally, out of the wreckage, they'd have beautiful, fascinating conversations. They'd begun to make peace, it had seemed to Gina, the year before Lois's death. Then Lois had died, and her dad had gone back to being almost the way he'd been before they'd ever started rubbing each other up the wrong way, a gentle, intimate ally. She hadn't understood (and didn't now), but she'd recognised a similar reversion in herself. After Lois's death, the antagonism towards him that had been a perpetual, nagging imperative faded away, first into negligibility, then into non-existence. When she thought of it now, the arguments – her navel piercing, *Bad Lieutenant*, a joint discovered in her handbag – it was obvious they'd chosen things they both knew didn't matter. What wasn't obvious was why.

34

She read at random.

> If at his counsel I should turn aside
> Into that ominous tract which, all agree,
> Hides the Dark Tower. Yet acquiescingly
> I did turn as he pointed; neither pride
> Nor hope

Nathan stood it, made himself stand it. Whether they'd rather it had been her. They'd watched *Sophie's Choice* the Christmas before Lois's death, had the film's hypothesis imposed on them. I'd ask them to take all three of you, Nathan had joked, evading. It had been Gina who'd asked, *stirring*. Later, in bed, he'd said to Cheryl, don't talk about it, it's disgusting. To consider some things is disgusting. But people have had to make such choices, Cheryl said. That obliges us to consider it. Nathan had nearly lost his temper. Yeah, well it doesn't oblige *me* to consider it. If someone sticks a gun to my head, *then* I'll be obliged. Until then it's disgusting. Craven of him. He did consider such things, secretly; they plagued him. But he couldn't bear bringing them into dialogue. Not least because he was afraid of the part of Cheryl that insisted on looking at the world no matter what the world had to show. How can I write if I'm not prepared to look? she wanted to know. I don't care, he said. It's disgusting and I do *not* want to talk about it.

You knew Gina must have asked herself that. And Luke. You knew you should have said something. Why didn't you? (He knew the answer, too.) All the things you should have done. No: only the things you *knew* you should have done.

The pull of her was terrible but so was the heat of her life if he went too close. It was an appalling beauty, the livingness of her, that she'd come out of Cheryl and him, that lust and habit, love and boredom, the transport and comedy of fucking and all the nameless places of their marriage had hauled her up through the knit of their genes and flung her out into being. It was too good; unbearable.

university I'll be streets ahead with all this death under my belt. No point having the death without the sex.

Which led, Nathan picked up, to Matt, and her not having let him fuck her yet, or not, as they said, 'properly'. Matt couldn't see that the delay was because she hadn't decided whether he was likely to make a hash of it for her, her first time. He, *boy* that he was, thought she was holding on to it the old-fashioned way. Susan at college had been sent a birthday card, a cartoon drawing of two sperm, one of them asking, 'How far to the ovaries?' the other replying, 'Miles. We've only just passed the tonsils.' Not funny, Gina thought, but then less and less was. (Or more and more was. That was the way of it, getting older. The world was either less and less or more and more funny.) Well, anyway, that was her. She'd *sucked cock*. She'd *swallowed*. She'd done it experimentally, for herself, not for Matt, though obviously he wasn't complaining. She'd wanted to see if it would make her feel sick. It hadn't, at the time; but then later, the thought of what semen *was*, millions of little creatures swimming, swimming, with their own life . . . Not sick, exactly. Something. Sad, possibly. Unprotected exchange of bodily fluids. Well, it was her fucking life.

This was hard on Nathan. Not the sexual details (although the image of her *sucking cock* gave him a little fracture of sadness, while part of him stupidly grieved that she wasn't exempt, that if she wanted all that palaver – *men* – she'd have to have all the trouble and conflict and doubt that went with it), but the thought that he'd been forced to trade his former position – having to guess what was going on in her head but none the less being able to act on that guess – for his current one: knowing what was going on in her head but being unable to do anything about it. All the life he'd have to see from this side.

Presumably, Gina thought, it was wrong or at least a sign of disturbance to turn over sex thoughts (*cocksucker*, there was a joke in *Sophie's Choice*, Meryl Streep describing a suit as 'cocksucker' instead of 'seersucker'; they'd watched it that Christmas and her mum had laughed at the joke and looked over at her to see if she'd got it and she had, and another flake of her childhood had dropped away in their mutual recognition) to be turning these thoughts over on the day of your dad's funeral, but she didn't care. She thought of herself wondering how he was going to breathe in the coffin and marvelled at the stubbornness of mental habits.

Her complexity settled Nathan, slightly. He thought of the period of warring with Gina. Don't worry about it, Cheryl had said. It's puberty. It's so the love won't be romantic. A girl knows she's in danger of falling in love with her father so she sets her will against him. Chooses war. I should know. Nathan had always responded to such diagnoses with the same joke: Yes, yes, if you go *in* for that sort of thing. They joked about it, weren't alarmed, followed the educated directive not to be alarmed if a thing made sense. Cheryl, The Writer, or rather Aspiring Writer (their own satirical capitals) especially. (You need to marry someone like me, he'd said to her, because if you marry someone like you you'll end up in an asylum. They joked about that, too, that he left the glamour and glamorous thinking to her, that Cheryl was the dinner party star.) None the less, it had depressed him, the unspoken but implied other half of Cheryl's theory, that Gina's puberty made her a sexual being, that he was fighting her to avoid a Freudian pile-up. He thought of the rows, of how pure certain moments of antipathy had been. And the relief afterwards, as if they'd discharged an unpleasant duty together. Then Lois's death. The arguments had dried up and blown away.

At Lois's cremation, Gina remembered, she'd wanted to follow the casket behind the curtains into the furnace. She hadn't quite believed that something else – some secret resurrection – wasn't taking place in there. The closing curtains had evoked magicians. It always annoyed her that there had to be a cloak or a cape. If the transformation was really happening, why have the cape? Why not just *show* the woman disappearing?

Lois was dead and now her dad was, too. Which meant your thoughts strayed further from the script. You saw how going shopping and television and exams and buses and holidays and huge companies and banks – the whole thing was . . . What? Just an agreement between people. What happened to Lois was outside the agreement. Her dad had been taken outside the agreement, had been shown. The horror was that there *was* anything outside the agreement. They'd had an open coffin for him. It had amazed her, his face utterly not him any more because of the life gone out. She'd thought of the euphemisms: asleep; at rest; at peace. Ludicrous, with his head and body and limbs and closed eyes bearing absolutely no resemblance to him asleep, or at rest, or at peace. Your dad becomes a body. Extraordinary, the tangle of blood vessels, the weight of bone and skin, a graveyard of nerves. As a child she'd found a dead rat on her great-granddad's farm. She'd put a stick in its mouth and prised it open. When it snapped shut, the teeth had made a little *tick*, striking each other. That, more than anything, had confirmed its deadness. She'd remembered this, looking down at her dad's closed mouth. Was there something that held the jaws together? A pin? An adhesive? It hadn't mattered how hard she'd tried, all her thoughts seemed inappropriate. Thinking at all was. What you needed was to be put into a state in which thinking was impossible. Could you grieve without thinking? Could you *feel* without thinking? The problem with thinking was that you never knew what any given thought might end up being attached to. It was like a giant net. In fact, like the internet. Madness was someone with attention deficit disorder surfing the internet. Sanity was the ability to stick to your search.

The urgency of the need to comfort her went through Nathan like an inflammation. There was nothing to scream with. Nothing to do anything with. Imprisonment without a body to imprison. He went nearer. Saw her stiffen. Stopped.

Careful. It'll hurt her.

Someone knocked.

'Yeah?'

'It's me.'

Matt.

Gina sat with her back to the door, staring out of the window.

'I'm coming down in a minute.'

'Can I come in a sec?'

'Okay.'

She said okay brightly enough, but it was a defeat, born out of another neural heave, an effort not to condemn Matt for not seeing that nothing he could do or say or ever become would make any difference to what she was feeling, which was at the moment a delicate curiosity about herself, about what all this was doing to her. She thought of herself as a prisoner being transported in a windowless vehicle, with no idea of her destination or what she would have to become to survive when she got there.

The door opened and Matt came in carrying two glasses: brandy, which neither of them, as far as she knew, liked. As soon as she saw him she knew everything he'd do or say just now would be derived from the script.

'You okay?' he asked, handing Gina the glass.

'Not really,' she said. 'But . . .' Script shrug. She took a sip, then put the glass on the desk. It was in the air that normally when they were alone together they were physical with each other. That was what being alone facilitated. Now what?

Experimentally, Gina went to him, put her arms round him and kissed him. She felt his shock when she used her tongue – then his determination to respond. She could feel him wondering whether to step up a sexual gear, put his free hand on her breast or up her skirt. She stopped, hugged him, chastely, knowing he'd be thinking: Yes, that's the way it is if someone's in this state, grief or whatever, all different feelings going mad and crashing into each other. Be flexible. Fit whatever shape she makes. Don't fuck it up.

She moved away from him. 'I just need a few minutes,' she said.

Matt was relieved. He left a pause meant to indicate that he was weighing up whether to override her, manfully – you don't know what you need right now, Gina (he imagined himself doing it in an American accent) – then said, very quietly, 'Okay. I'll be downstairs,' before turning, exiting, and closing the door with calculated gentleness behind him.

Gina waited a few moments, then went out onto the landing. Nathan stayed put; he knew she was coming back. (He was acclimatizing. Bits of their intentions flitted around people like butterflies. He saw Gina seeing herself in the bathroom, then back in her bedroom. He assumed she was going to use the toilet, freshen up, draw solace from the room's white ceramics. She was like that, sensuously spontaneous, rested her face against things, curled up in odd nooks.) She came back with a packet of Nurofen and a glass of water. Nathan could feel around her the curiosity about herself, a detached spirit of enquiry. Also a slight annoyance at the insistence of her body: armpits firing up then cooling, scalp tingling, fingertips wide awake. Sitting at the desk, she popped all the pills from their foil pods and lined them up along a sheet of handwritten notes. Twelve. Apostles. Days of Christmas. Angry Men.

He froze. First fear – but then a suspension of all thought and feeling. There was nothing from this moment, no possibility in any direction.

Twelve Nurofen'll kill you, Gina had heard. Seemed hard to believe with the dozen little pills laid out in front of her. Also presumably a sort of compassionate joke on the part of the manufacturers that you actually *got* twelve in a box. She looked at the open book, where, against the poem's first stanza, which began 'My first thought was, he lied in every word,/That hoary cripple with malicious eye', she had written: 'Openly unheroic: contempt, suspicion, boredom, fatalism. Not knightly qualities.' She'd asked her dad once: what's the most important virtue? He'd thought about it, then said, Truth. But her mum had shaken her head when Gina reported this. Courage, she'd said. No good knowing the truth if you haven't got the courage to speak it. (There was a troublesome knowledge between Gina and her mum, that they were like each other, that they felt slightly sorry for her dad and Luke, the *men*.) It occurred to her now that if she left the book open people would take it as a literary suicide note. She almost laughed aloud, then checked herself because the laugh wouldn't be genuine. No laugh alone in a room was, unless you were mad. Nathan had once read (secretly, with shame and pride) a page of her journal, in which the effusive way her peers greeted each other in the town centre on Saturday afternoons – with falsetto endearments and theatrical embraces – was taken apart with delighted loathing. The page had ended: 'I'd rather have the Devil than that shite. Even the Devil isn't fucking *pretentious*.'

Gina closed the book and wondered if her dad had ever wanted to have sex with her. Or Luke with Cheryl. Over the last couple of years she'd found herself able to bring these speculations out and have a look at them, to be intellectually interested without the moral queasiness called for by the script. Immediately following Lois's death the locks on her most disturbing thoughts and memories were doubled. But gradually, one by one, she'd opened them, found them innocuous. In the very earliest days of masturbation (how old had she been? Eight? Nine?) she'd gone through a phase of filching her parents' underwear from the dirty laundry basket to rub her face into when she touched herself. After the phase had passed, she buried the memory of it deep (and in any case her shame was required for the next development, her having been introduced by the boy across the road to his dad's porn mags); but in the years after Lois's death she brought this and other things back into consciousness, where they shrivelled in the light of her looking at them into objects of pathos or comedy.

In spite of himself Nathan came out of suspension with a mixture of voyeuristic guilt and pride in her courage. This was beauty. He forgot everything else, even the pills on the desk. This was his daughter, in full flight. She was so like Cheryl, the way Cheryl used to be, the curiosity that wrecked and elevated her. Again he thought how utterly astonishing it was that she, Gina, had come into being via his and Cheryl's (most likely casual) desire; casual desire and a little biological flurry: Gina, in existence.

But the thought of existence returned him to his own, and to Gina's hands at rest around the glass of water. Don't, darling. Don't go near this.

There were other unlocked secrets. In Lois's obituary, the *Express & Echo* had misprinted the word cremation. The *m* had gone missing. Creation. Everyone noticed and no one said anything. She hadn't said anything, either; but she knew it would have been better if she had. Lois would have laughed herself. There was no shame in it.

When her mum had told her her dad was dead the two of them had stood and stared at each other. Another recognition, this time that the first feeling in the queue was curiosity. Lois. Now Dad. She and her mother had looked at each other and shared, it seemed to Gina, the same thought: someone's experimenting on us. To see what it does to us. To see what we become. Was there a feeling of excitement? Wasn't there always, despite any *other* feelings, a part of you designed to respond only to the excitement of something new, to change? Was there shame in that?

One by one she replaced the pills. It had been a moment, but it had passed. Anything else would be performance. Most likely even this was. She hadn't wanted to kill herself. Just been curious about what the mechanics of preparation

would feel like, whether the world's immediate details –
desk, wall, books, carpet – would be given special clarity.
(They had been, but it was obvious that only the real thing
would deliver the real thing.) She sat back in her chair and
looked out of the window.

Mrs Lloyd

Halfway down the stairs Gina crossed the blonde woman from the funeral, coming up. Both of them slowed, knowing a friendly gesture was required but knowing too they couldn't produce it. There was an awkward exchange of looks as they slowed almost to stopping but then speeded up again and passed, slipped back into their private worlds.

Stay away from her.

Nathan still didn't know who she was. He watched her coming up the stairs. As a child he'd had a recurring nightmare: he was in his pyjamas in a high-up bedroom in a strange house. It was his house, in the dream, his room. He was at the window, looking down onto a big, tightly cropped lawn. It was a bright, hot day. On the lawn stood a handsome man in a dark suit. The man looked up at Nathan and smiled. 'I'm coming up now,' he'd say. Just that. Nathan screamed or whimpered himself awake. He watched the blonde woman's knees and long shins as she climbed the last of the stairs with the same familiar dread. I'm coming up now.

He knew he knew her. Second-order recognition, he'd read somewhere. Like second-order desire, wanting to want something. Could he have had an affair with her? Did he want her? In the absence of the body . . . What was the amputee's tumescence? God only knew. (Maybe that was why Cheryl terrified him now. It had been good with her, when it had been good. He remembered *that*.) In any case, he felt nothing much about this woman. The way in would have been the haughty face and the whiff of greed. He would have had to find it, it would have taken imaginative energy, working himself up. Whatever she had, it was nowhere near enough for him to have cheated on Cheryl.

Not that, then. Her and the young man driving the car? Drunk. Manslaughter. In which case what were they doing here?

It didn't feel right. He bounced set-ups from Chandlers and Columbos off himself, blackmails, love triangles, wills, cover-ups – but he was still a history teacher pushing fifty living in Exeter with his wife and daughter, one son at university, one daughter dead. No room for strangers.

The woman reached the landing. Coldness spread from her towards him. He daren't let it touch him. In the park when he was small there'd been a stagnant pool, scummed and littered. You were dared to walk in as deep as you could, bare-legged. It would be like that. He backed off.

His and Cheryl's bedroom was across the landing. He'd get in there. Rest for a minute. Think it through.

The woman paused and looked down over the banister into the hall, where the young man was standing alone with a drink and a canapé, rocking on his heels slightly. Then she crossed to the bathroom door, opened it and went in.

Whether they'd rather it had been her. Of course Gina had wondered. To consider some things was disgusting. To be made to consider them worse. He thought of the beauty, Gina growing to accommodate herself, the strange becoming familiar, the shameful negligible, the occult known. It came to him afresh that he wouldn't see this, the continuing adventure of her becoming who she was, or if he was allowed to see it he'd be denied sharing it, living it. You took it all for granted.

His and Cheryl's bedroom door was closed. He hesitated for a moment, then passed through.

Mistaken. This wasn't their bedroom. It wasn't a room at all.

Neither dark nor light, but he knew if he held his hand up in front of his face he wouldn't be able to see it. Unease and familiarity. Nothing to see nothing to hear nothing to smell feel taste and still consciousness persisted.

Lois?

Nothing.

Soon the next thing would happen. He didn't know how he knew.

Now he noticed, with only mild incredulity, two pearly, quivering, unidentical rosettes of light there with him. Emerged from nothing like the funeral's rain. One was there (his old version wanted to say) to his right, the other to his left. That wasn't quite it, until he forced the thought, then it was, quite it: one to his right and one to his left. The thing was to go to one of them. But they exerted equal pull, or generated the same desire — which left him where he was, suspended. The two desires worked in gentle friction, until eventually the effect was like a pair of hands being wrung, incessantly. Mild anxiety became agitation, agitation discomfort, discomfort unease, unease – and when it happened he realised he had known it would – dread.

There had been dreams in which he'd murdered someone. When he woke, the first moments would be filled with a feeling of indelible responsibility, the nausea of knowing that nothing he could do now would erase what he'd done. Then he'd realise that it was only a dream, that he was still clean, innocent, free, and relief and joy would flood him. He'd turn and put his arms round Cheryl, kiss her shoulder, inhale the smell of her hair, wallow in his deliverance from dread.

This was the dread, or something very like it. He had the feeling of having known it would come to this, in this place, from the moment of entering. Hadn't he known, but distracted himself from knowing?

Get out. Get—

Sheer will back-pedalled him. The radical amputee limbs dream-dragged, strained, flailed – the greenhouse irrigator mist – then he was out.

Their bedroom was as he remembered it, white walls, wooden floor, a high ceiling and a big bed. Red and gold kilim rug in front of the dresser, dark art-deco wardrobe in the corner. The window looked out over the front garden and hedge to the road. Quiet. Cars were distinct events during the day, reassuring at night, ominous in the small hours. He and Cheryl had just begun learning the new sounds. Fox barks. An *owl*, for God's sake.

Habit turned him to the mirror. Not being visible put pressure on the radical amputee gut, as if a blunt blade were being pushed there. If this were a film, he thought, there'd be the sound of fruity, sadistic laughter.

Something had happened. He'd come across here . . . He'd come across here and . . .

The thought trailed into nothing. Enervation. The living hurt. He had a reservoir of tolerance for pain. Finite, though. Pain would empty it, eventually.

A slight disturbance in the room began to impinge like the sound of a housefly.

Don't you remember?

No, Missy, I don't.

Stopped short. Held absolutely still.

Lois?

Nothing.

Lois? Come on, Missy, it's Dad. Lo?

He waited a long time. Silence. Clouds dimmed and undimmed the room's light. There were bits of blue sky if he looked, but remote. Don't you remember? It hadn't come from him. He hadn't imagined it, had he?

Lois?

But the room had reasserted itself with its somewhere pocket of disturbance. A cloud moved, let sunlight onto the wood floor, brought its knots and grain up, the silver threads of the rug's fringe. On the digital clock a seven turned into an eight. When they arrested you you got one phone call. It gave him a stab of loneliness. Who would he call? Cheryl? Lois? The living or the dead?

Don't you remember?

I'm trying, Lo.

Tiberius's reign ended in AD 47. The Bastille fell in 1798.

He remembered *that*. Presumably just so whoever it was could enjoy the joke. Cheryl would have. Historians, she'd quoted, pissed, one evening with friends, are like deaf people who go on answering questions no one has asked them. Tolstoy, she'd slurred, then burped. (She was a wild drunk, terrifying to men, especially, who, courtesy of the booze, morphed into her father.) Nathan had been drunk, too, and had defended himself in a quiet aside: And history *teachers*, God help us, just repeat the answers historians have already given; you could train parrots to do it. No one had heard. Later, in bed, Cheryl, still drunk, but rough and penitent, had made extravagant love to him. It was often like that. She hated the predictability of herself, but knew life probably wouldn't be long enough for her to grow out of it.

All this as he moved around the room trying to track down the houseflyish interference. If it was a sound it was one only he'd be able to hear. (These stones, he'd teased Gina, they *hum*. Subsonically.) It came and went, depending on where he was. Like the game with the kids where you hide something and then say Warm or Cold. That he wasn't thinking about what happened back there, nor, properly, about the blonde woman and the young man, dug at him, but he ignored it. He felt weak from Gina. The living hurt the dead. He didn't have the strength, just for the moment.

Cheryl's black blouse hung on the back of the bedroom door. There was a white bathrobe underneath it, and on the hook next to it a leather shoulder bag and two or three chiffon scarves. There was a kind of tinnitus around the items generally, but the blouse – held off, he realised, by his own will – was a strong signal waiting for him to tune in. What had been the housefly interference. This how it works, Lo? Did you bring me here?

He was afraid of it. You go into it, he thought. Or not into, but close. You angle yourself, maybe; signal's like a spiralling galaxy and you hook onto one of the outflung——

'Now that, mister, is a sexy item.'

Cheryl, the birthday girl, has unwrapped The Main Present: a black satin blouse cut to fit close. It's from Marianne's, and signifies – since they'd had their phone cut off last month and been forced to take a handout from her father, The Capitalist, The Wilcox – reckless spending.

'My God.'

The cut doesn't permit Cheryl to fasten it where she normally would, so it's the button below.

'Christ,' Nathan says. 'I don't think that's strictly fair on Adrian.'

This is 1982, four years after graduation. Nathan's lifelong friendship with Adrian gave Cheryl pause, initially, the thought of taking it on and failing; but, after much stumbling and wincing, it's been assimilated. Of late the three of them (plus Ade's girlfriend, Marsha, a non-academic non-politicised waitress) have had a lot of long, late-night conversations about Men and Women, in which it's transpired that Ade's realised (sadly, since it's unlikely he's going to have what it takes to get better, he knows) his membership of the misogynistic patriarchy. Cheryl and Nathan aren't deaf to all this, but they do consider themselves (it's their dirty secret) above or beyond or piggishly beneath it. Cheryl's occasionally bothered by something she read somewhere: 'Feminism suffers when thinking women make exceptions of their men. Remember: there are no exceptions.' She knows. She's taking the easy way out. Always the same with her, the private, the personal, the particular. She's selfish, she reminds herself for the umpteenth time. A selfish little egotistical hedonist with delusions of grandeur. Never mind. When she's published, she'll start living right.

'My knockers are fantastic,' she says, in front of the mirror. The bedroom's a mess. They're both untidy, and hoarders, and enamoured of their slovenly life.

'Yes, they are.'

Nathan's recently moved into a new phase of desiring her. In this phase (he'll come out of it, they both know) there's no one on the planet, film stars and porn models included, he desires more. Her desire for him, they both also know, is a trickier thing to track.

'I don't think you should keep that on if you don't want to be fucked to within an inch of your life,' Nathan says.

'I'm someone men don't look twice at in the street,' Cheryl says. 'Don't contradict' – at his reflex – 'but there you are: Look at those breasts. Superb.'

Cheryl's come late, thanks to Nathan, to the enjoyment of herself as an object of desire. She wasn't one of 'the pretty ones' at school; her sister Lynn had the looks, her father said, not deliberately within her hearing but not deliberately out of it, either. None the less, she's grown up with a feeling of entitlement. She's never competed with the attractive girls, but she has waited, with patient fury. Hence relief now that Nathan's seen what she has, but also vindication. Secure in his desire, she simultaneously indulges and satirises her vanity. It's a sort of sex toy for both of them, never to be taken too seriously.

'Well, I'm not taking it off,' she says, and after a collusive glance at him in the mirror, unzips her skirt, steps out of it, turns and sashays over to him on the bed. It's done in the half tongue-in-cheek way they employ to segue from the mundane into the erotic, and it works. Nathan feels the soft touch of her breasts and belly on his skin, the shape of her waist between his hands, her mouth on his. The lemony perfume she's taken to of late does its thing, but it's an accent, filigree on the main desire, which isn't for her body but for her look of knowing him, and the force which grows up between them as a feeling of invincibility——

Nathan was flung out. The memory had ravished him like a classy drug. Instantly addictive. More, no arguing. This was the pill that offered the good dream. Reality's always too high a price to pay, Ade used to say. Miserable Socrates has it over the happy pig every time. Nathan hadn't been sure then, and sure or not he didn't care now. He wanted more, and moved closer, waiting for the signal's hook. They'd loved each other——

Wrong angle. Wrong spar, frequency, whatever. It sucked him in and rooted him. A different bedroom. This one, here, the new house. Curtains half drawn, sunlight coming through the gap. Motes drift and flare. Cheryl sits facing away from the dressing table, leaning forward, feet planted, legs apart, elbows on knees, wrists loose, hands dead. She's wearing nothing but the black blouse. There's a sheen of sweat between her breasts. A cigarette smoulders between the first two fingers of her left hand.

Across from her, on the edge of the bed, Adrian, naked, sits with the same posture. The room's rich with recently spent energy. A cloud turns the sun down, then up again; details re-ignite, a slew of coins on the floor, Adrian's belt buckle, the hairs on Cheryl's forearm.

'Where is he?' Adrian says. He's said it, Nathan knows, instead of all the other things he wants to say.

'At the dig,' Cheryl says.

A long silence. Adrian's resisting the urge to jump up, pull his clothes on and run from the house. It's his ethics, Nathan knows, to resist whatever he most wants. His failed ethics, this morning.

A car approaches, slows for the bend, accelerates away, a reminder to Adrian of The World.

'Why've we done this?' he says.

Nathan feels Cheryl shift into impatience. She wants Adrian gone. (A stab of love: he, Nathan, still knows her, recognises her, understands the way she works with another man. His wife. A history had grown up between them, fabulous, a delight. Their first child – Luke – coming out of her body, gore and miracle. She'd been private all through that pregnancy. The bloody delivery under the warm lamps had returned her to him, her face stripped by pain to its essence. They'd both looked at the infant, then at each other, having seen the same thing, all the future's boundaries blasted: what've we done? It had brought them back together, that they were both doubtful of their potential as parents, that they'd leaped without looking and were now at the mercy of a terrifying momentum.)

'Cheryl?' Adrian says.

'Because I collect perversions.'

Which will silence Adrian because it reminds him that his motives are irrelevant. The explanation's all Cheryl. Adrian's been wondering whether she will leave Nathan, finally, for him, after all these years. It's seemed a reasonable thought: Nathan and Cheryl are each other's curse since the loss of Lois, and all three of them know Adrian's always been in love with Cheryl. He's been thinking, sitting looking down at his discarded jeans and shirt, that he might be the next thing for her, something against which the next phase of her transformation can proceed. He's been thinking, too, that he'd be okay with that, if it meant he had her for a while. (Nathan isn't surprised or much disappointed. It's been understood between himself and Adrian that Adrian wouldn't be strong enough not to forfeit their friendship if Cheryl made herself available.)

'What are we going to do?' Adrian says to Cheryl.

Cheryl bows her head and moves it slowly through a tension-easing arc. The golden wedge haircut hangs forward, revealing her sturdy neck and upper vertebrae. (Kiss my neck, she'd said to Nathan, one night early on. It had been one of the most arousing things he'd ever heard.) Her impatience is thickening into boredom. This is the way it is for her now, lots of different streams, hurrying initially, then slowing, hitting silt, backing up.

'That's the problem with being alive,' she says, staring at the floor. 'You've got to keep thinking of what to do.'

Loop. He let it run through five times, then withdrew. When you wanted to see it again you were thrown out and when you wanted out you were allowed to see it again. He'd known it was too good to be true. You're woken prematurely from a delicious dream so you go back into sleep to finish it. But there's something else there instead. You don't chose the dream, the dream chooses you.

The coming out entailed at the point of cross-over a sort of vertigo. Now here was the new bedroom again. Where, sometime in the recent past, she'd fucked Adrian. He let the words hang in him, meat hooks. Had he known before? He wasn't sure. There was a weight at the centre of him, a little stone of sadness. Because I collect perversions. Faint memory of anger, too. Trying to get hold of it, he wrote the possibilities as tabloid headlines: BEST MATE FUCKED MY WIFE THEN KILLED ME. Or better still: WIFE KILLS HUBBY AFTER FUCK-ING HIS PAL. Why not, if she collected perversions?

It ought to have transformed her in his mind, Ade, too, bankrupted their history together. That it didn't intimated he'd known, anyway, in the life before. The tabloid idiom was apt, since he knew the story it offered was false. Adrian didn't have murder in him. Cheryl most likely did but certainly not for adultery's convenience. It gave him with a sort of boredom the thought that this was in any case the thin end of the wedge.

Adrian used to say: Nate, how about you let me sleep with Cheryl? She'll like it, you know. It'll spice things up between you. You'll thank me for it in the long run.

Not just now, Ade, thanks.

What about if I made a deliberately bad job of it? Then you'd look like Casanova.

It's awfully decent of you, Ade, but not just now, thanks all the same.

They'd had to joke about it. What was the alternative? Cheryl would go along with the joking up to a point, then get irritated or angry. There'd been one crockery-throwing row, years ago, in which she described herself as the thing with which Adrian and Nathan vicariously fucked each other. All taken back the following morning, written off as the foul mouth on her, pissed. She'd felt doubly sheepish, Nathan had known, because she'd not long before teased from him the confession that there had been a handful of homosexual fantasies when he'd first hit puberty. He'd been loth to admit it to her (he was too young to see it as anything but regrettable confusion), but Cheryl had laughed and kissed him and told him not to be such an idiot, then fucked his brains out. She'd always been ahead of him.

Nathan waited for something, rage, perhaps, but it didn't come. Instead a dismal sense of having joined another league of ordinariness, all the men and women who'd been cheated on. My wife had an affair. My husband was unfaithful. There was the little nugget of his own particular sadness, but he saw beyond it, out into the dully glowing mass that all such unique griefs collectively formed. The betrayed, the cuckolded, the duped, the abandoned, they shared the same depressing common denominator. He was part of that, now, that quiet league. There ought to be a way of saluting other members, a secret handshake, a password.

He went back to the blouse. Nothing. No signal, no pulse. Depressing as a spent firework. Fuck this. He wasn't going to feel any better. Energy spent among the living was non-regenerable. The reservoir had been opened and now it was just a matter of time.

Slightly disgusted – though with whom or what he wasn't sure – Nathan turned and passed out of the room.

Across the landing the toilet flushed. He watched from what felt like a safe distance as the blonde woman emerged and crossed to the head of the stairs, at the top of which the young man in the grey suit met her.

'You all right?' the young man said.

'Yeah. Look, I'm going. I feel weird. Christ knows what we're doing here, anyway.'

'Yeah, I know.'

'If I don't see you before I go, we'll speak next week, yeah?'

'I can give you a lift if you like. I'm not staying, either.'

'I've got a cab coming. Thanks.'

A pause, awkward, Nathan thought, drawing nearer. An exchange conducted without looking each other in the eye. Whoever they were, they were being forced to share space and find things to say. Coldness radiated from them, nudging Nathan like the lip of a lake. Reaching their perimeter, he was convinced they'd be able to see him if they bothered to look.

'Loo in there is it?' the young man said.

'Yeah,' she said. 'Listen, I'll call you next week.'

He lifted his hand for her to shake, but she didn't see it. She went past him, down the stairs. For a moment he kept the hand stupidly raised, then waggled the fingers in a humourless acknowledgement of the gaff, then dropped it, and went into the bathroom. Nathan, with lessened drift now, followed.

But at the closed bathroom door stopped. He'd assumed the events in his and Cheryl's room (what was that other thing? Hadn't there been something just before that?) had made him reckless. But at the bathroom door he met the cold force-field and drew back. He didn't have what it took. Which means you'll never have what it takes, since you're only getting weaker. Fuck. Can't. I *can't*.

The tone of the last thought was the frustrated child's. It had taken him a long time to learn to ride his first bicycle. There were falls. I *can't*. And his dad's implacable it's-the-only-way-you'll-learn. The hatred for the bicycle was like the hatred now of his fear of the blonde woman and the man in the bathroom, a hatred that entailed knowing there was no other way. It's the only way you'll learn. Someone did this.

He listened to the young man peeing, zipping up, flushing, washing his hands. The dank radius rippled. Any second

58

the door would open, Nathan would be taken by it, gulped down. The thought appealed, briefly, threatened swift seduction – then he was backing wildly, flailing, all the new orientation skills gone.

From where he came to rest, ashamed and furious just beneath the landing ceiling, he watched the young man come out of the bathroom and go downstairs. Knew that he knew him. Strained. Knew him, yes, but not well. Same whiff of greed as the woman, a banknote stink, business. Insurance? *Life* insurance? But that was Cheryl's. She was the murderable one, the one with the money, and he, Nathan, was the beneficiary, or the kids if they both went. Rubbish. His mind was going. He couldn't shake either of the bedroom vignettes. Now that, Mister, is a sexy item. They'd loved each other so much. Now there was fear waiting if he went near her. Why? He knew about her and Adrian. Had probably known before. What was there to be afraid of?

There'd been a dream after Lois's death. Him standing on an empty beach with his back to the sea, looking at what appeared to be a completely deserted town, wondering, vaguely, where everyone had gone. A creeping, unnerving realisation that there was something wrong with the light. Then the most elemental horror. It's behind you. Turning, he saw a wall of water a thousand feet high, busy with thrashing creatures, drowned cars, shipwrecks, corpses and industrial filth, coming towards him.

And?

Nothing. Just the rising and falling fear. What else was there? Cheryl had had a Jungian interlude in her mid-twenties, had interrogated him about his dreams. Everyone in your dreams is you, a way you see yourself. He went along with her long-sufferingly, trotting out lost wallets, talking animals, terrorists, having to resit maths O level. She'd known he didn't take it seriously. Didn't take it seriously herself, really, just played. One Sunday morning, half-heartedly masturbating him, she'd stopped (inspiration having struck) and said: Only the dead understand their dreams. They were young, and so sexually confident of themselves in each other that Nathan had waited a moment, then said: Possibly, but could I just have my hand-job without having to consider something like that?

Fear subsided. He would have laughed. There'd been gold with her, moments of sickening satisfaction. They'd ploughed through half a dozen stages of love, bashed and made use of each other. The marriage had been a disordered heap of treasure and junk.

Suddenly, he missed her, their shared history. The way they remained tuned to each other across a room full of people. He'd look up and see her green eyes glance at him. Yes, I know. Us. They'd known there was nothing novel about it as far as the world was concerned; they'd known it was only love, which the world had seen billions of times before. Or rather Cheryl had known. He'd never considered it. Having fallen in love with her he'd realised love was what he'd been waiting for. The question of what he *wanted* out of life had been answered. Whereas Cheryl had space left over. It was one of the differences between them. It was what kept him striving towards her.

Sanity was the ability to stick to your search. Murder or not the couple knew something. Not couple. Whoever the fuck they were. He'd have to be stronger. Try her again. There was a place with two lights. Nathan James Clark, born 6th February 1953, died . . . He didn't know. Hadn't even looked at the headstone. (The pupils' revenge. Spinning

Mule 1779. *Always* give dates – this is *history*, Jason! C+.)
Gina was still eighteen which meant this was 2003. Summer.
August? See if there's a newspaper lying around. Or in the
study, the Ansel Adams calendar . . . How long did they
keep bodies before burying them? Had there been a post
mortem? An inquest? He should have tried the coffin
(though an instinct told him no, not allowed), searched the
body for bullet holes, stab wounds, poison.

His body. A pang of sadness for the loss of it. Only kids
bothered with their bodies in the right way, sniffed a knee,
sucked a knuckle, studied a fingerprint whorl in the sun. You
grew up and lost respect. Or developed anxiety if you were
a woman. He told himself stupid – but they'd been through
it with him, shins, hands, elbows, clocked-up his tally of
bruises and scrapes, knocks. Cheryl's kisses and the handled
weights of the kids. All his time.

The reservoir was emptying, apparently. He felt it in the
churned struggle to get downstairs, that certain movement
cost him dear. Either that or the drain was proportional to
the number and nearness of the living. Not with levity but
with a sort of grim lack of surprise, he thought: avoid
crowds. Nothing changes.

Downstairs, people had drunk enough to have abandoned
the egg-shell walking of the first hour. Food hitherto
morosely nibbled was tucked into without apology. Man's in
the ground; not eating won't bring him back. He didn't
take it personally. It comforted him, grimly, turned what had
been a reluctant assembly into a warm-blooded collective
with an instinct for life

or you could do something funny, like just have your cock and
balls buried and leave everything else to medical science. A little
casket

eight-and-a-half stone since she was sixteen
yeah and please for fuck's sake make it a large one will you
don't love him any more. Funny how you know

He couldn't see the young man, but the blonde woman was in the middle of the lounge with Luke and Jake, Lynn's husband.

'Actually, I was looking for your mum, to say goodbye. Can't seem to spot her.'

'I think she's in the office. Into the hall and then right.'

'Thanks. I'll just . . .'

She moved off with a pained smile. Nathan in her slip-stream tried to summon something, courage, he supposed, since the dead-water aura still unmanned him. Self-made money, he told himself. Chain of boutiques, maybe. One of Thatcher's poster girls if the squinting baroness could be bothered to look these days, poor cow. Adrian would fancy her. Women with power. Adrian had confessed to fancying Margaret Thatcher. Essentially masochistic. And so Cheryl, eventually.

All to keep his mind off the fear. In spite of which a sensationalist documentary-style American voice asked: Is this the face of a killer? He ignored it, concentrated instead on keeping a safe distance. She had a long neck and a long body. Very white skin. That would be another way in, sexually, the breasts and thighs being faintly veined (which he liked and for which taste Cheryl accused him of latent vampirism). She wasn't used to moving this way, tentatively, unsure of her place. At each doorway she paused and peeped in. Coming to the end of her tolerance of being here, Nathan thought. Through the cold he could feel her need to get out, do something anonymous and mundane. She'd go to Dartington for glass. Spend some money. One of those paperweights you could get lost in. And the hour's drive to let all this shit drain away. It surprised him that anything should come through.

'Oh, hi. Sorry.'

Cheryl was with her father, George, in a room at the end of the hall which had been set up as an office. She stood with that same look of her limbs having come loose. George sat on a two-seater green leather couch, facing her. They both looked up.

'Hi,' the woman said. 'Sorry to disturb you. I just came to say goodbye.'

Cheryl came towards her, and the two of them stepped out into the hall.

'Thanks for coming,' Cheryl said. 'I know it must've been weird.'

'I wanted to be here.' A pause. 'Are you . . . No. Stupid to ask. Sorry.'

'There's nothing to say, so please don't try,' Cheryl said.

'No, I know.'

'We'll speak.'

'Yeah, of course.'

Another moment of two people not knowing what to do. After a hesitation they stiffly and with minimal contact embraced. The awkwardness reached Nathan in a jangle. Then the blonde woman turned and came towards him preceded by the radius of dread. He told himself this was it. Stand. Let her pass through. Now and at the hour of our death—

He couldn't. Backing was reflexive. Even then he nearly went under, dragged at by the weight that swelled ahead of her. He had to shelter in the kitchen till she passed, telling himself, Go after her, go *after* her.

No good. All the body that wasn't there resisted the will that was. Like trying to clench your fist first thing in the morning. He put it like that to himself, but argued back that it was just fear, just *fear*. Not that he'd come away entirely empty-handed.

She was there. At the hour of our death. She was there.

Watching? Was that what he remembered? A shutter opened and he was looking up from under a deep red veil and seeing her standing above him. Was she holding a gun? She was holding something. Her face in precise detail but most of the rest blurred. There might have been someone else standing behind her. Then the shutter closed. Nothing more. He tried to force it. Got nothing.

She watched me die. Stood and watched.

Frank

He could feel sorry for himself. There it was, suddenly available, a welter of self-sympathy the little flicker of sadness
about his lost body had only hinted at. It would be a long
feast if he started eating and there'd be no stopping until it
was all gone and he found that he was empty. No point. He
made a decision to resist it. Cheryl had read him a poem
years ago (who was it? Auden? Lawrence?) about little birds
dropping frozen from trees without ever having felt self-pity.
It had affected him strangely at the time, had felt like a little
frozen thing itself, dead, but valuable. Years before the kids,
that was. Before Lois. Cheryl sat up in bed with one anthol-
ogy or another, him with his head in her lap, both of them
ashamed of how easy it was to hide from the world in the
pleasure of each other.

He made his way back down the hall to the office.

'Come on, love,' Cheryl's father said to her. 'For God's sake.
That's *nothing.*'

'Tell me how much the contract's worth.'

'Cheryl, don't be stupid.'

'Come on, tell me.'

He sighed. 'You know how much. But there's no . . .' She stared at him. He wasn't going to be let off this, whatever it was. He closed his eyes slowly, then opened them. 'I don't even know,' he said. 'Two and a half million?'

'Yes, that's right.'

'Send Ken to the fucking meeting. Why are we even discussing—'

'They don't want to deal with Ken, they want to deal with me.'

Silence. Nathan tried to feel his way in. She was holding her father still and making him suffer. George couldn't look at her. This was excruciating for him, whatever it was. Whereas she stared at him, bored.

'You need to stop all this, now,' George said, to the floor.

'All what?'

'You know what. All this. This rubbish.'

'Rubbish?'

He closed his eyes again. He was trying to force himself to keep in mind that this was because she was suffering. But he was a selfish man, and he was suffering himself.

Cheryl let 'rubbish' hang for a moment, feeling him searching for a way out and knowing there wasn't one, then lost interest. Whatever this had once been, it was played out, Nathan saw. She was going through the motions. After perhaps a minute had passed, she turned and walked out of the room.

Nathan followed.

Reached out to her, tentatively.

No response. She was holding herself shut, not only to

him. A different pain, this, not her aliveness, but that her aliveness was locked away. Since Lois's death, of course. People who hadn't known her before would have described her as just the opposite, wide awake, able to enjoy things, a woman of will and appetite. But to her family it was as if she'd put on a personality like an expensive new dress, a young woman's dress to show she was too old for it, or a thin woman's to show fat. Inside her, he knew, there was penned energy, her history compressed and made to fit into a narrow place where it could be kept away from all the life she had left to live. She's gone away, Gina had said to Luke one night. (Nathan had been outside Luke's bedroom door, halted on his way back from a small-hours piss by a bright oblong of moonlight on the landing wall. Cheryl had been downstairs, awake, with the television on.) She might as well go physically, Gina had said. I think she will. She'll go to some other country and leave us money. There had been silence, Nathan half lost in the light, half listening. Then Luke had said: What'll Dad do if she goes? Gina had sounded impatient when she'd answered. Fuck knows. He's waiting for something. Trouble is she's stronger than him. Twice as strong. Nathan had gone back to bed, alone.

'Cheryl?'

Cheryl stopped in the doorway of his father's room. It had been a little boy appeal and it had called up a flicker of disgust, the first real thing Nathan had felt from her. None the less she'd stopped.

'Yes?' she said.

Frank was standing in the middle of the room, bent slightly forwards. He looked as if he'd been deposited in a waiting room then abandoned. Nathan felt both sorry for him and, in his amoral self, tired of him, his continued existence. Lois's death put the living on trial, the old especially. Cheryl had felt it, too, though neither of them had ever said anything, and she'd had no love for Frank to start with.

Killed. It had been the old man's thought and here was the old man.

'Can I do anything?' Frank said.

'Like what?' Cheryl said. This was her way with him, a refusal to go along with his current myth of himself as a frail old man hurt by his own uselessness. Nathan had heard it in his small voice, that regardless of the rest of the day (or the world) the true object of pity was himself.

Cheryl stared at Frank, who looked up at her from under his brows, then away, then up at her again, like a dog seeing if the whip was still there. There were tears in his eyes. He'd worked himself up to tears so many times in the past that now, Nathan knew, even he, Frank, wouldn't know which ones were genuine. They're all genuine, Cheryl had said, because they're all for himself. It wasn't that she hated him. It was that she knew what he wanted, which was – had been for years – continuous attention and unconditional love from everyone. He went after it by affirming, incessantly, that he wanted nothing. Your dad's a monster, Nathan, Cheryl had said once, matter-of-factly. It had made him laugh. I'm serious. He's a bottomless pit of ego and need, and it'll only get worse as he gets older. Listen to the anecdotes. Find *one* that isn't self-congratulation under the guise of self-effacement. Fuck knows how your mother stood it. Nathan hadn't ever thought of his father in that way, but once Cheryl had said it he found it hard not to.

'It's not right,' Frank said, face trembling, hands not knowing what to do. 'It's not *right.*'

For a moment, Cheryl said nothing. Nathan found himself wishing: don't hurt him, love. You're right about him,
but don't hurt him. He's just an old man.

'Frank,' Cheryl said, 'what happens now is up to you.
You can go on living here as we planned, or not, whichever
you prefer. You're welcome here, always. If you want to go
into sheltered housing instead, that's fine, I'll pay. If you
want a live-in helper here, that's fine, too, the money's there
for it.'

Frank stared at her. 'Is that what you think I'm bothered
about?' he said.

'Yes,' Cheryl said.

'My son's *dead*, and you think . . . It should have been *me*,
fucking useless old man.'

'Yes, it should. There's no justice. As we know.'

Frank stared at her with weak ferocity, then turned away.
The top drawer of the dresser was open. It was where Frank
kept the few odds and ends that had been Nathan's mother's.
She'd died of leukaemia twenty years ago.

'What've I ever done to you?' Frank said, again in the
small voice.

'Nothing.'

'Nothing. Then why d'you . . .?'

He'd banked on Cheryl interrupting. She never did what
he needed her to do.

Nathan could feel it coming off his father, the compulsion
to reify the myth of himself: battered hero; selfless soul;
lonely old man. He could feel that some part of Frank knew
it was useless with Cheryl, that she didn't believe in it,
rejected it, wholesale; but could feel too that Frank didn't
have a choice: to accept that Cheryl didn't believe he was a
good, kind, generous and now fragile old man was to accept

the possibility that he wasn't. That was unbearable. It was easier to refuse to believe in Cheryl's disbelief. Easier to assume she'd come round in the end. So he went on, playing the same card, over and over again.

'Let's leave it, Cheryl, love,' Frank said, sighing, sitting down on the edge of his bed, a spring of which twanged. 'I don't want to upset you. I'm sorry. Don't take any notice of me.'

The bulk of Cheryl's consciousness had withdrawn, but the little that was left registered tired revulsion. This version of himself – pitiful old nuisance – was no less sly than the others, in fact harder to attack. It was what he retreated into after every failed attempt to convert her.

'We're both upset now,' he said, staring at the carpet.

Baby talk. Cheryl stared down at the top of Frank's head. A few silver strands swept back from the widow's peak over the oily scalp. She had options. Pity. Contempt. Compassion. Boredom. The great relief for her was that the sexual man in Frank had stopped surfacing some time back. (Nathan went closer.) Age, presumably, wore even that out. He'd never done anything obscene, no inappropriate behaviour. But she'd always been appalled at the way the sexual man in him rose up and made its silent appeal to her whenever the two of them were alone. Never threatening, just there. As if it was an entitlement, as if Nathan by definition was his sexual proxy. She'd been slightly fascinated by it, by how astonished and ostensibly (perhaps even genuinely) offended Frank would have been to be to be accused of something like that. Lucky she didn't find him remotely attractive. (Nathan looked more like his mother, if he looked like either of them, and not much even like her.) In spite of which she'd occasionally been invaded by sexual images of herself and Frank. She'd known it was nothing, just the perverseness of imagination. As at school when a teacher had said: I want you all to think of anything you like as long as it's not Napoleon's white horse. Perverseness had never frightened her, but she'd got sick of it, the open-endedness of it. When they cut me open, she'd said to Nathan, they won't find a heart, just a lidless eyeball the size of a grapefruit. He understood. It was why she wrote. There was nothing else to do with it. They'd all found it impossible to lie to her, or impossible to lie convincingly. It was Nathan the kids came to with ropey alibis and baroque explanations.

'Don't take any notice of me,' Frank said again, getting up from the bed, knees giving off a tick each.

'Think about what I've said,' Cheryl said. 'You'll always be made comfortable here.'

Frank nodded and smiled with what looked like discomfort. It was meant to convey that he didn't believe her. He did believe her; but the belief compromised the myth of his suffering. It wasn't welfare he wanted, it was her (and everyone else's) continuous attention and unconditional love. That he didn't have it and never would drove him nearly mad, though of course he didn't know that *was* what he wanted. Sometimes – Nathan picked this up like a little neural flare in the darkness – Frank told himself he was in love with Cheryl, not knowing whether he was or not, only that the idea gave him a satisfactory shock and seemed to explain the pain she gave him.

He stood in profile to her. 'Let's not argue today,' he said, looking at the edge of the dresser.

Cheryl said nothing, just watched him. After a moment, she turned and walked away down the corridor.

Nathan had lost momentum. How much of this had he

known? The thoughts felt familiar, but had he had them before? Was there a limit? After a point it would fuck you up, melt your brain. The Man with X-Ray Eyes went mad – plucked them out, didn't he? Ray Milland. Cheryl said he played every role like a man in a foul mood, as if he had terrible indigestion.

The thought flitted in that this was potentially endless. Hell, in other words. He'd always imagined Hell as a place you knew straight away. One minute you weren't in Hell the next you were. On fire. But maybe part of Hell was how long it took you to realise you were in it? He asked himself how long he'd be able to do this without going mad. If this was Hell madness wouldn't be an option. There were no options in Hell. That was the point.

Meanwhile Frank stood looking down into the dresser's drawer. Lil's clothes had gone to charity shops when she'd died, but he kept a handful of mementos in here, a couple of silk headscarves, her rosary, a bundle of letters, her address book, some photographs, the legendary reliquary.

There was a signal. As from Cheryl's black blouse, but a different note.

Unsure whether he wanted this, Nathan hung back. It had stopped raining. The window showed a corner of the garden glistening in sunlight, a laburnum blinding. It occurred to him for the first time that he'd never get to know this house. Then his father reached into the drawer, and the reliquary's high whine lashed out and caught him——

It's a small mother-of-pearl box in the shape of a cross, and his father's holding it up in front of Nathan's face as if he's about to brand him with it.

'Do you know what this is?'

Rhetorical. These are the questions of the whisky- and tobacco-flavoured front room on Sundays after church. Nathan loves the mysteries they tow in, from space, from God, from long ago. At the asking of these questions the bay window comes into and goes out of existence, and in the moments of its dissolution Nathan might see anything out there: whales; galaxies; Lucifer dripping fire; soldiers.

His father springs the box's hidden catch and the lid pops open, releasing a smell of old pennies and felt. Inside there's a cavity snugly holding a phial of clear liquid, which his father removes and holds up to the light. 'Lourdes water,' he says. Nathan knows all about Lourdes water. There's a plastic bottle in the shape of the Virgin Mary (Blessed is the fruit of thy womb, which he doesn't understand but which evokes a bunch of dark and slightly sinister grapes) in the bathroom cabinet, three quarters full of it. Saint Bernadette saw visions of Mary and now a spring poured out of the grotto, twenty seven thousand gallons every day, as his father's pointed out, the water of which has the power to make cripples walk and the blind see. Nathan's always wondered what effect the water would have if you didn't have anything wrong with you. A recurring fantasy is of unscrewing the plastic top (Mary's crown), drinking the water, and being able to fly or turn invisible as a result. The profanity inhibits him, but the truth is he's not tall enough to reach the bathroom cabinet.

His father replaces the phial and directs Nathan's attention to the back of the cross-shaped lid, into which a small dark fragment of something has been fitted, framed in what looks like copper, and sealed under a thin sheet of glass. When his father speaks, Nathan's overwhelmed by a feeling of recognition, as if he's known this was coming, something from a former life he's been waiting years to remember.

'A splinter of the True Cross,' his father says. Nathan's scalp tingles. He's never heard the term 'the True Cross' before, but already the bay window's showing one moment the cobbles and facing terrace, the next a dark hill and lowering sky. He feels dizzy. 'This is a tiny splinter of the actual cross on which Christ was crucified on Golgotha two thousand years ago.' (It's always 'Christ' with his father, bloodier and more urgent than his mother's 'Jesus', who might be a family friend.) The word 'Golgotha' forms a portal through which Nathan's sucked, accompanied by a distorted or horror-filmish version of the line from 'The Lord of the Dance': 'I danced on a Friday when the sky turned black/It's hard to dance with the Devil on your back.' He's at the foot of the cross, looking up. Warm rain falls on his face. He's never imagined it from this angle before. He can see the soles of Christ's feet (dirty), the outer edge of one long leg (thin, bent slightly at the knee), the scrawny hip and bloody ribcage; shockingly, an armpit full of dark hair. Worst, the thorn-crowned hippy face, foreshortened, looking down at him——

Frank closed his fist around the reliquary, a surge of anger that had pulled Nathan out, spun him back into the room with a feeling of . . . what? The bends? A mild version, he supposed, having never experienced them. Never having been scuba diving. (Or hang-gliding, or abseiling, or windsurfing, or jet-skiing. All the things you never got round to that people given a second chance made sure they did. What would he do with a second chance? Put his arms round Gina more often? Talk to Luke. Try to bring Cheryl back.) Frank's relationship with God was like his relationship with everyone else: he, Frank, was at the centre of it.

I warned you. Told you I wouldn't be responsible for my actions if anything else happened to this family. But you didn't listen, did you? Nothing's enough for you. Nothing's ever enough for you.

This was Frank to God. Nathan listened with growing impatience.

'Fuck you,' Frank said aloud, to God. The room's carpet and curtains swallowed it. He'd insisted on contraception with Lil, despite her stauncher Catholicism. The shop that sold Durex also sold porn (foreign and under the counter in those days), glimpses of which had sent him back to her with new desires, all of which featured in the moral game of snakes and ladders he played with God. If something bad happened — to him, to Lil, to Nathan or the car or the guttering or at work — Frank punished God by, for example, going on at Lil (always jokingly, at first) for not giving him oral sex. Lil thought it was disgusting, had actually vomited on more than one occasion afterwards; but could always, eventually, be browbeaten or emotionally blackmailed into at least attempting it. It had surprised him. She was stronger than him, generally bossed him, in fact. And yet in this matter of the bedroom she could be made to concede, against herself. He wondered if it gave her the martyr's pleasure, if she offered it up as a penance. In any case, Frank's attitude was that this was primarily between him and God. Lil was just the means to a punitive end.

Cheryl knew, Nathan thought: female nose for female discontent, especially that kind. Holds it against the old man. Can't blame her. Poor Ma. Hadn't he known, himself? Sometimes there was a look to her when she sat at the window; she might have been looking out of jail. On the other hand, he remembered the two of them laughing, seeming in cahoots. She'd loved Frank, Nathan was sure. The mix of it dropped another layer of tiredness on him.

The edges of the reliquary were cutting into Frank's palm, so he relaxed his grip.

She didn't even know me.

There had been Lil's illness, those stretched times between morphine shots where her pain was so bad she didn't recognise him, her husband, he might as well have been a stranger. Frank had seen this as God playing by the same rules, making Lil suffer to punish him. He'd offered up all sorts of promises in exchange for the relief of her pain. God had ignored him. Then Frank had been afraid. Lil's suffering was too extreme to have come about in payment for anything he, Frank, could have done. Or anything Lil could have done, for that matter. From which the thought had risen up like a tidal wave (Nathan remembered his dream of the deserted beach, the light going wrong, having to turn to see) that God had a scheme of things to which he, Frank, simply wasn't privy; the whole history of his and God's tiffing and making up, of rewards and punishments, of sinning and forgiving, had been a creation of his own wilful imagination. You're nothing to Him. He's got other fish to fry.

Lil's eyes didn't recognise him. The pain was nothing to do with him. They were human and alone and the only person to blame for all the ways he'd mistreated her was himself.

Which was as far, Nathan now saw, as his father was capable of going. Here he stopped and bounced back to the tempestuous tit-for-tat vision of life with God in which his, Frank's, soul and moral account were the central issues. But it hadn't ended with Lil's death, had it? There'd been Lois taken. And now Nathan. Wife, granddaughter, son. Next to which his little hoard of sins was nothing.

God.

The word went off like an underground bomb. Nathan realised he'd been using – thinking – it all along without for one moment considering what it meant *now*. In his life, his adult life, it had meant two things: a deep habit of imagination and emotion; and an awkward but clean and dignified space left behind by rigorous deconstruction.

Now?

The absurdity of the lateness of this thought would have made him laugh. (Apparently the dead didn't laugh, not while they were among the living.) None the less he was only just having it. It didn't yield much. He didn't sense anything, no Presence, beneficent or otherwise. On the one hand (the thought of Lois flashed; he reached out . . .), there remained his suspicion that something was being withheld, a feeling of *not yet*. On the other, the idea that somewhere beyond where he was now (some . . . what? place? dimension?) there was a Being waiting, something with a benign personality . . . He just didn't feel it. Nor did he feel he'd discovered anything momentous. Suppose your death delivered neither Reality with a capital R nor Truth with a capital T, but was simply relative to your life? No God for *you*. Perhaps his mother had gone where there was one? Paradise, with prelapsarian animals and the lame walking straight.

Frank dropped the reliquary back into the drawer. Cheryl had said of it to Nathan: It's not whether it's authentic, it's whether it's *disgusting*. Frank couldn't leave a difference of opinion or belief alone. Brought them up in front of Cheryl. She'd stand it as long as she could, then turn and demolish him. She always felt guilty afterwards, obliged to explain to

Nathan. It's bad enough a whole fucking religion based on someone being tortured to death. But then to venerate the . . . the what? . . . the *apparatus* . . . Does it get holier the more blood it's got on it? Tears? Sweat? Shit and piss? They don't see it like that, Nathan had said. I *know*, Cheryl had insisted. I don't *mind* them not seeing it like that. I just wish your father would stop minding that *I* see it like that, for fuck's sake.

Certain objects, places. There were things of Lois's.

Things of mine.

A second thought he couldn't believe hadn't surfaced before. You miss the obvious. What things of yours? Clothes? Wallet? Diary?

There was a feeling he was on the edge of recognising. Things of Lois's.

Then he did recognise it. Something wrong with the light. *It's behind you.* You turn and there it is.

No memory of how Lois died.

Luke

An indeterminacy of time and place followed or didn't follow but held him still and spinning. Peripherally he was aware of Frank moving about, but the bulk of consciousness was being rushed through by everything he could remember, round the things he couldn't. Ought to give shape to them, water rushing round rocks. The not knowing generated what might have been heat. Images came and went: Gina at the dining-room table at the Roseberry Road house, flicking through the *TV Times*; a police car pulling up outside the bay window, Cheryl getting out, her face with a post-coital look, a bandage round her hand; himself in a windowless room, a manila envelope on the desk in front of him. The blonde woman standing, looking down at him. These and countless others yielding phantom fever heat, phantom pins and needles, prickle of phantom sweat and the contraction of the phantom scalp.

Then back. He was outside his father's open door. Frank

was at the window, hands in cardie pockets, looking out into the garden, eyes wet and wide, eyebrows raised. Nathan felt sorry for him. He was all that Cheryl said he was, but there were other things, too. He was generous, he loved – genuinely *loved* – doing practical things for people. Loved being useful. Fixing a thing. He'd spent a day fixing Nathan's car and in the evening when he came in, quietly fulfilled, a lovely atmosphere of peace came in with him. They sat and talked. Cheryl gave him a tray supper of homemade soup and toast. They all wondered, afterwards, why it couldn't always be like that.

Concentrate. Jesus. Thought was a loop: he started with the reach for the memory of how Lois had died, curved, went through darkness, returned to the starting point. Or rather two loops, joined, the figure eight on its side symbol of infinity: he returned not to the start but to a second reach for the memory of how he had died. How did Lois die? Curve, darkness . . . How did I die? Curve, darkness . . . How did Lois . . .

Put gall in the way of despair. The double loop was giving someone a laugh, him going round; Luke's Scalectrix.

Not knowing what he was looking for, he went to the study. He and Gina had put inverted commas around it, 'the study', in ironic allusion to his working-class childhood. There was a desk, bookshelves, filing cabinets and a lot of things Cheryl (having traded hoarding for consumption) would have thrown out. In one corner was a standing mahogany case of twenty slender drawers for Nathan's amateur archaeology finds. Cheryl had bought it for him at auction a month ago. He'd been going to sort through it this summer, mount the finds, make it something he could show people, if they were interested.

For what it was worth, the tear-off calendar on the desk said 28 August, with which month at least the Ansel Adams on the wall concurred. He'd wondered, after they'd bought the place (after Cheryl had bought it, since it was her money), whether there might be the faintest pleasure in material acquisition, this being the sort of house formerly known only via fiction or Sunday supplements. Nothing. Cheryl had drafted one of the Fenn Industries crews in to paint the whole place white, had antique furniture she'd been accumulating brought in from storage. She'd asked him, occasionally, if he thought a thing was better in this corner or that (he'd invented preferences), but by and large the new home had taken shape with him barely noticing. He wondered how Cheryl's having made a lot of money would have affected him had she done it in their old life, the life before Lois's death. An impossible thought-experiment: the Cheryl of their old life couldn't have made a lot of money.

He took himself round the room. Come on, give me something. Give me *something*.

POTTY TYCOON TO DIG FOR GRAIL, LOCAL EXPERT SAYS

There was a file open on the desk and the *Express & Echo* clipping was the first thing in it, Urquhart being dismissed by the head of archaeology at Exeter University as an eccentric with more money than brains, certainly more money than archaeological nous. The dig was one of a dozen he'd under-written around the world. Happily for the headline writers, his fortune had been made in, among other things, the design and mass production of bathroom suites. Politely, he was an extremely wealthy man with a passion for occult and ancient artefacts. Crudely, a multi-millionaire Grail twit.

Nathan had heard of him, and though like everyone else on the dig he found the notion that the Holy Grail (a) existed, and (b) was likely to be found in South Devon utterly risible, he jumped at the chance to spend the summer getting paid to do what he loved doing for fre——

'It's over.'

'What?'

'Just got the call. Urquhart's pulling out.'

It's mid-morning up on the hill. Nathan, Louise and Tom have stopped for a cuppa. The last two hours have turned up the usual stuff: Roman coins; bird bones; a spade handle. The week's seen temperatures of 28 degrees and today looks set for the same. All morning Nathan's been aware of a migrainish flutter in his peripheral vision. Now this.

'So what now?' Louise says.

Team leader John has brought the news and looks happier for having delivered it. Nathan understands: the aesthetic or ethical issue of working for Urquhart, a man professionals regard as an irritating brat, has been resolved for him. He can go home with a clean conscience without feeling he's missing out. 'Now nothing,' John says. 'We pack up our troubles and toddle off home until the next multi-millionaire in search of eternal truth comes calling.'

There's a dismal atmosphere when he's gone. Nathan, Louise and Tom finish their tea, then stand around, not knowing what to do. Nathan shudders.

'What's wrong?' Louise says. She's a divorcee in her late forties, very English, straw-coloured hair, no make-up, brittle blue eyes, the look of a farmer's wife taken to booze. Sadness where sex used to be, although the rumour is she's started sleeping with Tom. She's got a grown-up daughter with whom there's a rift. Ex-husband's remarried to, in her words, 'a vacuous little tart'. Nathan likes her, thinks of her as civilised. There's an Iris Murdoch in her rucksack. Sleeping with her (or anyone other than Cheryl) hadn't occurred to him until the Tom rumour sprang up, but it wouldn't have worked even if he'd wanted to. They're too sad for each other. Tom, on the other hand, has wolfish middle-aged good looks and an appetite for life. Nathan hopes Louise is getting something out of it. Hopes, but doubts it.

'Feel a bit fluish,' he says. 'Maybe I've got sunstroke.'

'Bugger,' Tom says. 'I was just getting into a rhythm here.'

'Yeah,' Louise says. 'Although I'm not sure how much fun I'm having in this heat.' She and Tom exchange a look. The last few days they've been wondering what the fuck is wrong with Nathan, who's been a humourless automaton.

Meanwhile it's dawned on Nathan that for some days he's been entertaining himself with the ridiculous daydream of digging up the Grail. In his fantasy it's late afternoon, the site workers gone, only him, Louise and Tom left. Silent, intent work. Heat and the rasp of crickets. Then a trowel scrape, his fingers plucking off loam to reveal one pale hemisphere of what can only be the bowl of a goblet. Earthenware, no gold; each repeat of the fantasy dulls the vessel down, authenticity inversely proportional to ornament. Gina's been calling him Indiana.

Now the rest of the summer spreads out around him like an empty plain. He feels dizzy.

'Nathan?' Louise says.

He turns to her.

'D'you fancy a pint? We can come back after lunch.'

'You look worried about something,' Nathan says.

'Do I?'

'Yeah.'

She looks at Tom, then back at him. 'Well I'm not,' she says. Then, after a pause. 'Or rather, yeah, we were slightly worried about you, actually.'

'Me?'

'You've been a bit quiet.'

Tom raises his eyebrows and purses his lips, half endorsing, half offering male allegiance if Nathan wants to dismiss this as *women*. Nathan sees Tom and Louise's relationship: Tom can't be counted on for anything. Again he feels sorry for Louise. But he *isn't* feeling well. They're both looking at him. He keeps seeing what he calls to himself 'the summer' expanding in every direction around him, flat, going on for ever, distance beyond imagining——

Flung out this time. A controlled explosion brought him from where he'd been to where he was now with a dead stop and the quality of film sped backwards.

Not clues. Indiscriminate bits. They're only clues if someone's leaving them.

Don't you remember, Dad?

Oh, Jesus. Lo?

The door opened and Luke came in. Bright-eyed, apparently wide awake, but Nathan knew it was exhaustion. The boy looked like him, the way he'd looked at that age, dark eyes and hair, thin face, the habit (Frank's, too) of looking out from under his brows. Nathan went close, felt his son's contained disturbance. He'd been a nervous child. That phase of nightmares. Sometimes when he woke up he didn't recognise them. You're *not* my mummy! They'd have to go and get Gina, whom he always did recognise, who could bring him back from wherever he'd gone. A doctor had said, They're just powerful dreams; he'll grow out of it. And he had. Physics now, up in Manchester, Nathan baffled by the choice since neither he nor Cheryl had anything like that in them. Now here he was with his own chaos inside.

It's all right, Luke. It's going to be all right.

The 'all right' carried a sarcastic echo. There'd been a place, those Hubble pictures, the Horsehead Nebula, Luke had said, years ago. Two white lights like roses.

He made himself stop. He was losing it. Get a grip. (Lois? Missy, are you seeing this?)

Cheryl had made up one of the spare bedrooms on the second floor but Luke had said, No, *this* room, please. Cheryl hadn't argued. The days of looking into the whys of things like that were gone. In one corner he'd unrolled a Karimoor mat and sleeping bag. His rucksack leaned against the desk.

Nathan was remembering the day they packed all Lois's things from Roseberry Road. Cheryl had ordered the boxes, just ordinary cardboard, but plain, unused. He'd come in from the site one day and found she'd started, and without saying anything he'd helped her. He'd thought, This is the first time in ages we've done something together.

Luke mooched around the room, putting something off, Nathan knew, holding out against eruption or fracture with an effort that left him high-wire tight. For a while he stood at the bookcase, head on one side, reading the spines. *Alexander the Great. History in Education. Birds of Britain and Europe. Exeter, Roman City. The Past All Around Us.* (Nathan remembered moving in. None of the usual pleasure unpacking the books. Other moves, it had been the best bit, licence to take a leisurely wander back down his reading life. This time he'd done it quickly, barely looking at the titles.) Historyman, the kids called him, encouraged by Cheryl. They meant, as in Batman, Superman. He liked it, that they bothered, that it made them laugh.

Luke went to the desk and sat down, thinking of the funeral. Its concrete details had been surreally vivid: the stone flavour of the church; the candles' lozenges of flame; the soft wet grass and mist of rain. He'd been a pall-bearer. All the times he'd seen it on television it had looked a fuck of an awkward thing to do, carrying a coffin – and it had been, the men slightly different heights. There'd been missteps, jarring, a moment when it seemed as if everyone apart from him had let go. You noticed all these things. Your mind had no decorum. One night in the pub he'd heard a medical student claim corpses farted, the natural expulsion of residual gasses from the gut as the internal organs began to decompose. He'd thought about that, too, lugging the casket, listening. Presumably, morticians had some way of making sure it didn't happen during the funeral. You'd think Nature would give you a fucking break when you're *dead*, the medical student had said. Dearly beloved, we are gathered— *paaaarp*. Luke had laughed – genuinely – but had heard in the split second before he did so the rest of the table not knowing how he'd take it. They'd all laughed; but they'd been waiting for him, the licence he granted. The medical guy must have been one of only a handful on campus who didn't know who Luke was.

These thoughts and others like them had along with the day's perceptual details seen him through the service, the burial, the drive home. Now, though, the wake's booze had prised other parts of him open: Dad's dead. The great experiment in subtraction continued. It hadn't surprised him when Gina said she felt like pissing herself laughing. Survival was absurd to the point of hilarity. Every moment you carried on was like putting your foot out not knowing whether there'd be a stepping stone there. Every moment a part of you announced: Still here. Still here. Still here. Sometimes with a laugh, sometimes with defiance, sometimes with nothing, just robotic observation. After Lois's death he hadn't felt anything. Or hadn't known what to feel. Was there a difference? They'd all existed in a state of extremity for so long that none of the old soundings for feeling told anything, at least not to him. There was, first, a gram of relief that it was over. And there was the fascinating spectacle of his mum and dad's faces and voices suddenly revealing aspects of themselves he'd never seen before. She's dead. He'd said the words to himself in his head. Lois is dead. It was as if an invisible weight had been taken off. As if his head had cleared. How could that have been an acceptable feeling to have?

Nathan, so close now that there was an effect like the transfer of body heat (it loosened him, let him unspool slightly into Luke's thinking), could tell there was something against which all this was pitched as a diversion.

It's all right. Whatever it is, it'll be all right.

It wasn't all right. It required constant self-distraction. Luke was trying to remember at what age he'd stopped kissing his father goodnight. Eight? Nine? Had he made some formal declaration? Then the big gap through the teens, everything awkward. Then, with relief, curiously undifficult hugs at the hellos and goodbyes of visits home from university. They'd been comfortable with that, thank God. They'd navigated both being men. That was the sort of thing time was for, to allow you to come to the right level of physical contact with your dad. Something, at least, that they'd come to that.

Nathan remembered it, too, the withdrawal of the boy's body with the onset of puberty, no more clambering or jumping. He'd missed keeping the casual check on muscle and bone, strength, skill. (Some genetic directive, he supposed, to make sure you were sending out good stock.) Cheryl had teased him again with Freud: he doesn't play with you any more because he wants to kill you. And sleep with me, she didn't need to add. Yes, of course, Nathan had said, if you go in for that sort of thing. That sort of thing or not, he'd missed the contact, the way Luke used to come in with red cheeks and cold hands and the smell of clean mud or freezing pavements on him. It was pain not to be able to scoop him up, to feel the life and trouble of him, to stay (literally, he now realised) in touch.

Luke lit a Marlboro, thinking briefly of the photograph he'd seen not long ago of a pair of cancerous lungs. At the funeral service, the priest had said: All of you will have different memories of Nathan, and though today it's the memories that make his absence acute, in time those same memories will be a great comfort. Luke had thought it a strange thing to say, since the priest knew nothing about Nathan, nor what memories any of his family and friends might have of him.

Luke had nearly laughed out loud in his pew. He'd been thinking of the day his mum had walked in on him wanking in the bathroom. Her face, then her saying, Oh shit, then covering her mouth with her hand too late, then, Shit, sorry, sorry, and all the while looking and trying to not look, in fact turning away but of course seeing everything. Couldn't have lasted longer than three seconds. How old had he been? Eleven? Twelve? He'd spent the rest of the day self-imprisoned in his room, hot with shame. Cheryl had come up and knocked, saying, It's all right, love, honestly, but he couldn't face her. Eventually, late in the evening, after ignored calls down for tea, his dad had come up and demanded, quietly, to be let in. And because he'd assumed this was it, that *punishment* was coming and it was better just to get it over with, he'd unlocked the door and let him in. (Nathan remembered. Luke's face warm as a new loaf, the look of surrender to deserved fate. The room had been filled with evening sunlight, everything still. Nathan had had to stop himself putting his arms around his son and telling him that he loved him.) Luke had sat on the bed with his knees up, fingers laced around shins, head down, face hidden.

It happened to me, too, his dad had said, then laughed.

Half horrified, half fascinated, Luke had listened as his dad, standing looking out of the bedroom window with his hands in his pockets, told him how, when he was about Luke's age, he was walked in on in his bedroom – 'doing what you were doing today' – by *his* mum, Grandma Lil, whom Luke had never known. The story went that he'd heard her coming in at the last second and leaped off the bed, made a dash – trousers still unfastened, private parts still on display – for the box room, which adjoined his and which was where the washing was hung to dry on a clothes maiden.

Luke had sat with his head down and listened with a mixture of relief and horror. Relief because obviously nothing bad was going to happen to him, nothing punitive, but horror because the thought of his dad doing what he'd been doing today was . . . what? Shocking? Ugly? Deflating?

Definitely an admission of weakness. Could *Mum* know? It was incredible.

That wasn't the worst of it, his dad had continued, still not looking at him. Grandma Lil had followed him into the box room and begun hanging the washing. The only way he could keep his back to her was by facing the window. He couldn't fasten his trousers without her seeing, so he had to stand there, holding his trousers up with his hands in his pockets, exposed, in full view of anyone passing in the street below. For ages no one did pass. Meanwhile Grandma Lil chatted away, asking what he'd done at school and whether he had any homework . . . Then Mrs Clements from the fish and chip shop walked by and looked up.

'Got quite a surprise,' his dad had said, chuckling, 'to see me standing there at the window. Flashing.'

Luke had laughed. Couldn't look at his dad – and if he had been able to he would have seen that his dad, though smiling, couldn't look at him, either. It was extraordinary. A new shameful allegiance against Mum, Gina, Lois. Him and his dad – then The Girls. The notion that any of The Girls might do what he'd been doing today (or that there might be a female version of it at all) never entered his head. Instead, he was filled with a new sense – something funny and weak, exciting and only very slightly dirty – of being male; the first real recognition of a giant denominator common to him and his dad. Something to be proud and ashamed of.

At the door, his dad had said: 'It's all right, you know. It's nothing to worry about or feel guilty about. It's normal. Everyone does it. Just got to make sure you're in private, that's all.'

Luke chain-lit another Marlboro. He'd wanted to tell the

story at the funeral. In church. From the fucking pulpit. Fucking priests.

The good memory, Nathan could feel, had dragged anger up with it. Or fear. Something, the thing it was taking all Luke's energy to avoid thinking about. Nathan was afraid himself. There was a signal from somewhere. It had begun, like the houseflyish interference of earlier, to register on him, peripheral but insistent. Potential to drive you, if untraced, mad. Luke looked terrible. He'd left crying behind a long time back, to judge from the face and the dead shoulders. His lips were dry and the afternoon's wine had blackened them. Fingernails bitten to the quick. On top of the fear, Nathan was irritated: what the fuck was Cheryl doing about this? Was she talking to him? To Gina?

Luke reached down, opened the rucksack, and took out a small wooden box.

Signal source.

Nathan, uneasy, went closer.

The wood was cherry, hand-carved, inlaid with dots of what looked like ivory. Not the sort of thing Luke would be interested in owning. Signal strong and mean, now, full of barbs. Lois had been the one for natty little things. He was stalling. Luke opened the lid to——

Nathan doesn't know the shop. Looks like it's in an arcade. Wood crafts and silver jewellery. Interior lighting of tiny, pinkish, headache inducing spots on steel rails that give the place a Christmassy look. Five or six browsers, but it's small enough for that to feel like a crowd.

Luke's in there in jeans and a second-hand parka, looking hot and tired, a plump stye on his left eye. His hair's longer, the way it was a year ago. (Gina'd teased him that he was turning into a hippy a generation too late. Even at the time Nathan had thought, no, it's just another thing he's forgotten about.) He's thinking, among other things, of the way Lois's face used to look when he told her highly improbable (but often true) Amazing Facts of Science. The planet Saturn would float on water, if you could find a sea big enough. She wanted the most outlandish things to be true. That was the face: the look of wanting something to be true but not wanting to forget all the times before, when it had turned out they were making it up. They. Him and Gina, that was. When she was very young they used to tell her she was adopted. Which summoned a different face: watch her slip incrementally into horror. Never satisfied until she was on the verge of tears. Cruelty. He used to be amazed they could do it. Convinced he never would have on his own if it wasn't for Gina. Once Gina started he had to join in. But they were kind to Lois, too. Made things for her. His origami fad. Birds, fish, little paper boxes. He'd given her endless piggybacks, skinny legs over his shoulders and hard little belly pressing against the back of his head. Used to pretend he'd gone blind and start staggering about, veering away from things at the last minute. She loved it. Her giggle was too old and husky for her, slightly obscene. Lois laughs like a mad old granny, Gina said.

Without really thinking, he's picked up and opened a little wooden box. Miniature dominoes packed into the inside of the lid, miniature backgammon in the main compartment. All very prettily made. Sort of thing Lois would have loved.

As soon as he thinks this he knows he's going to have to steal it. That's the way it's been: a moment comes when he knows he *has* to. Adrenalin floods him. He knows how it'll feel, the point of no return as he pockets the box and makes his way to the door. That's the thing, the essence of it, the addictive element, that feeling that once you cross the threshold you've done it, you're guilty. If they catch you certain things will happen, certain things . . .

He doesn't even look round to see if he's being watched.

Nathan came out to find Luke sitting back in the chair with the box open on the desk in front of him, some of the dominoes scattered near his right hand. Second Marlboro gone. Had he known? He *done* anything about it?

Luke replaced the dominoes, closed the box and returned it to his rucksack. For a moment he sat still. Then, remembering the way at primary school if you said you didn't feel well you were allowed to sit slumped forward with your head on the table, he bent and rested his cheek against the desk. Nice, that smell of old wood, cold, too, like balm. There were all these sense memories, everyone had them, you couldn't get rid of them. What were you supposed to do with them? They went nowhere when you died, unless you'd told someone, and even then it wouldn't be the same. Before the day his dad had told him jerking off was nothing to feel guilty about, he'd been convinced there was something wrong with him. Then the epiphany: no, it was all right.

Luke raised his head, slowly.

There was something else, Nathan knew. He couldn't get it, couldn't get any closer. It was worse than with Gina. He didn't know how much longer he could stand it. And when he couldn't stand it, what then? How much worse did it get?

The dead can see everything, Luke thought. Or would be able to, if there were an afterlife. He hadn't been brought up with one, except for Grampy's rubbish about Heaven and Hell, which in any case had been completely undermined by his mum and dad's obvious non-belief. Or his mum's obvious non-belief, anyway. His dad hadn't quite shucked it, he thought.

He reached down to the rucksack, one of the outside pockets, brought out an old brown envelope.

Can you see this, Dad?

If you look in the right places, Dad, you'll see.

The door opened and Frank came in.

Luke's eyes closed. He'd loved his grandfather as a child. Fishing. Boxing tips. Every now and again the old man made an appeal to all that. Sometimes Luke could fake a response, other times, weighed down by all the ways he'd changed, he couldn't. In which case he'd get irritated by Frank, snap, feel like shit afterwards.

'What you doing, Cool?' Frank said.

'Nothing, Grampy.'

Without urgency, Luke bent and returned the brown envelope to his rucksack pocket. Frank didn't notice.

'I keep turning it over in my mind,' Frank said. 'Keep looking at it to try 'n' see, you know?'

'Yeah. There's nothing to see, I don't think.'

'Are we cursed? D'you think there's such a thing as a curse?'

'I don't know, Grampy,' Luke said. He wasn't up to this. The 'Cool' had rankled. *Cool Hand Luke.* Frank was the only one who still used the nickname. They'd all called him that, for years, long before Luke had seen the film. He'd been about thirteen when he finally did, one Easter when Frank was staying with them at the old house. BBC2, late; they'd all stayed up. Luke had surrendered to it completely, the cruelty of the prison, the violence, the repeated crushing of good-ness, the triumph and sadness of the egg-eating, the moment of appalling eroticism when the girl washes the car. But the scene that had brought him back into the living room was the one in which the screen Luke's dying mother, Arletta, comes to see him. She tells him she's leaving the farm to his brother, John, not because he's earned it, but as compensation for not having been loved by her as much as he, Luke, has been. Sometimes you just have a feelin' for a child, she rasps.

Luke thought about it now, how *his* mum and dad hadn't looked at him, or at each other, or anywhere except at the screen, and how none the less the room had filled with them not saying anything. It was as if he'd caught them doing something dirty. For a few minutes the atmosphere had remained, then the narrative had taken them again and it had been all right.

But 'Cool' had faded from use. Only Frank persisted, and now that Luke was old enough for irony it didn't matter. Just made him feel sorry for and irritated by Frank.

Frank didn't know what to say. He'd wanted to make a connection but the moment had come and gone. He sud-denly felt dog-tired, unwanted, sorry for himself. A lot of his good intentions ended up like this these days.

'You should eat something,' he said. 'There's all that food your mum's put on.'

'Yeah, I will in a bit, Grampy.'

'Come and have something to eat.'

'In a bit.'

'Come and pour me out a drink, then, will you? I can't see to do it properly.'

Luke squeezed his jaws together for a moment, then relaxed.

'Okay,' he said. 'We'll make it a double, shall we?'

Nathan stayed put after they'd gone out. The envelope? Hadn't liked the shift in Luke just then.

But nothing came.

Sometimes you just have a feelin' for a child. Nathan had forgotten the *Cool Hand Luke* evening. Or buried it. You think they don't pick up these things but they do. He caught the zooish smell again, around himself, his own shame – and from it an acute feeling of his visibility to Lois. She'd had three years to watch them all, find out who loved whom. How much.

Some things are disgusting to consider, he'd said to Cheryl. You mean terrifying to consider, she hadn't needed to correct.

From which came a feeling of the exact dimensions of his failure, as a father, a husband, a teacher, a man, a human being. He thought of a fancy gift box unpacked flat so that its whole area was visible at a glance. There you are, that's all of it, nothing exceptional. Ordinary. He remembered Gina, her expanding to accommodate her own strangeness. This was shrinking to fit your own deficiencies. One was for the living, the other for the dead. It relaxed him for a moment. Was it comfort?

Whatever it was, there was still Luke. The stealing didn't matter (as long as he didn't get caught), only the misery that drove it. Although of course he *would* get caught, just a matter of time. Survivors committed crimes to get caught and punished for the worse crime of having survived. Pop psychology, but Luke was the type for it, he supposed. Those nightmares when he was a kid. Plus that phase when he was maybe six or seven or eight of holding on to his shit, refusing all attempts to get him to go then eventually more often than not messing his pants. The doctor had said he'd grow out of that, too (standard line in those days; no doubt all sorts of alternatives now) and he had, but Nathan and Cheryl had known it was their fault, and had been relieved when the phase passed. Cheryl had left Freud out of it. Freud was for teasing Nathan, not for real life.

If it was just the stealing Nathan wasn't worried. Gina'd get him to stop, even if Cheryl wasn't doing anything. (Did she know? Was she talking to him? To Gina?) But it wasn't just the stealing, obviously. Can you see this, Dad?

The rucksack was where Luke had left it, down by the desk. Nathan approached it. Amazing what you couldn't do without hands, or feet, or anything else. Not knowing what would come of it – staggering compression of all his son's journeys or some phantom correlate for the stink of his socks – Nathan sent himself through the pack.

Nothing. Faintest version of the irrigator mist. He circled, looked for a trailing spar. Still nothing.

If you look in the right places, Dad, you'll see.

Her, or himself supplying her voice? Maybe she was trying to show him but they wouldn't let her? They? The powers that be. Whoever ran the withheld place.

Listen to yourself now, will you.

What *are* the right places, Lo?

His diary was in the top left drawer of the desk. If you keep a diary, Cheryl had said, I'll read it. Just so you know. It's wrong and disgusting, but I'm telling you if you leave writing lying around I'm going to read it. I can't help it. He hadn't worried. He'd had nothing to hide, and in any case it was only an appointments diary. But if Lois had been sick, or in and out of hospital, it might show. And if he'd had to go somewhere or meet someone close to the end of August.

He tried to open the drawer by thinking it. Come on. Nothing. Come *on*. Jesus. Fuck it.

Hadn't believed for a moment he could, which was perhaps the problem. Either way, he didn't have what it took.

There was a welter of feelings available to throw over the one he didn't want (fear: the longer you go on not remembering, the worse it's going to get); he chose irritation: the study was dead. Nothing. His own place and it had given him nothing. So he worked on a local dig. *And*?

Lois? Is there something here I'm missing?

He didn't expect an answer – but he didn't expect what he got, either: a vivid image of the Roseberry Road living room at Christmas, all of them seated looking at Lois, who, mouth tightly closed, was shaking her head and making indecipherable gestures with her hands. Charades.

The image vanished, but the feeling remained. No words, only actions. He and Cheryl drove the kids mad, they were so hopeless at charades. Luke was hampered by shyness, but he was orderly. Gina was quick at guessing but deliberately oblique in her mimes. Lois was the best, but was driven to shrieking distraction by the grown-ups' inability to stay focused, to keep the words they'd got, to remember the order, not to throw out so many guesses that when one of them was right they'd already made three more by the time they realised and then had to be dragged backwards.

He still wouldn't let himself believe it. If he committed to the belief she was with him and it was shown false, the loneliness would drive him mad. He thought of the two voices in *Psycho*. Norman Bates needed his mother so much he gave half himself over to becoming her. Nathan Clark and his daughter. He didn't want to think about need. There's what you need and there's what you want, Cheryl had written. There may be a universe out there in which they're one and the same thing, but it isn't the universe I live in.

Conceding that the room had nothing else for him, Nathan turned and headed for the closed door.

Wrong again.

There ought to be a smell to go with this, he thought, camphor, or whatever the dentist's was full of. The two rosettes of light appeared within moments. They didn't retain their shape for long but stretched and straightened into ingots, one (once he'd managed the trick of imposing spatiality again) to his left, the other to his right. *Bricks* of light now, the one on the left lying flat like a bed, the one on his right standing upright like a domino or a door.

No, not *like*. On the left, the light resolved itself categorically into a fiercely starched, white-linened bed with one corner turned back, while on the right it hardened into what was beyond doubt a door. In fact, this was a room: floor, ceiling, four walls, all white, frostily lit by a single overhead bulb, no windows. Institutional neutrality. And there now *was* the fug of camphor.

He wanted to get into the bed and go to sleep. The sheets looked to be the unnaturally crisp and papery sheets of hotel beds. The rest he'd enjoy reached out to him and filled him by degrees with the promise of its quality. All he had to do was get in, lie down and close his eyes. He luxuriated, turning the possibility over.

On the other hand there was, it couldn't be denied, the door. Wooden, four-panelled, white gloss, brass knob;

friendly, all in all, but absolutely not responsible for what you might find should you open it.

There was a philosophical story about a hungry ass faced with two equidistant and identical bales of hay. Unable to decide which one to tuck into, the animal starved to death.

Agitation, unease, discomfort, dread. He'd always had a particular fear of being burned alive; the time, long or short, which must surely be spent having to imagine the heat before the heat reached you and imagination was no longer necessary.

With an effort, Nathan took the third way and back-pedalled, understanding that there'd be only so many times he'd be allowed to do this.

Adrian

Emerging on the other side of the study door (was he imagining it or was there abrasion and the fizz of depletion when he did that now?) he almost collided with Cheryl. She was walking away from Adrian, fast. Adrian took three longer strides and grabbed her elbow at the foot of the stairs.

For a second it looked to Nathan as if Cheryl was going to slap Adrian. Her face said it, and the stiffened hand. But she just looked at him and he let go.

'Sorry,' Adrian said.

'There isn't a conversation waiting to be had,' Cheryl said.

'Not now I know but—'

'Not ever.'

She looked at him for a moment, then turned away and started up the stairs. Nathan knew the face: self-containment that made whether you lived or died a matter of indifference. (Well, he *had* died. Now what?) Adrian followed her. He's desperate, Nathan thought. She shows you two-thirds of herself and keeps the rest. Serves you right, Ade, you lousy bastard.

These thoughts, yes, but not much of the jealousy he'd been expecting. The rancour was partly for show, for himself, for *form*. Maybe he'd spent the genuine bitterness before he died? The study's irritation worked here, too, its grist this time Ade's twittering masculinity still wanting something from her (and still as she went up in front glancing at her arse big and hard in the funeral dress for flashbacks to that morning, the way all the years of having to imagine her had been finally knocked over like a stack of coins and there she was on all fours, naked, necessarily disappointing until he'd let the idea of her and her adultery take over) still bothering about his own guilt in a way she'd left behind years ago.

'Cheryl, for fuck's sake.'

Adrian, queasy from going up too fast on the morning's booze, halted on the first-floor landing. Cheryl, two stairs up the next flight, stopped and turned. Sun came in from the landing window and shrank her pupils, upping the proportion of green to black. Pepper and emerald, Nathan said. Gina, too, that joke feline streak. Lois and Luke had eyes like his own, dark as prunes.

'Listen,' Cheryl said, coming down the two steps, close to Adrian, frightening him. 'We know everything there is to know.'

Adrian was leaning slightly away from her. She looked exhausted, scraping the empty barrel of tolerance for men. 'Don't ask me to talk about anything. Understand.'

An instruction Adrian couldn't follow. Nathan knew. He was still in the old world where, no matter what, you talked about it, believed words were up to the job, tried.

Cheryl turned from him and went up the next flight of stairs without looking back.

Adrian wandered into the middle of the landing. He looked old. For a few moments he just stood there, hands hanging. Then he went to the door to the spare room and pushed it open.

Nathan followed him in.

One window, east facing, stripped floorboards, a dress rail on wheels occupied by Cheryl's clothes, half-unpacked boxes, shoes, an ironing board. Two or three faint signals, one strong from one of the boxes, but something from Adrian, too; Nathan didn't know if he wanted it.

Adrian lit a cigarette, shakily

nothing we can't shit on that's our great achievement oh get off your fucking high horse it's not humanity its you

Meanwhile the box's signals swiped at and missed Nathan like giant hands. There was a finite amount of dodging available.

The shame-stink off Adrian was terrible, pathetic, as when you caught the whiff of a tramp, close up. Underneath the revulsion sadness because you recognised suffering, whatever else was true.

Signals like the Gorgon's snakes around the poor bastard's head. Sooner or later, Nathan supposed he was going to——

Same room, same bits and pieces, different time. One difference is that the window's roller blind is down, softening what would otherwise be dazzling sunlight. The other is that Adrian's in here, struggling into his clothes. Voices from the room next door. Adrian's thinking, all these years, all these *years*, and in particular he's thinking of the time he and Nathan went camping with Victor Gibson from school, who, they discovered, talked, nonsensically, in his sleep. One night they'd slept in a barn. (Smells of hay and dried dung; summer night air; a hole in the roof showing Prussian-blue sky and a scatter of stars.) In the small hours, Adrian and Nathan awake, talking quietly, Victor had sat up in his sleeping bag, blinked a few times, said: 'He was like a peanut. He kept falling over,' then lain back down and returned to silent sleep.

It was the little pause, the second of rapture before they both burst out laughing, that united them in absolute joy. That moment was the jewel in which time stopped, perfecting everything, including the knowledge that they were young, and that the world hadn't yet got its hands on them.

Afterwards, with the laughing and Victor waking up and the further delight in having to tell him the story, self-consciousness crept back in, and though it was still very good it wasn't the perfection of that one moment before. But there had *been* that one moment, and each of them had added it to his treasury, to be drawn on . . . to be drawn on when . . .

Well it can't be drawn on, now, Adrian thinks. He feels better with his clothes on. Getting dressed had been ugly and sad beyond belief. You wouldn't think socks and a pair of shoes could make such a difference. What you've got to do now is work out whether it's better to stay or go. Go. Get the fuck out——

Off the back of which imperative Nathan threw himself out (he was alone – had Adrian's exits past and present synchronised?) not because it was painful (he'd felt sorry for Adrian; he remembered the barn, Victor, the pause before the laugh like a big ruby) but because the signal from the cardboard box was now overwhelming. Something of Cheryl's. Sooner or later he was going to have to face her, whatever it was she had. He'd struggled with something, coming up the stairs; Adrian's flick of lust, the flash via his playback of Cheryl's sexual self. Nathan had sensed the damage that might do if he let it loose on himself, the memory of how thick they'd been, husband and wife, years of it, the greedy pigs they'd been with each other in the sack, carnal surfeit and the nuanced places beyond. For a moment on the stairs the fear of her coldness had split and given him a glimpse – an alternative fear – of what the pain of wanting her in that way now would be like. He remembered the stab of belly-hunger the thought of his lost body had brought on. A version of that. Worse. The unbearable rubbing of wakefulness and exhaustion, an insomnia, open-ended.

Cheryl's perfume was in here, on some of the clothes; her history in shoes. She'd gone through a phase of not minding keeping her shoes on for sex, then had got slightly depressed at the gimmick's repeated efficacy. She'd never minded doing things that turned him on. She'd just minded their infallibility. Sexual repetition depressed women, Nathan thought (circling the open cardboard box, around which a signal rotated like a single blade of a fan, cutting the air with a *whup*), whereas sexual repetition gratified men. Ditto Indian food (he knew this was absurd and that he was just waiting to catch the blade's swing right): men found a curry they liked and ordered it every time. Women, having found one, kept risking disappointment by trying other things on the menu. How many times hadn't he been through it with Cheryl? Have the pasanda – you *like* the pasanda, for fuck's sake. But no (there was, he saw, a slew of manuscript pages and publishers' letters in the box), she'd do something insane. I think I'll try the Keema Genghis. And then see? *See?* I don't know why you can't stick with what you know you like. Because it's anti-life, she said. That was her handiest reduction, for life or anti-life——

Catching the blade hurts, in the phantom insides. None the less the tangent throws him into the living room at the Roseberry Road house, winter, five o'clock, dark. One set of fairy lights across the mantelpiece (Christmas over but they've all agreed they like them there so fuck it) and a scatter of pine needles in the bay window. New Year. The millennium's been and gone and the world's just the same. Gina's in her penultimate year of St Catherine's, sneaking her self round the edges of the claret and grey uniform via streaked hair, jewellery and mascara. She sits at the dining table peeling an orange and browsing through the *TV Times*. Luke's got five-a-side. Lois has gone swimming. An hour and a half in which Nathan, with a cup of tea, can relax with the *Guardian*'s review section from Saturday before he'll have to go and pick her up. Her, Claire, Gayle, and the other one with permanently raw nostrils whose name he can't for the life of him remember, and who's in real danger if she but knew it of being addressed by him in a lapse as Nostrils.

There's a piece about Holocaust denial he's been saving, but he can't concentrate. In a minute, Cheryl'll be home from work and there's the letter. There have, of course, been letters plural over the years. *Thank you for showing us your novel.* (One now legendary, with the typo *navel*) *Unfortunately, it's not really what we're looking for at the moment. We wish you the best of luck in placing it elsewhere.* Umpteen variations thereof. Nathan's watched Cheryl's evolution as a rejectee. These days she can tell from the weight of the envelope, she says. He gets very wound up, waiting, and ostensibly more depressed than Cheryl when it turns out to be a No. It's made her impatient with him. Look, she's said, this is the way it is: I won't die if I never get published. It's not the be-all and end-all. Just let me get on with it and accept that I can handle these letters without you flinging yourself around and sighing and kicking the telly. But he knows her better than that. It isn't the be-all and end-all, but without it she's still burning, slowly. He wants it for her, because he loves her, but because he loves her he's scared of what'll happen if she gets it. Her other life, her *writing* life, is already like a succubus or extra-marital lover.

'What's on telly, Gee?' he says, giving up with the Holocaust.

Gina's got GCSEs next year. (Not at Nathan's school; all three kids have gone to St Catherine's. None of them could have stood the trauma of sharing a classroom with their dad.) She'll get nine or ten, the family knows, but still, she's visibly heavy of limb since term started. Her tolerance for authority expired a year ago and now, confronted with teachers she believes she's got the measure of, she's silent and contemptuous. If they tell her off she just listens, staring at them. For this reason, and because the idea of having to divide his colleagues into those who would and would not fuck his daughter given the chance (the boys don't fancy her yet but the men would be seeing what she had about now), Nathan's relieved she's not with him at Whitecroft.

'Rubbish,' Gina says. 'No films.' Then after a pause, 'They shouldn't put the films on at Christmas. They should wait till bloody mid-January when everyone's ready to slash their wrists.'

He doesn't bother about the bloody. She's lately been

admitted to his and Cheryl's (and Luke's) swearing fraternity: All right, but not in front of Lois. And be sparing with *fucks*. *Cunts*, it's been tacitly given out and understood, are for moments of combative extremis only, and certainly not to be used on anyone you're related to. Like your real cunt, Gina's reasoned, though she's stopped short of suggesting the analogy, tacitly or otherwise.

Cheryl comes in from work chilled and damp. (She's gone full-time at the Exeter Volunteer Bureau, where she gets paid to co-ordinate volunteer workers and the organisations that need them. I'm not doing Good Work, she insisted when Adrian teased her about finally having developed a social conscience. I'm just the person who tells the people who *want* to do Good Work what number to ring.) Nathan and Gina hear the front door open and close – then the pause, which means Cheryl's seen the letter on the phone shelf. The two of them look at each other, Gina with an orange segment halfway to her mouth, Nathan with his face screwed up.

Cheryl coughs. They hear her pulling off her gloves and unzipping her coat. Then the rustle, tear and unceremonious yanking out of paper. Silence. Five seconds. Ten. Twenty. Nathan can't bear it. Half a minute. Gina's eyes have gone wide. It doesn't usually take this long.

Cheryl comes into the living room holding both letter and savaged envelope in one hand.

Nathan knows before she says it, because in her eyes there's triumph and sadness and an apology that it's so separate from him and means so much to her.

'Ma?' Gina says.

'They want it,' Cheryl says——

Out again, he couldn't tell whether he'd withdrawn himself or been as before centrifugally flung. Either way there had been a weird . . . what? Visual effect? Something at the tail end. He'd seen himself turn to the window, into which in a silent second his image had stretched, like pulled chewing gum, while everyone else in the room remained normal. The image origin – himself, sitting in the armchair – was clear and distinct, but the stretched aspect was an unrecognisable blur of colour and line. It went out through the window into the dark and cold, following the route he'd have to take in the car to collect Lois and her friends from swimming.

He loved her after swimming, hair cursorily dried and never combed, eyes big and her skin's ghost of chlorine. How many lengths, Missy? Twenty-five. She'd be sitting in the passenger seat eating a KitKat. She could swim for ever, he believed. It gave him a feeling of great calm to watch her.

Tiredness wrapped itself round him, increased its pressure. Can't be much time left. You find you waste it. Like life.

Exhausted, he turned and went sluggishly (until a surprising abrasion hurried him) through the wall.

A slat of sunlight lay across the landing.

Aside from the bathroom there were three rooms up here: the spare he'd just been in, the master bedroom, and the room directly opposite, the one they'd made Lois's.

Lois

There had never been any question of getting rid of Lois's things. In the Roseberry Road house they'd kept her room intact, and when they moved here reproduced it in the bedroom across from theirs. They'd done it without discussion, morbidity or delusion. It was Lois's room, that was all.

Nathan noticed how quiet it was. The weather had brightened. The rain had stopped and the clouds begun to break. Sunlight threw the shadow of the window's cross at a slant along one wall. From the window, Frank was visible, taking the young man in the suit on a tour of the garden, the latter very attentive, hands in pockets, asking questions, listening, nodding. Nathan could see at a glance Frank was telling his story, the worn and elaborate narrative of being eighty and horrified by the notion of interfering in The Young People's lives.

At first there were no signals. Nothing here where everything should be. He'd half expected to find Lois sitting on the bed, bored. Where've you *been?* You've been *ages.*

But nothing.

Then there was a signal, and the effect of his sudden reception was like the time years ago when he'd at last managed (with the aid of drops that fizzed and a curious rubber water-squirter) to dislodge from his left ear a plug of wax which for days had made him partially deaf. Sound had rushed back in and upset his balance. He'd lifted one leg off the floor and almost fallen over. Cheryl had nearly choked laughing at the look on his face. Now, as then, the effect was vertiginous, and for a moment the meanings of walls, ceiling and floor went missing.

He adjusted, angled himself to turn it down. Chasm howl quietened to seashell whisper. It was coming from the dressing table by the window. He knew what it was.

Why do kids like stories? he'd asked Cheryl. Because there's a beginning, a middle and an end, she said. The same, every time.

You've got to concentrate.

I'll try.

As if in response the door opened and Gina came in. Another Scotch, and now (Cheryl either not in the know or past caring) a cigarette. Nathan bristled. She'd been caught smoking two or three times and on each occasion had promised after his and Cheryl's steady, reasoned, loving pleas that she not do this to herself (undermined, Nathan pointed out, by Cheryl's actually smoking a cigarette at the time), never to take another cigarette in her life. But here she was, dragging away like a veteran.

The signal dropped out of range.

He'd had an inkling even at the time that his and Cheryl's parental currency had been devalued by Lois's death, that as the surviving daughter Gina believed she'd have to absorb

Lois's share of their worries as well as her own, and that therefore half of what they made a fuss about could be taken with a pinch of salt. Now he knew the inkling had been sound. But there was more. Part of Gina saw Lois's death as his and Cheryl's failure. No reasoning behind this view; it was disinterested and structural, hard-wired, as the phrase was these days: to outlive your child was to fail as a parent. Asked, Gina would have dismissed the idea with contempt. But the contempt belonged to her conscious self. In the subconscious or impartial self, in the pure *offspring*, the logic of it was beyond question, and her loyalty to it was evident in dozens of ways. The smoking, Nathan saw, was part of it. By surviving Lois they'd forfeited a share of their authority. Fallibility which might otherwise have remained hidden for years was hurried out into the limelight for the whole world, including Luke and Gina, to see. All right, darling, shshsh, all right, it'll be all right. The bump, the bee sting, the burn. It didn't matter what: as long as either he or Cheryl was there to tell them through the pain that it would, eventually, be all right, that the world would come back to normal without them being destroyed, they'd hold on. They'd 'Be brave' – but only because no real bravery was necessary in the light of the parental promise. Shshsh, it'll be all right. But Gina and Luke had learned that it wouldn't be all right. It could be all wrong, and there was your mother down on her hands and knees with her face pressed into the carpet, shaking uncontrollably, and there was your father crying like a hysterical child, so that even in the middle of your own horror there was a further or secondary one, the meta-horror of continuing to notice things.

These, Nathan felt Gina thinking, as she sat down at the dressing table (smoking suited her, he conceded; of course she was going to smoke, she was that sort of person – ah but Christ her lungs . . .) were the two horrors at the end of *Heart of Darkness*. Everyone else in her group had agonised over it. 'The horror! The horror!': what did it mean? She'd sat in class watching Mrs Edmunds trying not to look at her. (Mrs Edmunds spent a lot of time trying not to gawp at her, and more time praying that nothing in any of the texts would come too close to what had happened.) The first horror is that there's horror. The second is that you bear it. She'd been tempted to submit just that; fuck the 2,000 words.

She's magnificent, Nathan thought again, phantomly fractured down the phantom centre of himself by love and pride. How can I have made something like this, my ordinary genes? *The Miracle of Life*. (That was the sex education film when he was at school. Cartoon sperm scurrying along a tunnel, an eerily lit Perspex model of a foetus in a womb, and, worst of all, yellowed footage of a woman sweatily giving birth. They'd started off sniggering but had been reduced to mute awe.) It *was* a miracle. Look at Gina, all the life, all the *life*.

Gina sat very still and finished the cigarette. Nathan felt her annoyance at having to get up and open the window to flick the fag-end out. She wasn't going to kill herself, all right, but my God there were all these irritations. Open the window. Think of what to eat. Consider the problem of narrative voice in 'Childe Roland'. What you needed to do was spend more – *much* more – of your life sitting still and thinking and not being bothered by anyone. If the millions ever materialised, that's what she'd do.

He edged closer. Gina was going to a memory then pulling away from it in annoyance, not at its content but at her own inability to let go of the idea that it was meaning-ful. She kept going to it and veering away in the way he'd veered away from the sexual Cheryl. Either everything meant something or nothing did, except that was just one of those things that sounded more profound than it was——

The stone circle sits on a barrow, surrounded by a shallow ditch. Six dark uprights ring a small, rectangular, stone-lined cavity at the centre. Gina and Lois stand on the perimeter. Luke's a few feet away with their parents, setting out the picnic. It's summer, hot but dull. Thunder and lightning later, if they're lucky, which will terrify their mother and make her swear, majestically. Their dad drags them to places like this. History, he goes. History, you dullards, you *dolts*.

'These stones,' Gina says, 'they've got *eyes*.' She's nine years old and afraid of them so she makes things up to frighten Lois. (Making things up about the things she's afraid of gives her power over them. If there's a vampire under the bed she gives him a name, a mum and dad, a favourite colour.) 'They're really small, like pigs' eyes,' she continues. 'They only open and look at you when you've got your back to them.'

So saying, she steps into the ring and turns to look at Lois. 'They don't like people coming in here. They're against humans. They *hate* us. Every time someone steps into this circle, these stones get *angry*.' She waits, watching Lois. 'You'll feel it when you step between them. It's like breaking through an invisible wall. Unless you're too scared to come in, which you probably are.' She turns her back on her sister, and goes towards the smaller pile of stones at the circle's centre——

★

Nathan, precariously at the very tip of what he assumed was minimum safe distance, felt Gina pull back from the memory *the awful things you said and did but it's nothing in fact it's a sort of pathetic arrogance and indulgence*

'That's a cist,' Nathan says. 'A burial chamber. In other words, there used to be bodies in there.'

Lois, who's been standing looking down into the little tomb with her hands on her knees, straightens and draws back. (She says those words give her a headache, Gina's claimed. Cist, menhir, barrow, quoit, sarcen. She's so *soft*.)

'More than four thousand years ago,' Nathan says to her, with his hands on his hips. 'What do you think of that, Missy? No one knows what they're here for.'

'Human sacrifice,' Gina says.

'Could be,' he concedes.

'See?' Gina says to Lois. 'Blood was spilled here. That's what these stones still want. *Human blood*. The blood of the innocent. The blood of the youngest child!' She darts and lunges for her. Lois screams and runs, half laughing half crying, with her sister in hysterical pursuit——

Gina tore free again, bringing Nathan with her. Outwardly no change: she sat with slumped shoulders and one arm resting on Lois's dressing table. Inwardly savaged, she struggled to compose herself. As a child she'd soaked up meanings everywhere – all the available superstitions and beliefs plus a plethora of occult principles she invented herself – yellow cars, third, fifth and eighth steps, dead flies. Cheryl had capitalised, made up insane logic or absurd myth. For a year at least Gina had believed that a devil lived in the hot-water tank in the upstairs landing cupboard, incarcerated for some mischief, and that the occasional *tonk tink tank* was him trying to hammer and chisel his way out. She'd grown up ravenous for stories and signs, the difference between her and Luke obvious: he wanted knowledge, she wanted meaning. Nathan had watched Cheryl watching Gina, seeing her own younger self and feeding it. (And thinking this, now, it stunned him that he hadn't realised how much Luke took after *him*. All the boy's science – like all his, Nathan's, history – was a fee paid so that he could be left alone with love. Luke was waiting for love just as he, Nathan, had been before Cheryl. Romantic about nothing except love; but *to* love the dedication was absolute.) Gina's model of the world had been that it was full of disguised, encoded or concealed meanings and that it gave clues to them, eccentrically. All the individual meanings accrued to a totality. You gathered as many as you could. You'd never get them all but if you devoted yourself to the quest the totality might reward you with glimpses of itself now and then. Her mother's model, genetically inherited, Nathan believed. All the deconstruction academia had pounded them with hadn't made a dint in Cheryl's transcendent moments, nor in her commitment to writing as the surest method of gathering clues. And Nathan had read Gina's journals; they might have been Cheryl's.

Then Lois——

Gina lies in the cist with her eyes closed and her hands folded on her chest. Lois and Luke stand on the edge of the burial chamber looking down at her. Gina opens her eyes and sits up. 'She is risen,' she says (as Luke has, before her), then scrambles to her feet and pulls herself out onto the grass.

'Now you,' she says to Lois.

Lois shakes her head, without much conviction.

'It's up to you,' Gina says, looking away. 'But it's the only way of breaking the curse.'

'You're making it up,' Lois says.

'Okay, I'm making it up. Last year, in the hotel near the B&B, a seven-year-old girl was found dead in her bed one morning. Her and her brother had been out here on a visit the day before. He'd gone in the cist but *she* hadn't. They found her, in her bed, the next morning, stone dead. All her hair had gone completely white. Do you know what turns your hair pure white?'

Lois doesn't.

'Terror,' Gina says, businesslike. 'Absolute terror turns human hair snow white.'

'I'll ask Mum,' Lois says.

'Mum won't know about it, stupid,' Gina says. 'The whole thing was covered up.'

'Well, how do you know about it, then?'

Gina raises her eyes in the give-me-strength manner. She puts her hands in her jeans pockets and sighs. 'Lois,' she says, 'if you don't want to do it, that's okay. It's up to you. But don't say I didn't *tell* you when you wake up in the middle of the night and find your bed surrounded by these stones, with their eyes open, *looking at you*.'

Lois, obviously miserable, peers down into the grave. She can't do it. Gina's known all along she won't be able to, and has thus brought Lois to exactly the point of agony: the antidote she must take but daren't. Lois starts to cry, quietly.

Gina pulls Luke by the hand and the two of them back away. 'You're dead,' Gina whispers, shaking her head in disbelief. 'You're *dead*.'

★

Nathan went nearer – but Gina immediately sat up straight and looked over her shoulder, up, around the room. He backed away.

Gina sat, feeling she was in a film, someone being driven off her rocker. In the last few minutes she'd forgotten her dad was dead and this was his funeral. Her black blouse and skirt reasserted themselves; she'd forgotten she was this version of herself, formally dressed, given a wide berth by people. She had a sudden intimation of the future, of herself as someone impossible to shock. She hadn't grown into it yet but it was there, the logical extension of who she was now. What mattered more than whether she'd put a curse on her sister was that she was going to stay alive to think about it, to let it have its effects. She was sure that was what Lois would want, and even if Lois didn't, she'd stay alive in defiance of her. That was the future, she realised, herself, staying alive, regardless. Your sister's dead. Your dad's dead. Your mum's gone mad. Horrors lined up in front of her like petitioners: Look at *me*. Now, are you going to die? Nope. Next.

She got up from the chair. Suddenly she wanted things: another cigarette, another drink, to see Luke, eventually Matt. She felt sorry for her Grampy, who'd been wandering around all day like an overgrown toddler, not knowing what to do with himself. She'd go and find him, ask him about the flyweight days, the old leaden gloves, the way your chin was hot-wired to your knees and you went straight down like a sack of spuds. She could talk to him about *that*.

Nathan watched her go. Her back was strong and lovely; broader than average shoulders and there were those reliable Cheryl hips. Physically strong, thank God. From what he'd seen of Matt she could snap the willowy little bastard in half. These thoughts (as she reached the door, opened it and went out) gave Nathan such an access of love that he nearly went after her. It seemed enough to forget everything else. Enough only to be around them, this way. If he'd lost the life he'd had, wasn't he entitled to this one? The moments alone with Gina just now: had he been that close to her before?

He didn't move. The signal from the dressing table was still there and it was still an act of balance to stop himself falling into it. No, not balance, resistance. Its gravity stirred irritation, as when just past the bearable level of having your hair pulled. It had taken him a moment to recognise the feeling. It had surprised him. He'd wanted Gina to stay. If you were buried alive maybe you'd spend your last air singing a song or whistling a tune. If the fuel was finite, wasn't there always the temptation to spend it on your own comfort?

The signal dipped, lifted and turned up its throb. He thought of a black hole, the slew of matter being drawn in. There were other items on the dresser: a soft shoulder bag covered in purple spangles; postcards and photos Blu-Tacked to the mirror; a hairbrush (Lo's dark hair still in it); a scatter of pesetas from their one Spanish holiday; a Piglet soft toy; a cheap jewellery box full of cheap trinkets. Nathan went everywhere around the source of the signal, holding off, testing (he told himself) his will against it. But it was pointless.

Eventually he let out the slack and drifted within range. The little stone was just as it had alwa——

They're on the beach in Dorset. A shoestring holiday, as usual, the kids if they knew it furnished with more spending money than the adults, courtesy of Cheryl's father, who uses his grandchildren to launder handouts to his daughter. It's got harder to refuse since Lois, who came too long after the other two to benefit from hand-me-downs. Generally these days Nathan and Cheryl just take what comes and swallow what used to be pride and is now habit. In any case, it always seems worth it once they see the kids let loose in big spaces where land and weather mean something.

This being one of them. Under a textbook sandstone cliff there's a long shingle beach dotted with glistening knots of kelp and bladderwrack. Litter, too, since this is England. Luke's already brought a viscous condom on the end of a stick for parental identification. Gina's had a headless Action Man and a rusty wing mirror. But there are, cheerily enough, a hundred or so partially clothed Brits displaying dreary thighs, bellies and backs, either untouched by sun or roasted by it, and as far as Lois is concerned this is heaven.

Here she comes, one tentative step after another, crunch, crunch. Long pause as she weighs for the umpteenth time the question of whether walking on this stuff isn't, in fact, *painful*. Then crunch, crunch, crunch. Nathan, lying on his back with his face turned to look down his children's wake, observes her progress. He can hardly bear it. She's six years old. The new context of sky and water re-creates her, gives her her particularity afresh. Her small head, skinny legs and faint web of veins in the ribs when she stretches. Watching the careful stepping, the concentration, he gets the twinge in his abdomen, what he's come to think of as the phantom male umbilical. Desperate love. Too much. The world's full of—no, he can't let that in. That thinking makes him frantic. The way to deal with that is to not think it. Not to ask how much do I love her and what would happen if – and you see? That thinking's cunning. It loops back in using love's gravity. Which reminds him of the Apollo 13 fiasco, those poor bastards having to slingshot round the dark side of the moon and hope for the best. But they made it. Thank God. Thank *God* – and by this stage his relief for the astronauts is just another of a thousand versions of relief that every second, every minute, every hour, his kids are still there, living and breathing, having not been run over or drowned or kidnapped – you see? That thinking in again like a slippery sonofabitch. You can't give it an inch. Not a fucking *millimetre*.

'Look, Daddy.'

Look, Daddy. He's in cahoots with her. They're interested in things together. Whereas Gina had been a peremptory little thing and his superior knowledge a temporary aberration tolerated with exaggerated patience. Gina would have said: What is this, please? Then would have all but folded her arms and tapped her foot while he explained.

'What have you got there, Missy?'

It's an unusual stone. White, flattish, but with a near perfect hole worn smoothly through its middle. Lois holds it out to him, and he notices that she's shivering. Her hair's been salted and rats'-tailed by the sea, into and out of which she'll go with him or Cheryl or Luke (not Gina, who's not to be trusted), up to her knees but no further. Nathan wants to grab her and wrap her in the huge, rough pink towel and dry her violently, to feel her shoulders and belly and feet and bum rubbed to warmth; but she's picky about being manhandled and he senses this isn't the moment. Beyond her, further down the beach, he can see Luke and Gina down on their haunches, examining something. He knows them. They're nefarious. They know what sort of things they shouldn't do, but do them anyway and accept the consequences with impatient fatalism. You *know* you're not supposed to be in here, don't you? The solemn nodding of heads, yes. But at the same time no real apology: This is our lot. Get on with the punishment, whatever it is. We've got things to do.

Cheryl, who's been lying on her front, reading, gets up and fishes out the pink towel from the beach bag. She and Nathan are sexually greedy for each other again at the moment. It's ludicrous, Cheryl jokes, at our age. Ludicrous and *obscene*. He's got it worse than her. Desire ambushes him when she's brushing her teeth or fastening Lois's shoe. Just now a glimpse of his wife's bare armpit stiffened him. He daren't look at her heavy backside in the lilac bikini bottoms. The holiday's partly responsible, salt skin and alien bed-clothes, but also the shared relief of having the last of the kids at school, finally, socially integrated without disaster. On top of which, Cheryl's started writing again. He remembers what it was like before. The Writing, and around it a hand-ful of needs she fulfilled like an animal: food, sleep, sex. The received wisdom (although where he received it from remains a mystery) was that creativity sapped energy which would otherwise be sexual. Not so Cheryl. Sometimes, in the old days, the typewriter would go quiet and within five minutes she'd be unbuttoning his pants. Fuck me. Now, please. I need it. Afterwards: Thank you. I'm off back to work. The typewriter chattering again before his cock had gone soft. He'd wanted a church to go to, to give thanks. Several times in the staff room he'd felt close to just blurting it out. Listen, my wife . . . Of course he'd told Adrian. Adrian had just said, with mock gravitas, This will all have to be paid for, you know.

'There's a towel here for you,' Cheryl says. She's good at getting them to do things. Nathan sees it time and again. She could have said, Come here and let Mummy dry you. But

122

Lois doesn't like being passive while things happen to her. This way she gets to wear the towel like a cloak. Cheryl's honed motherhood. And there's that little scribble of varicosis in her left thigh that drives him mad. Christ. How long before they can get back to the hotel?

'Look,' Lois says to Cheryl, since Nathan hasn't yet taken the stone. Cheryl wraps the pink towel round Lois's shoulders. A cloud moves in front of the sun and the beach darkens. It's been like this all day, dull silver or tepidly bleached, gooseflesh coming and going.

'What's that, then?' Cheryl says, peering at the stone but not taking it in her hand.

'A stone with a hole in it,' Lois says.

Cheryl goes in closer. 'Is that a . . . No. I thought for a minute . . . Nah.'

'What?'

'Or *is* it?'

'*What?*'

Now Cheryl does take the stone. She holds it up to the light, looks through the hole, turns it in her hand as if testing weight and smoothness. Nathan knows she's thinking something up. Gina and Luke are getting past the credulous stage and Cheryl's all but given up with them. Lois, at six, is still the right side of the cusp. Another year or two and they'll have to start doling out the truth about things even to her. Cheryl's determined to milk the time that's left.

'Well,' Cheryl says. 'Unless I'm very, *very* much mistaken . . . It looks to me like a Hermes stone.'

'A Hermes stone?'

'Umm.'

'What *is* one of those?'

'It's a stone blessed by the Greek god, Hermes.' A pause.

Lois's face scrunched in concentration. 'Long ago in the ancient days,' Cheryl says, 'there were lots of Greek gods and demigods – a demigod's when you've got one parent who's a god and another parent who's a mortal, a human – and Hermes, he was the Messenger of all the other gods on Mount Olympus.'

Lois is familiar with Greek gods. Norse, too. We've already had bad dreams about Loki under the bed. Cheryl's gently sadistic with myth, says it'll do them good in the long run, nightmares notwithstanding, but the truth is she can't help herself. Thor, Medusa, Beelzebub. The kids just stand there taking it all in. It fits. Perseus, Coca-Cola, Odin, hoovering, Jack Frost, *News at Ten*. A continuum.

Cheryl continues, 'If Zeus – he was the main god, remember? who controlled thunder?' Lois nods. 'If Zeus wanted a message taken somewhere, he sent his son, Hermes, who could run faster than the wind, to carry it. So Hermes was the god of messengers.'

Lois stands with one foot on top of the other, teeth chattering. The cloud moves away from the sun and the beach flares again. Her shoulders relax. For a moment Nathan's revisited by the old feeling of guilt that he's been given everything he wants, that he has love, that he's surrounded by honest flesh and blood – and no contribution to the world required! The teaching, yes, but he's on autopilot half the time. No *big* contribution, he means. No art, no politics, no religion, no making the world a better place. Yet here he is neck deep in wealth, all these unearned treasures.

'Now, Hermes always carried a staff,' Cheryl says. 'Do you know what a staff is?'

Lois doesn't.

'A staff,' Cheryl says, 'is a long stick, like a walking stick, but longer, about the size of a spear. Anyway, Hermes's staff was a long stick with two snakes wrapped round it – not real snakes, metal ones. The whole thing was metal. Actually, it might have been wood . . . but I think it was more likely metal. Anyway, whenever Hermes stopped for a rest on one of his journeys, he would lean on his staff, you know, to take the weight off his feet. Some of his journeys were incredibly long, thousands of miles, and even he, god that he was, did need to rest sometimes. He had a winged helmet, by the way – did I mention that?'

'No.'

'Well, he had. A helmet with wings on it, and the staff with two serpents.'

'Could he fly?'

'No. Well . . . no.'

'Why's he got wings, then?'

'They were very small wings, not big enough to fly with. But – and this is an important "but" – he could run so fast, so *incredibly* fast, that it *looked* like he was flying. His feet moved so quickly that it seemed they were barely touching the ground at all.'

Lois is seeing it.

'Now, running at that sort of speed made Hermes incredibly hot. His head was hot and his feet were hot and his helmet was hot and his fingertips were hot – and because he was a god, this was much, *much* hotter than you or I would get. His staff was hottest of all, so hot that it glowed, not red hot, but *white* hot, which is what colour things go when red hot isn't enough and they have to get hotter.'

Cheryl pauses. Lois knows this is a space in which she might be able to guess how it'll all fit together, but she can't.

'Dry your hair, Missy,' Nathan says, without much conviction.

Lois adjusts her towel-cloak so that it drapes her head, prize-fighter style.

'The tip of the staff was so hot,' Cheryl concludes, 'that wherever it rested, it burned a hole.'

Ah. When her mother tells her things it's always like this. Not really learning something new but remembering something you knew long ago. The warmth's reached her scalp now. It makes her aware of her wet hair, and she begins to rub, gently. Cheryl holds the stone up between them and peers at her through the hole.

'This is where the tip of the staff made a hole,' she says, 'miles and miles away, thousands upon thousands of years ago. The sea's washed it up here, and now it's yours. Now you've got your own personal Hermes stone.'

She hands it back to Lois, who takes it, reverentially, but still, they all know, waiting for the payoff. Six years old: she wants to know what it'll *do* for her. For a moment, seeing her dark eyes ready (and greedy) for anything, Cheryl toys with telling her it'll make her run faster. But Nathan's warning radiates (he's leery of all this wild fiction) and in any case it can't be something Lois can put to the test so easily.

'Hermes stones,' she says, 'are very rare. Very rare, in fact, because Hermes very rarely needed to rest. Lots of people have never even heard of them. But long ago it was said that these stones were blessed, and while they won't make you fly, or even run faster' – flash of disappointment – 'they *will* keep you safe on journeys, because Hermes was the god of messengers and travellers, you see. Whoever travels with a Hermes stone travels safely, that's what they used to say.'

Lois turns the stone in her hands. She's been hoping for

126

something better. None the less an image forms in her mind: a tall man the colour of a sandstorm; a desert of white rocks; a dark sky and the rumble of thunder; the curious, gently twitching wings on his helmet.

'If I were you,' Cheryl says, 'I should treasure it, and keep it secret, and keep it safe. And always keep it with you when you travel.'

Lois likes 'when you travel', confirming that one day she'll do such things independently.

'Especially,' Cheryl adds (seeing the effect of the last suggestion), 'if you choose to travel by sea.'

Nathan was pulled out, violently, by the door opening. It sent him haywire. Deafening seashell noise, him wrestling for balance, then recovery, the noise manageable. He was above the bed, upside down.

'And this is another room,' Frank said. 'Oh . . . this is . . . Well that's a room we keep my granddaughter's things in. I thought it was the spare. I get them mixed up.'

After a third or fourth false start Nathan found a manoeuvre which righted him. Phantom blood rush. You jumped off too high a wall and it felt like your feet burst when they hit the ground. It defied belief, but Frank had extended the tour to the house's interior. The young man in the suit had followed him in and was standing jingling change in his left pocket, nodding.

'It's a cracking place,' he said. 'Solid as a rock. Are the fireplaces open?'

Not his natural idiom, Nathan knew, especially that 'cracking'. This was for Frank's benefit.

'Do you know, they are,' Frank said. 'But you can give me central heating any day. You don't think so much of open fires when you've grown up lugging coal in to get them going.'

Frank was loving this. He was – Nathan saw it for the first time with a touch of incredulity – house-proud. Superficially you couldn't find greater indifference to the Clarks' rise in material fortune. Underneath, to Frank's own surprise, a little furnace of pride.

Oh, for Christ's sake, Dad.

Dad, you're not concentrating.

'Anyway I'll show you, there's another floor. They were going to have the attic converted, although converted into what I don't know. All these bloody rooms already.'

They went out and closed the door.

Suddenly the stone's signal expanded, came up close (the scene in umpteen films where someone got diced by a pro-pellor) with a warning of its strength then drew back, leaving in its wake a tunnelled drop to itself that drew Nathan to its lip.

Sorry, Lo. Sorry.

Still he hesitated, remembering (was he?) something long ago, himself paused high up, holding back from a long fall towards . . . He couldn't remember. Dream, maybe. In any case he *wasn't* concentrating. Jesus. I'm trying, Missy.

But he thought it with a little shiver of duplicity: he was reluctant. He thought of the image he'd based his resolution on, to stay facing the living. This felt like turning the other way, to the drop.

He forced himself to think of Lois, waiting. One second of phantom nausea – then a plunge of supergravity, the room's other objects rushing up past him like fireworks and in his head the sound of himself screaming—

Lois and her swimming chums come out of the leisure centre and walk from the car park to a brick bus shelter where three boys on BMX bikes are waiting. Her hair's still wet and her head's cold in the January evening air. She's nervous, because her dad's expressly forbidden her to do anything when she's finished swimming except wait inside the leisure centre, either in the foyer or in the snack bar, until he comes to collect her. Disobeying makes her feel terrible because as well as loving her parents she likes them and knows they think of her as a good and responsible girl who wouldn't do anything stupid. Which she is and which she wouldn't, normally. It amazes her, actually, that she's out here, that all the love and liking and responsibleness isn't, when it comes down to it, sufficient to resist Gayle and Dominique, who've been slightly idiotic about these boys since they met them for the first time three weeks ago. The second week, Gayle went a few yards off with one of them and snogged him for what seemed to Lois an age but which was in reality only a couple of minutes. The whole thing had been bizarre and completely natural. All the conversation between them and the boys (although Lois and Claire were pretty quiet) took the form of sceptical questions and contemptuous answers, as if the last thing any of either group wanted was to be intimate with any of the other. And yet, when Nick (a dangerous-looking dark-haired boy with fierce green eyes and soft, moled skin) asked Gayle to come over there with him for a minute, there'd been only a cursory or pantomime rally of disbelieving refusal and contemptuous daring before she went. Last week, Dominique had gone, too, with Neal, or 'Nee' as they called him (not as good-looking as Nick, but cleverer, conscious, it seemed to Lois, of the ugliness of the way they had to go about all this); which had left Rob, who wasn't good-looking at all (flinty features and a blond skinhead, with earrings in both ears) and who sat on his bike with his forearms resting on the handlebars, smoking roll-ups and spitting through a gap in his teeth. Lois isn't going anywhere near him, and Claire isn't ready for any of them, but still, it's intriguing, the otherness of them, not to mention the fascinating spectacle of the snogging.

The bus shelter's backed by a bank of grass and a three- or four-deep line of birch trees. It surprises Lois that they don't bother going *behind* the trees. But they don't. There's Gayle and Nick a few yards to the left; Dominique and Nee a few yards to the right. In the middle, Rob, smoking and spitting, and her and Claire, standing with their arms folded under their burgeoning breasts and their wet scalps aching with cold——

Nathan struggled up but knew he wouldn't make it to full consciousness. There had been nightmares like this, dreams from which he'd clawed up to the overhang of wakefulness telling himself for God's sake don't fall asleep again, only to sink back down to where it was all waiting for him.

He had a couple of seconds. Lois's room returned, as if projected onto the inside of a conical screen surrounding him, then he was——

As yet there's no connection for Lois between the theoretically sexual world into which she's edging – boys, snogging, 'relationships', as the magazines call them – and her own private sexual life. She doesn't think of herself *having* a sexual life, private or otherwise. It's a curious state. She's been masturbating for a couple of years, but the fact hasn't made it into her awareness. She doesn't retain the concept between the acts. It's a third thing, separate not only from boys, snogging, 'relationships', but from her main body of sexual knowledge. She knows, courtesy of first-year biology and Gina's heartless sex quizzes over the years, what *happens*, what goes where, how babies are made and that for most people most of the time sex isn't anything to do with babies, that it *feels nice*. But still, the other thing (except when she's doing it it's no more than a blur on the edge of consciousness) seems altogether different. She knows that this – Nick, Nee, the kissing – is supposed to connect to the feeling nice, but she has no idea that the feeling nice is supposed to be like the other thing, the other feeling nice.

She stands, turning over in her mind what she does know, while Rob spits and smokes and talks about magic mushrooms and how someone at his school died the first time he took them because he was one of those people who had an incredibly powerful allergy to them, and have they had E yet, which makes you horny as a bastard? And apparently now there's this stuff for women like Viagra that makes them come like mad bitches, and he can get some.

Lois looks at her watch. Forty-five minutes, then she's going back to the leisure centre. They've barely been in the pool. Might as well not have gone in at all. Next week she's staying in and doing her lengths. The others can come out and have their heads freeze. She'd kiss Nick, or possibly Nee – but definitely not Rob and that's final. In any case she's worried about Claire, who doesn't seem to know *any-thing*, but who soaks up the boys' mere presence like a sponge. A lot of the time in their company Claire stares and frowns, not, Lois knows, in disapproval, but in an effort to make sense of them, to take in that they really are the way they are.

'Oh shit,' Lois says.

Claire manages to tear her attention away from Rob, who's still talking quietly about drugs, and look at her.

'What?'

'I've left it in the changing room.'

'What?'

'My stone.' She's grateful it's Claire and not the others. Dominique would have laughed, made a thing of it in front of the boys, something against which her, Dominique's, own superior sophistication would be patent.

'I'm going back for it,' she says. She knows where it is. In the hurry to get changed she'd dropped her bag and its contents tumbled out onto the cubicle floor. She'd put everything back except the Hermes stone, which was to go in her coat pocket for the ride home. She'd placed it on the little wooden seat in the cubicle while she finished dressing. Then Dominique had come and asked to borrow her lip gloss, cover for a quiet allegation that Gayle had let Nick 'get his fingers wet' the second time. They'd talked in whispers. She'd left without it.

Walking back, she has a weird impulse to leave the stone where it is. To lose it, let it go. Of course, the Hermes rubbish has long since bitten the dust, but she likes habit, things from the past. She's inherited her father's sentimentality about objects, and she shares the family's passion for its own mythology. Still, the impulse is very strong. She imagines telling her mother and father, casually, one day, when one of them mentions it: 'Oh, that. I lost it ages ago.' She's not sure why the idea gives her such a thrill, and wonders what's wrong with her, since underneath or alongside the impulse is a real sickening fear that someone will have found the stone and taken it. *That* thought, someone taking it out of her life, makes her weak with premature loss, and she hurries through a tunnel of cars towards the lights——

The lights of the building's façade flared and made a portal through which in the split second before it closed Nathan hurled himself, a wall like the dirty tidal wave having gone up in him to block the lights and Lois in her anorak with the hood up and hands in pockets moving between the cars.

Sunlight filled the room. He stared out of the window. The garden glistened. That was the way it was, rain then the sun's ravishment. Rainbows. He was going through the pointless business of trying to back away from himself, the reflex that overrode reason. Naturally, every time he looked there he still was. Me and my shadow. His mum used to sing that to him, creepily, to tease him; she widened her eyes and made strange movements with her meaty arms. Some sort of child prescience, he supposed, because now here they were, the Nathan shadow trying to form conclusions and the Nathan me trying to give it the slip, noticing the wet garden, the sunlight, all the time sidling away. There'd been an idiotic bestseller: *Wherever You Go, There You Are*, something like that.

What's the most important virtue, Dad? Truth. Cheryl's confident dismissal. Courage.

He turned from the window (more of a haul than a pivot, something that dragged time and burned fuel) again expecting to see Lois sitting on the bed, hands in her anorak pockets, hood up. I was showing you. Why did you go?

She wasn't there. If she had been, what look would she have given him?

Lo?

Nothing.

Lois?

Despite its creaking special effects her favourite film had been *Jason and the Argonauts*. The *Argo*'s wooden figurehead was the goddess Hera, who, when called upon by Jason, signified sentience by opening her wooden but heavily made up eyes. *This is the third and last time I can help you, Jason.*

Time wasting. At the end of it he'd got no further from himself, neither the conclusion – you were in it and you came out – nor the question it begged: why?

In the air-raid shelter his pulse had throbbed in his ears. The darkness and stink an intelligence that pressed him on all sides. He'd forgotten the two boys, the logistics, gone down to elemental fear. *I can keep you like this for ever*, the intelligence said, *and every moment worse. There's another moment . . . another . . . another . . .*

He stopped himself. The adult could, apparently, even the dead one.

Stop and think. Come on.

He put this tone on as he might have shrugged on a leather jacket that had been through a lot with him. It helped. Maybe he hadn't come out voluntarily? The signal was dead, after all, the stone on the dressing table returned to innocence. Lo's swimming night, Luke was at five-a-side and Cheryl got in late. Either he or Gina cooked or ordered from Murghal Spice. The night Cheryl got the letter.

Pause.

God, Dad, you're so *slow*, Gina used to say, when some quiz-show logic or soap sub-plot passed him by. You're so *retarded*. No wonder you're a teacher.

★

He didn't hurry, exactly, but what would have been adrenalin rushed him as he pushed through the closed door (which hurt slightly this time, like a plaster being pulled off) across the landing and through the door (again tearing; at this rate there'd be real pain soon) and into the spare room, where, like a violent booby-trap the box's signal smashed sideways into him and dragged him under——

In the hall he puts his arms round Cheryl and kisses her, though the truth is he's wondering how long he's got before the discrepancy this must establish between them – novelist and state comp. history teacher – will start to do damage. Her face is still cold from outside and even with his guts tightening the kiss detonates a small sensual charge. But the world he imagines she's now entitled to – parties, artistic men, recognition – rears up like a glittering and merciless dragon and there's nothing for him to do except stand and hope he's enough.

Cheryl knows all this. It came with the publisher's letter, along with a disinterested voice that said: A lot of this'll have to change. Novels don't come out of a husband and three kids. You and I both know you've been dreading this, the licence to live properly, by which you and I both know we mean dangerously, ravenously and with unstinted curiosity. Get out and hurt and beatify yourself, shove yourself through things. It won't come without damage and loss. Unless of course we're talking about a *hobby*. On top of which there's the fear, the sickness that follows in the wake of any bit of good luck, anything that suggests she has a destiny, that all these years she's been right about herself. And along with *that*, grown-up scorn for passion, the voice of Cheryl wife and mother of three backed by the weight of laundry and the long trail of ordinary days. Stop making such a fuss. It doesn't mean anything except that it's happened. It might just as easily not have.

The hall's overhead light's on and they're too close to the radiator. Cheryl's got her arms round him with the envelope and letter still scrunched in one hand. She wants to say, Please don't worry. He can feel her not able to. Instead they both laugh, and avoid looking at each other.

Gina's still at the table in the lounge. The thought of her mother as a published writer makes her slightly queasy. There'll be daughters in the books, sex, her friends reading all about it. Christ. She's always known that the challenge laid down by Cheryl is that she, Gina, live up to her, Cheryl. It's meant intelligence, a smart mouth, abstract thinking and guarding the little flame of passion for life. Now it'll mean this, too. Getting published. It's an unspoken understanding in the family, that Gina wants to write, too. At the same time she's excited by the prospect of her mother unleashed by success. Who knows what she'll be like? Will there be money? Perhaps she'll start drinking and shagging around. It'll speed up her own sexual development, Gina supposes. The pragmatist in her, however, thinks it'll just fuck things up. Her mother'll get more complicated, which means more depressed. Her dad'll feel small. Small*er*. The cosiness'll be like a sick room. They'll stop laughing, have affairs, get divorced. Her mother'll die with regrets and she, Gina, will lie awake next to her lover thinking about how one day the letter came and her mother was never the same again, and how she, Gina, is just like her, because nothing she gets (including this lover) ever seems to be enough.

'I've got to go for Lois,' Nathan says. He keeps his nose buried in Cheryl's hair, smells faint shampoo, the outside air

136

on her skin. 'I'll pick up some goodies on the way home.' Champagne, he supposes, which he's so far only ever drunk at weddings. What he really wants right now is a whisky, chucked down fast.

'Don't tell her,' Cheryl says. 'I want to.'

It's incredible how unnatural he feels with her. He kisses her on the cheek and she squeezes his arms. Then she backs and sits on the bottom stair, knees together, feet apart, still with the letter crushed like a flower under her nose. She's close to tears. He understands: all the years, all the bits of writing time snatched in lunch hours, docked from sleep, scraped from the edges of all the other things she's had to do. She's being given what she's waited for and it isn't how she's imagined it would be. Something else dawns on him: this won't be enough, either. He's relieved and therefore ashamed.

Cheryl for the umpteenth time in her life is asking whether human beings are free agents or merely links in a determined causal chain. An explosion fifteen billion years ago, Luke's told her, from a dimensionless point of infinite mass and density. Basically dominoes toppling ever since. That's it. Is it? If it is, what credit can she take for this? Or anyone for anything? Suddenly she thinks of her father, the phone call she'll be able to make. You never believed I could do this. Well, I've done it. As soon as she thinks this she feels sorry for him. He shrinks, becomes a frightened old man who's spent his whole adult life dressing insecurity and self-hatred up in self-made-man bluster. She has a vivid image of him down on his knees with his big-skulled grey-haired head in her mother's lap, crying like a baby. A memory or a dream?

And still she sits there on the bottom stair clutching the

letter, knowing that her husband doesn't know how to be, or knows but can't carry it off.

'You all right?' he asks, picking the car keys up from the phone shelf. He asks with a laugh, the implication being that it could only be a good sort of not being all right.

'Yeah, yeah,' she says. 'Go on, otherwise she'll be hanging around with a wet head. I'm going to run a bath.'

At the leisure centre Nathan finds Claire, Gayle and Nostrils in the foyer. They look uneasy.

'Where's Lois?' he says.

Cheryl

Nathan waited a while before coming out, but there was nothing else to see. He thought of police at accident sites. Come on, now, move along, there's nothing to see. Nothing to see here.

He'd gone quiet in himself. The churchyard seemed a long time ago. Fight's gone out of him, his dad would have said. He'd thought surrendering to fear would be the worst thing. But there were other things. This, the going quiet. The feeling of loneliness. He remembered his moment of defiance, the decision not to feel sorry for himself. He didn't feel sorry for himself. Just quiet. He'd thought he was tired before. Now he was beginning to get an inkling of how much more tired he might become. The potential for his own exhaustion spread out ahead of him like a parched plain. Fascinating in its way.

Where's Lois? he'd asked. Abracadabra for the unbearable magic of those days, though even now he didn't remember them clearly. Not clearly enough for either the billions dead or nothingness to claim him, since he was still here, confronted with the world from which he'd thought the soul excused.

Lois?

Silence. Her absence defined him even now.

I'm sorry. I'm sorry.

For breaking the contract signed in blood at her birth, that she wouldn't have to die before him.

Mr and Mrs Clark lost their little girl, did you hear? Someone took her.

He found Cheryl in the office talking to the young man, her in the swivel chair behind the desk, him on the couch opposite. The cold's radius had shrunk but it was wide enough to stop Nathan at the doorway. Not quite fear, but an intuition that crossing into it would take him to something from which there would be no turning back. It surprised him (along with the depressing surprise of Cheryl apparently pleasantly tête-à-tête) that he was so easily pricked awake. Pricked to something else, too, in spite of himself – referred Adrian-jealousy? He took it for granted that the young man found Cheryl desirable (in the matter of your wife's desirability other men were guilty until proven innocent, then put on perennial parole), but what about her? Could she possibly want him? Getting close enough would mean crossing the cold's meridian – for which he still, apparently, wasn't ready. Courage.

'. . . nine-to-fives, really,' she said. 'Bit of clerical here and there. It didn't seem to matter as long as both of us were working. Then three years ago – you know we lost our daughter?'

'Yes, I'm sorry.'

'I decided to get a proper job. So I asked my father for one.'

Nodding – but the flicker of *all right for some* undisguisable. Cheryl had discerned it, too, Nathan saw. Because I collect perversions. Impossible. The pale jowls and receding chin, plump – womanish was the word – thighs. In the old life she'd have said, r*epulsive*. It was what she said if you said, What about him on telly? R*epulsive*, as if you'd insulted her morality.

The phone rang. The young man hurried to his feet.

'Sorry, just a sec,' Cheryl said, picking up the phone with her left hand and making sit-down sit-down gestures with her right, ignored by him.

'Hello?'

The young man took a step towards the door. Nathan backed.

'Can you hold the line a moment, please,' Cheryl said, then covered the mouthpiece with her hand.

'Look I'll leave you to it,' the young man said.

'Actually I will have to take this,' Cheryl said.

'If I don't see you before I go . . .'

'No, no, I'll be through in a minute.'

He nodded, smiled, shoved his left hand in his pocket – looked for a moment as if he might bow – then came towards the door. Nathan backed into the hall. Not yet. Not till I've seen her. There are things she needs to know. He watched the young man disappear into the dining room, then turned and went into the office.

Cheryl was off the phone already, sitting with her back straight and her forearms flat on the desk. Now it had come to it he didn't know how to approach her. Absurd.

Everything they'd been through. He tried to summon . . .
what? Righteous indignation? That she'd . . . what? Fucked
Adrian? Let the kids drift into trouble? Not cried at his
funeral?

He moved closer. Was he ready if she was congratulating
herself? Making plans? Tallying up the ways he'd been a disappointment?

With an impulse part anger, part disgust, part need,
Nathan lunged into where he knew the broadcast would——

'She's going to drop it.'

Cheryl is *She* and Lois, slathered in blood, shit and
mucus, is *it*. The delivery nurse is in her fifties, abrasive,
with soft freckled arms and a meaty face. Twenty hours it's
taken (she's the third shift change), though time's something else in here, like God, omnipresent, omniscient,
definitely not morally good. Cheryl said no to the epidural
then changed her mind too late. I'm sorry, Mrs Clark, you
know, there's a window of opportunity. She'd felt the time
it had taken to say that. The phrase 'window of opportunity' had gone on for ever, syllables clambering over each
other to give the pain more time to do its thing. Language
was in cahoots with the pain. She'd wanted everyone to shut
up. She'd been aware of Nathan there, face wrecked,
making absolutely no difference to the pain. Breathing with
her, as taught ante-natally. He might as well have been toss-
ing pancakes or doing a crossword. Come on, love, that's it,
you're doing it, you're fucking doing it. She'd said, eventually, Don't talk, and he'd seen it, that she was in a different
universe, that nothing about him – none of the degrees of
empathy or guilt, the inner mantra that he'd swap places if
he could, the rage that it had to be like this, the pleading

with God for it to be over soon – was of any use or interest to her. He'd seen the exact dimensions of his negligibility. A tiny remnant of her still in this world had wanted him to know that he could get up and leave, for all she cared. Undoubtedly God was male.

She's going to drop it.

They're right. Cheryl's arms are wet sandbags. When her head falls forward the lights go out. Then somehow she lifts it and the lights come back on. She's going to drop it. The pronouns hurt, meanly, on top of everything else. They've had to cut her and now someone's stitching, white hot. She looks down at the baby, froglike on her belly, jellied with blood. She can see one shrivelled and strangely quivering hand, the miracle of fingernails and palm lines she'll maybe have read one day for a laugh. Cheryl thinks of the fat stone in the avocado she halved . . . When was that? Days ago? The pathos of the scallop left after she'd eased it out. Was that yesterday?

One of the sandbags starts to slip, then there's space where the baby was.

'I was going to drop her,' she says to Nathan, who's there, holding her hand. She knows the in extremis revelations have wounded him. As always he'd expected love to have it covered. She feels sorry for him, and knows now, outside the pain, that actually he *would* have swapped places with her if he could, and that that means something good. She thinks: That's why there's a world at all, so someone can feel they'd swap places to alleviate . . . so that the other person . . . But thinking's a greased weight and she's weak. Sleep comes to her like a dark angel every time her eyelids meet. It hurts when she swallows. Her body's struggling to add itself up to see if it's all there. The calculations float, drift, sharpen to concrete subtotals in shoulders, hips, knees, diffuse again. It's all right, she thinks. Nothing serious missing.

'Yeah, well I'm not surprised,' Nathan says, kissing her palm. 'You've just fought World War Three in here, love.'

His eyes fill up. Suddenly he seems a boy to her. 'Don't cry, Baby,' she says. It rakes her throat but she means it. Love doesn't have to cover everything. It's okay if the world's like that. She calls him Baby very rarely. It started as cod American, years ago, gradually shed its irony. Now it's for moments.

But he does cry, and laughs at himself. Holds her hand against his face. There's no gesture to express the tenderness he feels for her. She'd gone ugly and old in front of his eyes and it had shown him he didn't care, only let her not be in pain, please, please, please, anything but her in pain. Her face had strained and eventually surrendered her identity, and when her eyes had looked at him he'd known he might as well have been a stranger. He's crying because he wants to tell her he's so proud of her, that she had the strength and courage to become something else in order to get this child out into the world——

Coming out was a wrench through barbed wire, to lose the feeling of how good they'd been together with the new baby already a lovely particular ('Lois', they'd decided, not least because the name's origins were obscure and Cheryl had been put off so many others by their derivation), sharing the feeling that with this one the family was complete: Luke, Gina, Lois. Sharing, too, the disbelief that they were pulling it off, keeping jobs, making a living, running a home, lobbing children out into the world. Love. The kids were a sort of madness, because they couldn't afford them. It was evident to both of them that night in the delivery room that they hadn't grown up much, that they were still cobbling it all together, his only certainty her and the children, hers the same but with, too, an inner creative life like a troubling fourth unborn. Well, he could live with that. That was her, after all. That, if he was willing to own up to it, was the thing that kept her just out of his reach, made the distance for love to travel – and he didn't want *that* to change, did he?

Cheryl sat with her head resting on her arms on the desk, face turned away from him.

Cheryl?

She didn't move.

He'd started something now, he realised, a new fire in himself that would engulf all the others. There'd been love. He'd wanted it in life and he wanted it in death. She just wants the drugs, his dad had said of Lil when she was in the last, worst stages. She's just existing for the drugs.

It's why you stayed away from her. You knew this would happen. That she still carried it.

He didn't care. He wanted it. It was a shocking insistence. Like lust.

Cheryl got to her feet (as a brief image of Lois standing in her anorak with her arms folded—) smoothed the woollen skirt, looked around the room as if for help. Nathan could feel the way she was, exhausted and at the same time driven by furious energy. There was no help.

There is help, love. I'm here. Cheryl?

She looked down at the desk. An accounts department report. An uncapped Mont Blanc. Last week's TO DO list: Calls: Gunter re diffuser patent. Dad re Holloway bid. Jeff Niles re Colorado. Anderson's re Taunton development. They read like punchlines adrift from their jokes. She was thinking of the call to Luke at Manchester. Luke? It's Mum. All his intuition (and excitement?) packed into the space between that and her next words. Something bad's happened. Her own disbelief had made her calm. Luke had sounded very careful and quiet, as if not shock or grief had him but a kind of delicately balanced wonder. I'll come home, then. Simple effects of simple causes. You were relieved, for a while, of the burden of choice, of having to think what to do.

Nathan hung close, held in place under the monolithic insistence. Love. Remember love. Whiffs of shame came off him, he was so given over to the need, but he ignored them. *You're not concentrating.* He couldn't help it. He told himself he couldn't help it. It's beyond my control, as it said in that film, repeatedly, it's beyond my control.

Gunter re diffuser patent, Cheryl read again. Madness sent out little invitations to start with: just keep reading that and see what happens. She had to get out of the house, outside, air. It was physical. She'd got better at acting immediately in accord with her body's imperatives. Loss tuned you to yourself by bankrupting all the usual distractions.

Go. Now.

She'd had her shoes off all this time. She put them on (the young man would have noticed and inferred – oh fuck him anyway, the prick), switched off the desk lamp, which had been on, pointlessly, and walked quickly out of the room.

Nathan, with the new fire roaring, followed her.

The wake had changed gear. Cigarette smoke and the gold flavour of Scotch. The buffet with the sad look of having been ravaged. Pretty much everyone had forgotten why they were here. Belief in someone's death required effort or palpable reminders, otherwise habit kicked back in. Half of them were expecting Nathan to turn up any minute. Years ago Cheryl had come back from an aunt's funeral having seen it close up, that people answered death with life, food, drink, conversation. Must be why doctors and nurses fuck like rabbits, she'd said to him, undressing unequivocally, breath reeking of booze. Morticians must be at it like there's no tomorrow.

The young man in the suit was heavy with drink now, deep in conversation with Cheryl's brother-in-law, Jake.

' 'Course every month – Christ, practically every *minute* – everyone's saying it's got to burst, it's *got* to burst, you know? They think they can wait it out, buy next year, even the year after that. But the fact is, even if it does stop next year, income's still going to be miles behind, you're still going to be worse off for having waited. I keep telling them: It hurts, but it's going to fucking *kill* if you wait another twelve months.'

Throughout which Jake nodded and sipped his drink and paid, Nathan knew, not the slightest attention. He sold paint for Fenn Industries, so badly that even George's bald nepotism (for Lynn's sake) couldn't leg him up any higher than area manager for the South West. Cheryl had talked about sacking him and just giving Lynn the money every month. In the old days she would have added: Serve her right for being a size 10. Nathan remembered thinking at the time: she would've added something like that, in the old days.

In the Audi in the garage Cheryl sat with her handbag in her lap, head and hands resting on the steering wheel. Tired. He saw now that she'd been tired for a long time. Three years. All the energy had its root in her exhaustion. She hardly ever allowed herself these moments. Certainly he'd never seen one when he was alive. She lifted her head and sat back in the seat.

The door from the garage to the kitchen opened and Adrian came in.

Cheryl moved only her eyes at first, looked at him, said with the look, Stop, there's nothing to say; then leaned her head back against the headrest when it was clear he was going to talk anyway.

Adrian opened the passenger door, got in and closed it gently.

'Is there anything I can do?' he said, eventually.

Cheryl sat still, staring out of the windscreen at the garage wall. Two steel ladders hung there. A garden hose. Nathan could feel her thinking: I've run out of it, whatever it was.

It was obvious to all three of them that Adrian wasn't going to touch her. He'd touched her intimately for the last time that day in the new house. That might well have been the last of it, Cheryl thought, the fuel. Appropriate that she'd run out the same time as Nathan, right down to the day, maybe even the hour. Still in sync after all.

It gave Nathan pleasure that she thought this.

'D'you know what I'm addicted to?' Adrian said.

Cheryl looked at him. Nathan could feel what an effort it was for her to maintain even this level of engagement. Adrian felt it, too, and was embarrassed. It was as if he was belatedly awkward for having seen her naked, having fucked her, after all these years.

'Gardening, cookery and wildlife programmes,' Adrian said.

Cheryl got it, from her distance away: no politics. Maybe a joke, maybe not. She didn't care. He was only playing with the idea of being washed-up. He wasn't strong enough to be washed-up, nor weak enough. You needed extremity to wash you up if you were strong, persistent mediocrity if you were weak. If you were neither weak nor strong, you just didn't wash-up.

'I'm going for a drive,' she said. *Alone* the unspoken addendum.

'That woman phoned,' Adrian said.

Cheryl closed her eyes.

'The Lloyd woman.'

'And?'

'She's left her bag. Wanted to know if she could pick it up later. I said okay.'

'Fine.'

Still Adrian didn't move. Nathan felt Cheryl out of desperation stirring up something poisonous simply to get him out of the car. When she was on the verge of it, Adrian opened the door and got out.

'You all right to drive?'

'I've had one glass of wine,' she lied. 'Shut the door, will you?'

Watching her behind the wheel Nathan missed her, acutely. She'd always been a good driver, confident and quick. Occasionally impatient. I think this person in the Astra might actually be retarded. Delivered conversationally.

He didn't know where she was going because she didn't know herself, except south and east to where the coast's wrinkles smoothed out into Dorset. He was tired from Lois's room, and it was an effort to keep safe distance. He wanted to go close to her, the old habit tugged at him. Trees and fields went by in bright sunshine. The verges were blotched with dandelions, the roundabouts with buttercups and daisies. Cheryl let the driving absorb her and there was peace in the car, the first bit Nathan had known since coming back.

But not far from Woodbury she pulled over into a parking bay and turned the engine off, and he knew that whatever the driving had been doing for her had stopped working.

For a while she did nothing, just sat with her hands palms down on her thighs. Nathan worried: a woman sitting alone in a car in a lay-by on a country road. Surge of phantom nausea for his pains, together with self-derision, a version of his own voice asking him what he thought *he* was going to do, tough guy, if some bastard with a tyre iron and bad intentions showed up. Make ghost noises?

A stream of traffic passed and left silence in its wake. He went close to her. She was difficult. An awkward frequency. Come on, love. It was dishonourable, he knew, like trying to coerce her into sex knowing she didn't want it, but as with sexual desire this insistence wormed its way round honour, round the better self. In the memory of Lois's birth it had been as if he was alive. Miserable Socrates has it over the happy pig – fuck that and anyway Ade you forfeited your speaking rights when you——

In the living room of a council flat Cheryl sits in a green wing-backed armchair holding in both hands a mug of steaming tea. Opposite, on a three-seater couch, sit two women, also with tea. A third woman stands in profile against the wide window which looks out onto the estate. All three are smoking. The standing woman is overweight, with scraped-back and barretted bleach-blond hair and a jowly face of detonated capillaries. One on the couch is thin with a pierced nose and maroon hair in a ponytail. The other, in a pale pink jogging suit, has a full, cherubic face with heavy eyelids. Her wrists rattle with charm bracelets. Cheryl sits hunched forward, fingers laced round her mug. The gap between her and the other three is palpable and appalling. She'd be scared of them in other circumstances.

'Yeah, well they can't lock us up if they're not there, can they?' the woman in the jogging suit says.

Cheryl nods, slowly.

'Fact is there's been *nothing* done for this estate for fucking years,' the thin woman says. 'And now this? They fucking get away with it because the fucking police know about it and do fucking *nothing*. The police are on their fucking *side*.'

The standing woman continues to stare out of the window with a glazed look. 'I'm a mum,' she says. 'I'd kill to protect my kids. We all would, wouldn't we?'

'I'd fucking kill to protect mine,' the thin woman says. 'And if that's fucking wrong you can put the fucking hand-cuffs on now.'

'If you wouldn't kill to protect your kids, you've no right to call yourself a mother,' the woman in the jogging suit says. 'No right to *have* kids in the first place.'

Again, Cheryl nods.

The thin woman holds up a copy of the *News of the World*, which has been wedged between her and the arm of the couch. Under the masthead is the caption 'FOR SARAH', which the newspaper has adopted in memory of the murdered eight-year-old Sarah Payne. The front page shows the photograph they've all become familiar with over the preceding weeks, a pretty little girl, smiling. The woman holding the newspaper struggles to find something to say, but ends up just shaking her head. Cheryl thinks Payne. Pain.

The irritation of words. In the old days that would have whispered the threat of design. Now what? Nothing. Not even the possibility. It's gone.

It hasn't, quite. At the back of her mind she concedes the habit still flickers, trying to get her attention. Fuck you. If there's a design it's the design of infinite malevolence, in which case what is there to do except hate it?

'What the parents're going through . . . This must bring it all back for you, love.'

There's a short silence in which the three women reawake to Cheryl, her difference from them. They're experiencing a collective confusion, that someone they'd normally be against (the education, the class) has an overriding claim on their allegiance. Because it's happened to her, the mother's worst thing. It confuses them, vaguely, that this can't quite erase her as the enemy. She's an icon their logic's forced them to venerate. They must – it's beyond question – but still, they know what she'd think of them outside all this. They're fascinated by her and the way their feelings curdle around her. She's like a woman brought from another country, an alien beauty.

'There's nowhere to bring it back from,' Cheryl says, her throat dry. 'It never goes anywhere.'

Nathan looked at Cheryl, lying awkwardly across the two front seats. There was a patch of sun on the passenger side and the disinterested sensuous part of her had gravitated to it. The smell and warmth of the leather comforted. Gina gets it from her, Nathan thought, the ability to find solace in the physical world. What do the rest of us do? Unlearn it. Waste it. All the wasted gifts, Christ.

These thoughts somewhat to distract himself from the dirty

feeling of having tried to force something. The insistence was still there, like a skulking dog not quite driven away by a beating, but he'd been chastened into the strength to ignore it for a while. The weight of not knowing what happened – to Lois, to himself – had lifted a moment with Cheryl's memory of the birth. He hadn't realised the weight until it had gone, as if from the outset he'd been carrying his own and his daughter's bodies on his back without knowing and had had them suddenly taken away. Simon of Cyrene had carried the Cross for a stage of Christ's road to Calvary. Imagine the *relief* that must've been, Frank used to say, with a kind of erotic relish. And then to have to take it *back* on yourself.

Cheryl sat up, slowly. The sun had moved and the seat had cooled. A seam in the leather had left an imprint on her cheek.

She'd never told him about going to see these women, he thought, although he couldn't be sure. There was something it connected with, something of the same flavour, of the life she'd started living aside from him. She'd stayed out a lot in the evenings, business she said, meetings. He hadn't pushed it. She'd had a way of looking him in the eye as if to demonstrate her own impenetrability, to advertise her elsewhereness. Don't bother. He hadn't, after a while.

He saw the way it was for her. She didn't choose her memories, they chose her. Ringed her like standing stones. She was condemned to go from one to the other, time after time. He knew too that she didn't know how much longer she could stand it, that even her tremendous strength was finite, that she was tired.

It shamed him, the courage. He moved closer. Everything——

★

It's four in the morning and the party's only not over in that Nathan, Cheryl, Adrian and two others remain doggedly awake in the living room, furred with nicotine and hoarse from the night's bellowing. They've drunk themselves not quite sober but into a state in which none of them wants to let go of whatever this is, this small-hours momentum, tiredness and a shy aliveness to exactly where in their lives they are. They've made it through three years of seminars, lectures, essays, tutorials and exams, they've *graduated*, yes; but this moment, really, for the first time, is a glimpse of what they've got, an education, or the beginnings of one, the understanding that they're young and full of desire and that the world, against all former supposition, is actually theirs.

It's a student house, smelling of patchouli, electric fires and damp. There's a couple asleep on the couch with their hands up each other's shirts. A single boy in a black turtleneck also asleep where the tie-dyed curtains meet the floor. The house is pocketed with sleepers, which gives these awake ones a parental feeling of benevolent superiority. Adrian's rolling a joint. A couple of hours ago they'd all been sufficiently stoned. Now that's passed. This is a different phase, drugs without desperation, and Adrian goes about his business with tea-ceremony precision. It's a pleasure to watch. In fact, everything's a pleasure. There's a tape in the deck with *Rumours* on one side and *Blood on the Tracks* on the other, and for the last two hours they've just kept turning it over, repeatedly.

'You're going to be fucked tomorrow,' Cheryl says. She means Adrian and the other two, Greg and Cathy, who have what she and Nathan keep referring to as 'activist activities' scheduled.

'Not as fucked as Tesco's and Sainsbury's,' Cathy says.

154

Adrian smiles. The plan is to go round as many supermarkets as possible, loading shopping trolleys with South African products. Then let the checkout operator ring all the items up, only to be told that you're not paying for any of them because they're imported from South Africa. Jam up as many tills as possible. Adrian, Cathy and Greg are three of a group of sixty student protestors. Nathan and Cheryl are planning to spend the day in bed with chocolate buttons, the Winnie-the-Pooh books, Marvel comics and package holiday brochures. It's an acceptable joke, now, that 'The Lovers' don't care about the world. It's a toss-up for who's case is more objectionable: Nathan doesn't care about the world because all he cares about is Cheryl. He's obsessed with and in love with her, in that order, as Adrian says. Cheryl, on the other hand, doesn't care about the world because – Adrian can't think of any other way of formulating it – she doesn't *believe* in it.

'What's that quote?' Cheryl says: 'They came for the Jews, but I wasn't a Jew, so I did nothing. They came for the Communists, but I wasn't a Communist, so I did nothing, and blah-blah-blah until finally it's they came for me and there was no one left to help me?'

'Niemöller,' Nathan says.

'Bless you,' Greg says.

'Who?' Cathy says.

'Pastor Martin Niemöller. Nineteen forty-five. After he got out of Dachau.'

'If you say so,' Cheryl says. 'Anyway I'm the uncomplaining version. Fuck the Jews and the Communists and the queers and the fucking one-legged Peruvian nose-flautists. No one left when they come for me? It's a deal. Just don't bother me in the meantime.'

Everyone laughs.

'Cheryl thinks the world's an aesthetic battleground,' Adrian says, finishing the roll and looking around for roach material. 'Or is it a spiritual battleground? Or is it . . . a sort of aesthetico-spiritual . . .'

'I don't care *what* sort of battleground it is,' Cheryl says. 'I've deserted.'

'From which side?'

'Both sides. Any side.'

'Also known as nihilism,' Greg says.

'No, egotism,' Adrian says.

'The world's a political battleground,' Cathy says. 'You're on a side whether you like it or not.'

This puts the levity under threat. Cathy's recently started sleeping with Adrian and is aware of two things. One is that she has much more in common with him than he has with Cheryl. The other is that Adrian is still more attracted to Cheryl than he is to her. She can't see it, she tells herself, what they all see in Cheryl. She, Cathy, is after all much better looking. But she can see it. It's the indifference to the world. The otherness. The brazen involvement with the mystery of herself. All difficult for Cathy to admit to consciousness proper, because her politicised self feels guilty for being miffed that her good looks aren't enough.

'Egotism's the psychic correlate of capitalism,' Adrian says, inserting the roach.

'Then how come I'm not a capitalist?' Cheryl says.

'Because we don't have any capital,' Nathan offers.

'Because you've got *soul*, sister,' Adrian says. 'Because you know, deep down, that money fucks art.'

'Yeah, you watch me tell them where they can shove that Nobel Prize.'

'Money fucks art because art depends on friction and money removes friction. How many millionaires get round to writing that book they all say they've got in them?'

'I don't care about making money,' Cheryl says. 'Just as long as you lot stop going on at me for not reading the fucking *Guardian* every day. I've got a novel to write.'

'You don't think there's something bankrupt about that?' Greg says. 'Wanting to write a novel but not wanting to know what's going on in the world?'

'I *know* what's going on in the world,' Cheryl says. 'Politicians are corrupt, dictators are torturing people to death, the West's enslaved by money, the Third World's starving. What's going on in the world's what's *always* going on in the world, what's always *gone* on. The hairstyles change, that's all. Politics is like travel. It's for people who can't bear standing still and looking at themselves. It's the violent hobby of *busybodies*.'

'I hope you haven't written that down somewhere,' Nathan says.

'Václav Havel was imprisoned last year,' Cathy says.

'The guy off *Star Trek*?' Cheryl says. Adrian, having lit the joint, coughs laughter. Everyone apart from Cathy knows that Cheryl knows who Václav Havel is.

'The Czech playwright Václav Havel was put in jail last year for signing in support of Charter 77.'

'More fool him for signing,' Cheryl says.

'It was a document written to bring attention to human rights abuses,' Cathy says.

'Bollocks to that,' Cheryl says. 'D'you seriously think that Charter 77, or any other charter for that matter, is going to make a difference to the sum total of human suffering? Half the fucking planet doesn't enjoy human rights and half the fucking planet never will. We're not cut out for human rights. We're more interesting than that.'

'We know you're nice, really,' Adrian says.

'Maybe so,' Cheryl says. 'I just don't want to have to watch *Panorama* any more.'

Nathan, Greg and Adrian smile. Whenever they're worried about anything, they walk around humming the theme music from either *Panorama* or *World in Action*.

'Supposing you were God,' Nathan says, taking the joint. He pauses to drag, inhales injudiciously, and suffers a coughing fit.

'Supposing you were,' Adrian says. 'Presumably you'd be able to smoke a joint without that sort of performance.'

'No no,' Nathan says, eyes streaming. 'I mean, from God's point of view, being able to peruse the whole of history in every detail. Would the world look much different now from the way it did in, say, AD 1066, or AD 66, or 2066 BC? Purely in terms of good and evil, compassion and cruelty?'

Nathan hasn't asked the question rhetorically, but it brings quiet in any case. Coincidentally, *Rumours* comes to its end for the third time. Adrian flips the tape and *Blood on the Tracks* starts again.

'There's this theory,' Cheryl says. Her voice is different now, a tonal apology to Cathy, whom, actually, she likes and knows is a good and decent person, but on whom she can't help committing small acts of cruelty. 'The idea is that the amount of good and evil in the world is fixed. I can't remember whether it's fixed at equal portions, but it's definitely fixed. Anyway, the point is, if there's some horror – the Black Death, for example – then to compensate you get Shakespeare. Or if someone murders someone in New York, someone in Timbuktu lays down his life for a friend.

The quantities remain fixed. I can't remember whose theory it is.'

'Bit impersonal, isn't it?' Adrian says. 'Not much comfort to the mother whose child's just been killed by a bomb in Belfast: Don't worry, madam, a woman in Madrid's just given birth to a sculptor.'

'Yeah, well, it appeals to me,' Cheryl says. This and all the rest's been self-satisfied and pointless game playing, but suddenly she thinks that the idea *does* appeal to her. The challenge then would be to keep seeing the balance – or keep finding it, proactively, symphony for earthquake, love for hate. On second thoughts, not good. She'd be running around like a madwoman, rescuing kittens and kissing children, donating blood, giving money away. Chaos.

'What I'd love more than anything,' Nathan says, 'is a cup of coffee with two sugars and lots of milk.'

Again, a prosaic peace descends, because here they are, with their shared feeling of having survived and become powerful, and someone will, eventually, make the coffee. Cheryl thinks of her childhood, which means a flash of anxiety because she wants to keep hold of the way the seasons were giant characters and life was her shapeless and urgent quest; there was a pale blue cardigan with mother-of-pearlish buttons she loved and a pair of her mother's gardening gloves of which she was terrified; the world was personal and alive. That's why, deep down, she really does hate politics, because it says no, never mind that, that's not important.

Outside, a milk float rattlecrashes down the street. The boy in the black turtleneck wakes up, raises his head, looks at them all with an expression of profound distaste, then falls back asleep. Cathy and Greg go to make coffee. Cheryl lies down and puts her head in Nathan's lap. She picks up his hand by the wrist and places it on her head, which means she wants her hair played with. It's part of the confidence given to her by love, to demand things. Adrian lies on his back with his fingers laced behind his head and a smile on his face, partly the grass, yes, but mainly the comfort of intimacy with these two. They all know the relation in which they stand to one another, all the degrees of ambiguity. A gap in the curtains shows a rectangle of lightening sky. Nathan's thinking: We don't need much more than this, do we? To have eaten and drunk and taken a few drugs and stayed up all night talking and to be sitting with your best friend at the stereo and your girl resting her head in your lap? How do wars ever get started?

Cathy and Greg return, and the smell of coffee's a sensuous extravagance. Also, Cathy's found an untouched bar of Cadbury's Fruit and Nut in the fridge. Their childhoods come back as they sit eating the chocolate and drinking the coffee – and again they have it, that feeling of having arrived in a time and place which whether or not they want it belongs to them. There's Cathy's white knee showing through a hole in her jeans, Adrian's hair sticking up all wrong, Greg rolling a cigarette. The details command reverence. All of them feel the command and all of them obey——

Cheryl started the car. She needed to be moving again. There were necessities; they revealed themselves to her when they felt like it rather than when she needed them, which was unfortunate but you took what you could get, still, even after everything. She pulled out into the empty road, heading east. There was also, durable when the rest had perished, irony. Her fear had been that she'd be punished by political evil because she'd never been a force for political good. There'd be a war because she'd voted wrongly (or more likely forgotten to vote at all); England would become a totalitarian state and the kids would turn into the Parsons kids from *Nineteen Eighty-Four*; Nathan would be gunned down by neo-Nazis for having dinner with a Pakistani friend; Gina would be run over by a mental patient who should have been straitjacketed in the psychiatric unit the government she'd done nothing to stop coming to power had shut down. Everything would turn out to be political, as Adrian had always claimed, unable to claim it without the grin that was half tolerance half threat.

But if you could count on God for nothing else you could count on Him for irony. She'd been punished, but not by policy. Instead He'd sent one of His messengers, His or the Devil's – either way it carried His imprimatur. Out of the darkness, out of the void. Tell me how *this* is political, she'd said to Adrian, quietly, once. Go on. Tell me who I should have voted for, what march I should have gone on, what petition I should have signed.

Nathan listened, remembering the days in the Roseberry Road house after Lois's death. Cheryl had said, sitting in the kitchen at four in the morning, That's the pathetic fallacy dead, too. He'd understood. The whole family had indulged themselves in the ascription of sentience to the inanimate world. Now the washing machine, the back door, the dustpan and brush – all the dead rubbish they'd made quick between them (because they couldn't help it, because there was love in the house and love wanted life for everything) – defined the delusion, the idiocy of it. Nathan had thought of all the factories and materials and processes, car production lines, then of the way they'd thought of their own Viva: It's a dog, this car, Cheryl had said to the kids, a dog with no idea of its own degeneracy. A trip to Torquay, you say? This car gets excited. It has no idea that it'll be a miracle if it gets to the bottom of the road, never mind Torquay. (She forced words onto them. Degeneracy. Lois must have been six or seven at the time.) He and Cheryl had been sitting on the kitchen floor with their backs against the row of units. All the objects around them were homogeneously dead. He'd wanted to reach out and hold her hand, but he'd done that so many times over those days and it had made no difference to either of them, except to harden their separateness and reify their loss. Everything they said or did demonstrated the same thing: that nothing they said or did made any difference.

Cheryl drove smoothly, never breaking the speed limit. Consciously or otherwise she'd picked these roads for the gear-changes, something for both hands to do. The sun went over her cheekbones in slow-moving stripes; her eyes narrowed and relaxed, narrowed and relaxed. Nathan thought of the hard and soft of her thigh, how many times he'd rested his hand there as she drove. The sun crossing her face showed the summer band of freckles below her eyes.

After the graduation party that night in '78 they'd taken the first tube into town and gone down to the South Bank. Sunday morning, a pink and gold sky over the river, hardly anyone around but still the city's clutter of history and pent life present. Nathan had thought of the millions around them curled in bed (flying dreams, nightmares, half-awakeness or simple black sleep) and felt that he never wanted to do anyone harm for the rest of his life. Something had happened. He'd been delivered into a certainty, and now come what may he had to act on it. All finalities were at some level satisfying – even death, he supposed, as the waterside lamps went off – because they relieved you of choice.

'Cheryl?' he said.

'Umm?'

'Will you marry me?'

She hadn't been looking at him. She'd been looking at a cormorant on the river, savagely preening itself. When she did turn to him he saw her covering the remaining distance to certainty, a headful of lightspeed calculations. She knew herself: she wanted mystery and danger, passion and the sordid affair with language, to *make something* out of her life. There'd be infidelities. Lies. She was bigger and hungrier than him. But she would (he judged) need him. Whatever else was true, she did love him, or suffered enough inarticulable feelings to be reduced to the language of love.

'Yes,' she said. She said it partly to see what it sounded like, what it did to her. She liked it, but she was afraid, too.

He'd thought: There's a good chance she won't leave me. She *is* bigger, and wilder and riskier, but she's not quite the creature she'll need to be for the life she's imagining. She's not strong enough, yet, to really hurt someone, and sooner or later the life she's imagining will ask her to do just that. She knows it's no coincidence that so many artists are terrible people; carnage in their wakes because that's the price experience demands. She might never make it as a writer for that very reason. It's one of her fears. Which'll be worse, losing her to her success or being destroyed by her failure?

Did I really see all that? Nathan wondered, as Cheryl accelerated out of Sidford and a pair of herring gulls went wheeling up on the left. No. He couldn't have. Revisionism. He'd just wanted her. His. To make it certain, or as certain as could be. He hadn't known he was going to ask her until the river lights went off. Then the Thames blue silver and that rose-gold sky. Told her afterwards it was an aesthetic conspiracy.

That morning by the river the power reversal was complete. He was hers. He'd picked her out because he'd seen the unobvious beauty and bottlenecked sensuality. A cynical start. He hadn't been prepared for what came next, namely, her personality, her soul, *her*, the wealth of self she'd been hoarding.

Cheryl parked and switched off the engine. Branscombe, this was, a long curve of beach backed by sandstone cliffs. A pocket of people at the shop end, thinning out further down the bay. Cheryl pulled her shoes off and began to walk.

Nathan looked out to sea. Whitecaps, bright light, a couple of smoke-coloured tankers miles away. Salt air and gulls sailing out with sunlit feet dangling, curving, coming back. Cheryl used to be jealous of him because he was good at just being in days and places like this, uninterfered with by language, by what it was all *like*. I can't *get* to it, she used to say. Get to what? There's nothing to get to, you're already in it. To what it's got, she said. To what's *here*.

To what it *means*, he knew she meant. At which he'd always realise how much childhood Catholicism remained, how much, if he was truthful, it meant God to him.

And now? (The ranks of the dead observed gave him nothing. 'Withheld' had been the word from the beginning. Now in the image Lois stood in their front line, a stranger's hands on her shoulders. He's not doing very well, is he, dear? Not he isn't. He won't concentrate. He's like that. Is he, darling? Or is it just selfishness?) He remembered the question of God arriving (via Frank) what seemed a long time ago, his own sweep for a Being turning up nothing.

Now he wasn't sure (or didn't care); it was imaginable that a very great distance away, far past the first shadowy lines of the hominid dead and further still, far enough out for concepts to fold or dissipate, there might have been something, a core from which creation poured in all directions, a personality so complex and remote that only the crudest and most diluted aspects of it turned up now and again in beauty and ugliness like paltry or negligible strands of DNA. If the dead were any nearer to it, it was by too small an increment to show.

This is far enough, Cheryl thought. There was no one further down the beach to her right and she was fifty yards from the nearest person on her left. She sat down. Her eyes were narrowed against the sunlight on the water. She was turning her grandmother's ring on her finger, a habit, another of the thousand things his love had found its way into. Throughout her life she'd had a recurring dream of being the only person left after the mysterious disappearance of everyone else from the planet. In the dream she always found her way to the sea, sat down on the beach like this, facing the sun and the water, felt the desolation resolving itself into peace, as if she'd come at last into the correct relationship with everything around her, as if all the animals and plants, the sky, the weather, had been waiting for her, to let her in among them.

She continued turning the ring on her finger, thinking of the day she found it. She'd been, what, six? Maybe seven. The adults had given up looking for it, her gran brokenhearted because it had been in her family so long. Cheryl had found it by the stream at the bottom of the yard (into which water her gran sometimes tossed the heads and skins of butchered chickens or rabbits without a flicker of remorse) and run in with it to tell them. But on her way through the living room she'd accidentally kicked over her dad's whisky glass and he'd smacked her. By the time she got to the front room where her mum and gran were lining curtains she had a lump in her throat, not from the smack but from the day's betrayal. She put the ring on the sideboard, mumbled that she'd found it, then turned and went up to her room in tears.

The child was still there and Nathan felt sorry for it. Cheryl let the memory go, and instead turned the ring on her finger inwards so that the edges of the beryl dug when she squeezed. She laughed about it, inside, but not in the right way. It occurred to him that it was the sort of thing Gina would laugh about in a different way. The right way?

My dad never did anything to me, Cheryl had said, one night, early in their relationship, because she'd been slagging him off and had suddenly caught the viciousness in her voice. Never *did* anything, she'd repeated, for Nathan to understand that George had never interfered with her, sexually, since this was the late Seventies and even then it seemed there wasn't a woman alive who hadn't been molested by her uncle or brother or dad. They'd been lying in bed in Nathan's Halls room in the small hours. One of those conversations that marked the sloughing of another layer of privacy. They'd known everything would be slightly different afterwards, even breakfast in a few hours. Nathan had only been half paying attention. The other half was busy marvelling at the feeling of solidity she gave him. Before her he'd been ghostly. A centre of self barely worthy of the name. He'd read books, passed exams, had sex with half a dozen girls, had bizarre dreams and minor religious moments courtesy of clear nights or autumn dusks – but never with a feeling of urgency or actuality, a consciousness of really being in the world, himself, alive, unique. His life might have been *all* bizarre dreams. Nor had he, particularly, minded. He'd blown around, more or less a person, more or less continuous. He'd had a terrible tendency to assume other people's accents, tics or traits. History had seemed the sanest thing, facts, lives and deaths that had already happened. Lying next to her, listening to her talk about her dad, it was as if all the loose, unravelled, stray or floating bits of himself were reeled in and brought home. It occurred to him for perhaps the first time in his life that he was, in fact, himself, Nathan Clark. The miracle of it! Here he was, really alive in the world! (And the shock flipside: one day he would really die.) He grinned to himself in the dark, hoping she wouldn't notice.

He never did anything like *that*, Cheryl said of her father. It's just that he's always been a bully. Not physically violent. I don't think he's ever laid a finger on my mum. But he can't bear the possibility that there might be people completely different from him. That would mean there was an alternative to *being* him. Which would mean he'd need an excuse not to change, to get better. Because the truth is he doesn't want to be him. He's like all bullies: totally disgusted by himself inside.

They'd made love that night and it had been different, as they'd known it would be, as they knew the cornflakes and toast and coffee and first moments of the first lecture would be. They'd stayed awake, opened the curtains and watched it get light. There'd been a pale, green-tinted sky and a few dark, horizontal quills of cloud.

That was the first night he'd known he was in love with her. The memory was still there, whole, intact, of that little burgeoning of certainty. Years later, reading a second-hand copy of *The Good Soldier,* he'd found a passage underlined.

> For every man there comes at last a time of life when the woman who then sets her seal on his imagination has set her seal for good. He will travel over no more horizons; he will never again set the knapsack over his shoulders; he will retire from those scenes. He will have gone out of the business.

Someone had underlined it. A man, presumably, since it was the only thing underlined in the whole book. Nathan had paused, having read it, recognising himself. Cheryl was the woman, and he'd met her when he was twenty-one years old. A young age to go out of the business. But he had, and never regretted it. Apart from Adrian he didn't know if she'd been faithful. He supposed not. There'd been a couple of holidays without him from which she'd come back with a look. He'd chosen not to know. The thought of her fucking other men from time to time would have hurt, of course, if he dwelled on it; he wasn't insensible. He just hadn't dwelled on it. There were the kids, his and Cheryl's life around them like a roaring fire. That would incinerate anyone who came near. In any case, he, as *The Good Soldier* had it, had gone out of the business.

It brought the need up in him again, thinking of the times she'd come back with that look. She'd confessed infidelity by bringing her enriched self back and giving it to him. It's still for you. Still yours. It only gets better for you. He'd under-stood, he thought now (circling closer again as the shadow of a gull rippled over her); even at the time the logic of it had got through. There was no denying she'd fucked him with guilt, but with love, too. There'd been a temptation to resist it, to go along with his furious cuckold. But his understanding had got in the way. Then Adrian. That had been different, he supposed – had to suppose because he still couldn't remember how he'd come to find out about the two of them, assuming he had found out. All of which woke the insistence again, stupidly (maybe it genuinely was beyond his control?), like a second tumescence. Suffering again the dirty feeling of his own weakness he searched the spiralling slew around her, came very gently closer, knowing he might not——

It's three thirty in the Queen Victoria the summer of 2000, two weeks after Cheryl's brief arrest and release. There's been the usual rise in the pub's urgency as the ghost of the old closing time's shaped up, but it's passed, and now the place lazes again, ambered with sunlight and muscled with smoke. Cheryl sits opposite her dad at a corner table.

'I'm not saying no,' he says. 'I'm just asking why.'

George sits hunched forward, leaning on his forearms. He's long-boned and broad-backed, with a big ribcage and a monumental head. Still uses hair oil; the widow's peak liver-spots gleam. He tans easily but unevenly and the front of his cranium sports a patch like a birthmark. Cheryl's inherited the bones and the green eyes but nothing of the bulldoggish features. Her mother's wide mouth, he thinks, thank Christ, not much of a world for ugly women.

'Because it's what I want. It's what you can do for me.'

He looks at her, takes a sip of his Glenlivet, calculates, carefully. Obviously she doesn't want this, or doesn't want it for any good reason.

'What about your writing?'

She lifts her head and they look at each other, something they rarely do since it reveals all the things it's too late for.

There's nothing to be said about the writing. She's not going to laugh at the idea or break down in tears or bother lying that she'll keep at it in her spare time. She's not going to say what her look says anyway, which is just: Lois is dead. Lois is dead. Lois is dead.

George looks away first. He's not used to this, having no rights, no power, no room to cut a deal. Whatever she wants he'll have to give it to her because if he doesn't she'll unleash herself on him. This isn't a request, it's a threat.

'It's not as simple as—'

'Is it your company or not?'

The businessman in him suddenly realises she'll be good. Doesn't know whether to feel proud. Does know to feel scared. And excited. Danger excites him and she's the most dangerous person in his world. He thinks of the memo: As of next month my daughter, Cheryl Clark, will be joining Fenn Industries. She'll be working alongside myself and Ken Turner with a view to . . .

She's got something to build cruelty on, he knows: what happened to Lois. Whereas he's had to build it on nothing, on fear. He's had to do everything he's done in the true and certain knowledge of having no entitlement to do any of it. Not that he thinks much on these lines. Not that he thinks much full stop. Thinking's got only one end point – that he's going to die, and since the certainty of his death tows in the wrongness of his life that's him and thinking at odds with each other. Getting along now means distracting himself. A thousand distractions, from snooker at the club and occasional whores to the tunes and ad jingles that start up in his head the moment he's off the phone or out of the meeting.

In Bangkok for a contract he'd discovered the male ex-pat sex consumer community, men who'd thought they'd worked it out, that they weren't interested enough in women as people (nor attractive or wealthy enough to get anywhere near the women they wanted) in which case what the fuck was the point of living in England or Germany or Italy or America? None the less only those fuelled by very specific perversions could hack it for the duration. The rest went heavy, sat around hotel lobbies bitching about the fact that it was all fake, the affection the girls out here provided; and why was that? Because they couldn't get far enough away from their own death for sincere affection not to seem relevant.

George can't get away from it, either. Cheryl looks at him and the look itself's an emissary of death, an advertisement for its certainty. She's been able to do that since she was twelve or thirteen years old, since the brains and language kicked in. And now on top of all that Lois's death stinks on her as if someone's doused her in petrol. Careful: she'll set light to herself and throw her arms round you. There's a raft of questions she lets him know (without saying anything) she has the licence, power and malice to ask. How old were the girls in Patpong? Have you ever loved Mum? Do you wonder whether you'll be called to account for all the rule bending and intimidation, all the blackmail and backhanders, all the *business*? Do you ever, for one minute, consider that your entire system of values might be wrong? Does Lois keep you awake at night with the only question she was allowed to carry with her into death: How could you let this happen to me?

Now this. Give me a job. Teach me everything you know. Don't dare refuse.

He sits back and looks down into his drink. I've spent my life, he thinks — but the momentum required to carry him down the familiar road (I've spent my life building something for my kids with hard graft and the wits God gave me . . .) deserts him and all he can think of is that if he's lucky he's got maybe another fifteen or twenty years at most and he's not ready never will be for death.

'Let me think about it for a day or two,' he says.

Cheryl lay on her side, knees tucked up, hands between them. The sun was warm on the bare parts of her, feet, legs, throat, face. Nathan, above, looking down, could feel her wanting to dissolve into the heat, let her atoms trickle away like a sand sculpture's grains in the wind. It was what she craved, these days, to disappear into something. If she hadn't built up such a powerful image of God as essentially small and neurotically bothered about people, this might be the time she found Him. But God was the one thing that put her *off* dissolution. Eventually she'd have to become herself again in order to reject Him. A postponed but inevitable annoyance. She'd rather wait, reject Him once and for all, then be sent off to wherever the damned went, not Hell, she thought, for some reason.

Nathan, chastened again, felt sorry for her, aside from love. She was alone. He wanted to put his arms round her, to know at least the inadequacy of putting his arms round her; even that would be something they could share, the ordinary business of not being quite enough to each other to conquer the misery of what had happened. That he couldn't had the power to invoke the furious child part of himself if he let it.

Pointless. He held it back.

Cheryl went into her handbag for cigarettes, inwardly

taking her hat off to the power of addiction. You didn't forget the handbag with the fags. Whatever else was going on. Smoking didn't mind. Lost Luke to it, Gina, too, now. Nathan should have smoked. He'd have had the comfort of knowing cigarettes didn't kill him.

She rummaged, found the Silk Cut and disposable lighter. The contents of your handbag were cruel, lipstick, purse, keys, hairbrush, perfume, crumbs; they stayed the same no matter what changes you were going through. Cruel innocent little constants.

A breeze lifted her hair and cooled her scalp. She was exhausted. She could feel the mass of the sandstone behind her and the tilt of the sea thin-crushed at the shingle's edge. And for all this, she thought (summoning the quote without any of the irony she used to slap on), Nature is never spent. She used to corrupt it after particularly long and intense intercourse, whisper in his ear: And for all this, Nathan is never spent. Nathan, raw, throbbing, receiving his body's multiple signals of delighted outrage that he'd *overdone it, again,* would slur words against the pillow or her hot flank: Nathan *is* spent, actually. Spent to death.

Nathan could feel her state, a paradox of exhaustion and energy. He wanted to tell her he loved her and that he didn't know what the word 'love' meant. These two things in paradoxical simultaneity, like her exhaustion and energy. Thoughts lined up: Lois's death had ruined them. The ruin they shared was the palace. They ought to go away from it, on excursions, but always come back, keep seeing each other, carrying on. No other life was possible. They should go out and return, out and return, further every time but always back to each other because what had happened had made them each other's necessity. Starting afresh with a new identity was impossible. They wouldn't be able to fuck each other, probably, but it seemed to Nathan a negligible detail. That wasn't for them any more but they were still for each other. Were condemned to each other, in fact, and so must make it a sort of treasury from which to draw.

Near her like this it was easy to think with the wrong grammar, what they ought to do, how they might repair the damage. Easy to think as if he were alive.

But she was alone, with no idea what to do next, now that this phase of herself was coming to its end.

Cheryl fingered the scar on her thumb. Five stitches it had been, though Nathan couldn't remember how she'd cut it.

He didn't like this, that she lay there like something dropped from the sky. She was so desperate to go out into something and the heat was a heavy seduction, lying on her. He went closer, weakening again under the pressure of the insistence; he *would* have this. Love at one remove. He could wait. What else, after all (*me, Dad*) did he——

Cheryl's never been onto the estate, never imagined it, never had cause to. Now she's part of its movement, privy to its will.

It's dark and the air's all wrong, Continental heat picked up and dropped on England like a giant animal skin. She's in the middle of a crowd of fifty or sixty people and the heat of the throng surrounds her. Heat or power, she can't tell. Impossible to keep sensations and thoughts separate. She keeps coming to. Her self keeps returning from wherever it's been, and when it does she feels physically enriched. If she were to look down and discover that they were carrying her in a sedan chair she wouldn't be surprised. Two teenage boys walk with her, one a skinhead with a pale, eager face and a painful-looking Adam's apple, the other tall with waxed black hair and a nose ring. There's an elasticity or bounce between the two of them in which she feels cradled. Each moment has its nowness: walking, listening to the murmur. She looks up at the skinhead and he looks down at her, eyes wide, face beatified with purpose. He nods at her, and she nods back, feeling as she does that her own face is warm and over-alive. Miles away or in another time there's her house with Nathan and Gina and Luke in it. She thinks of it as a snow-shaker. It irritates her for a moment, then it's gone.

They walk through a precinct of failed shops. Boarded-up windows, broken glass, graffiti trailed over everything. Heat's eased out the concrete's history: piss, beer, dogshit. In the centre of the square are two raised rectangular areas of grass covered in litter. A broken toilet, a shopping trolley, a Calor gas heater. The crowd's torch beams shudder and swing. At the back, some mums and dads have brought their kids. She's seen a young girl on a pink bike with stabilisers, another carrying a doll missing a leg, a small boy in a plastic Roman soldier's helmet. The children have assimilated the mood. It's familiar to them, this state they can't believe it's taken the grown-ups so long to get to.

Everyone quietens as they approach the targeted flat. It's on the second floor of a six-storey block, each floor with a railed walkway. Cheryl sees kitchen blinds, the estate's standard blue front door, a solitary hanging basket of dead fuchsia. All the faces around her are lifted. The black-haired boy puts his arm round her shoulder and gives her a squeeze.

Cheryl notices the three women from earlier, nearby. The woman with maroon hair is looking up at the second-floor flat shaking her head, no, no, no. Her face crumples, recovers, crumples again, then she lowers her head and starts crying, quietly. The woman in the jogging suit puts her arm round her and exchanges a curious, tight-lipped look with the third woman. The third woman mouths, silently, fucking bastards, then lifts her chin and shouts: 'Get out here, you fucking pervert!'

Her voice is an ugly scrape across the silence, but there's an affirmative noise from the crowd, and suddenly a petrol bomb goes sailing over their heads, crashes into the front wall of the flat just below the window and bursts into flame. Stones and bottles follow, two or three of which smash through the kitchen window.

The boy with his arm round Cheryl squeezes her shoulder again and she looks up at him. His face is a mixture of concern and joy. A slight frown, nostrils flared, but a smile flickering. It's as if something to which he's never imagined entitlement – nobility, perhaps – has given itself to him, descended on him like the Holy Spirit.

'We'll get him,' he says to her, very calm and tender. She imagines that if he were to go to his girlfriend at this moment to make love he would astonish her with tenderness. He looks up at the skinhead, who nods vigorously, also with nostrils flared, mouth turned down at the corners. By which time men and women are peeling off from the crowd, racing towards the stairways.

Cheryl finds herself running with them. The thing she can't bear to think about is Lois, but the images persist: Lois laughing like a little drunk; Lois watching Nathan shave; Lois with soap in her eye, face scrunched going *Aaaaah* with deliberate melodrama. Each one springs something uncomfortable in Cheryl's chest. Adrian's avoided writing anything about paedophilia since Lois's death, but the paper's made it clear where it stands on these latest events. Naming and shaming drives offenders already on the register underground, making them harder to track and thereby increasing the threat to children. Cheryl's seen it, the logic. She thinks of it having a colour, a softly radiant pale-blue neon. Or there's the one about the causal relationship between shame and offence. You shame the reforming paedophile, the self-esteem crucial to abstinence vanishes, the feeling of worthlessness and exclusion takes over and he offends again. More pale-blue neon, more gentle illumination. It comes to her, running (these are muscles unused like this since school – she gets a flash of the green track, the lanes marked out in lime, summer), that thinking – reason, argument, philosophy, ethics – is beautiful. She thinks of the human mess back down the centuries – all the hacked corpses, the millions dead – and yet still the patient, thankless labour of thinking, the pale-blue neon structure delicately resisting madness, the great, angelic effort.

Adrenalin. Thighs and calves tingling. Amazingly, the door to the flat opens and a dark-haired man in his late forties looks out. Cheryl ducks with half a dozen others into the ammoniacal stairwell, lungs pounding. A siren starts up, though it sounds far away.

'That's the fucking police.'

'Fuck it.'

'Someone's called them.'

'Have they got him?'

'Can't tell.'

'Have they got the cunt?'

'Fuck the police.'

All as they jostle one another up the steps. Cheryl has

momentary out-of-body experiences, glimpses of herself from a position just above and to the left of her own head. She gulps air, thinks of all the breakfasts and dinners and teas cooked here, the perpetual tinnitus of children, the way the blonde woman's mouth went ugly when she'd said she'd kill to protect her kids. Must bring it all back, love. Detective Fowler had looked her in the eye when he'd told her, had somehow managed to get the words out, one after another. Cheryl had thought, there's grammar, verbs, nouns, pronouns, tenses, all still willing to lend themselves. Language refuses nothing. If it can do it, it will. We've found the body of a young girl matching Lois's description.

From sounding distant the sirens are suddenly very close. The man in the flat's managed to get the door shut, but they're close to kicking it in. If it holds much longer someone'll risk the kitchen window's broken glass. The stink of burning petrol reaches her, slows her for a moment. Years ago, Adrian had said to her, That attitude leads to capitalism. Then why am I not a capitalist? she'd asked. Because you've got *soul*, sister, he'd replied, grinning. She doesn't know why she remembers this now. The thoughts and images come and go like little birds. The door goes in with a crash, followed by a curious silence in the seconds it takes for the first members of the group to get in and grab him. So quiet she can hear the buckle and snap of the flames. She feels her throat tighten. Possibly a twinge in her cunt. An intimation of the howling emptiness if that persists – but it doesn't; it's just her body not knowing how to be, trying different things, short-circuiting.

A second police siren, doors slamming. Three or four men, her two boys among them, drag the man from his flat. The silence holds for a moment (it's as if he can't speak and try to get free at the same time), then suddenly he screams. Someone kicks him in the ribs. The skinhead thumps his mouth as if he's thumping a mouse that's had the audacity to poke its head out of a hole. Again silence and furious wriggling.

'Get him out of here.'

'Are they here yet?'

As he's dragged kicking along the walkway towards the stairwell the man makes a gargling noise in the back of his throat, nowhere near loud enough to attract attention. But any sound from him is intolerable. The skinhead thumps again. This time the nose bursts (Cheryl hears an alien sound; understands: cartilage) and blood appears like a flower on his face. She's hot, her scalp tingles, she remembers fights at primary school, the way your body swung and sang and you emerged with advance warnings of pain and your hair filled with static. Her childhood seems very close, in fact. But there are, too, flashes of her distinct and current self, forty-four years old, her body opened and closed three times for the kids, her hands' unfamiliarity with violence. When the skinhead thumped the second time it had felt like her own fist doing it. She feels the blow's imprint on the edge of her hand. She doesn't know whether she's dog-tired or filled with energy. Both. All the opposites are close at their extremes, she supposes.

Someone's brought a van round, a dark transit, and though there are what sound like police shouts and dog barks on the air they manage to get the man into the back. Cheryl, the black-haired boy and two other men in the rear, the maroon-haired woman and an overweight, bare-chested man in the front. The vehicle smells of old vinyl and damp boots. Their victim's sobbing, I'm on the register, I'm on the register, but the boy (all of whose movements are preceded by a quick glance at her as if for permission) kicks him hard in the balls, twice, and Cheryl knows from the quality of silence that follows that he won't be able to speak for a while.

'Your hand's bleeding,' the boy says to Cheryl. She looks down and sees that her left hand is indeed bloody. Now and only now she recalls a flash of pain getting into the van. Something sharp. She doesn't know. Her thumb starts to throb, and for a few moments she thinks she might be sick.

The woman in the front is crying inconsolably, craned round over the back of her seat. She's saying something, directed at the man on the floor of the van, but the tears make gibberish of it. The van swerves, mounts a kerb, dismounts. Everyone gets a shake and a bounce, there's a sudden acceleration, but it doesn't last long.

'Can't do it,' the driver says. 'They've fucking blocked it.'

The van comes to a halt, interior splashed by siren lights. There'll only be a moment before it's over. Doors slam. A dog barks. A walkie-talkie crackles, gives out indecipherable speech. For the first time in three years Cheryl finds herself regarding the world with something other than contempt. 'What it reduces to,' Adrian's editor had written, 'is a dull ethical truth no less true for being dull: you can't take the law into your own hands.' The other men in the back of the van are quiet, looking at her. They'd be touching the peaks of their caps if they had them. Her dark-haired boy has one foot pressing on the ankle of the man on the van's floor. The man lies curled on his side with his hands between his legs, unable to stop taking in-breaths. Each inhalation's visible in a jerk of his head and shoulders. The boy looks at her shyly. A dull ethical truth no less true for being dull. Bits of the pale-blue neon structure radiate light, and this is one of them. What happens if you take the law into your own hands? You go outside the law. Outside. Law. Become an outlaw. It's not that you can't do it, it's just there are consequences if you do. Cheryl steps over the man on the floor and turns to face him. He looks up at her and tries to speak, but he's in too much pain. Experimentally, she stamps on his face, not very hard. He seems to not react at all. She realises that's always been her bargain with the world: don't ask me to observe rules and I won't ask you for protection when I break them. An imprisoned sociopath interviewed on a BBC2 documentary had said the same thing. She remembers the man. He'd sat in a chair wearing an orange prison suit with legs and arms restrained. Bald, pendulous, and wearing blue-tinted glasses. The fat face had had a pursed, sensual mouth and the look of never having shared anything with anyone. He'd spoken in a gravelly Southern State drawl. You all kin do whut you want to me, but I'm juss doin' whut I do. Someone'll make a country and western record out of that, Gina had said. It had become one of the family's phrases for a while. I'm juss doin' whut I do.

A police hand bangs on the side of the van. 'Let's have everyone out, nice and easy, please,' a man's voice says, and to Cheryl it's as if she's just breathed in too big a breath of icy air. She lifts her foot a second time (feeling the boy's hand lightly at rest in the wet small of her back where her T-shirt's ridden up – it's partly to balance her, only partly, she knows), but suddenly she thinks of Lois again, the time in the bathroom watching Nathan shave off an experimental moustache and beard. What're you doing, Daddy? Cheryl had been lying in the bath, observing. Shaving my moustache off, Nathan said. Lois nodded and gave out having understood, though Cheryl and Nathan knew she hadn't, quite. And then the proof: When will you shave it back on?

'Go on,' the boy says to Cheryl, gently, as to a nervous horse. 'It's all right, you're all right.'

But Cheryl lowers her foot, reaches out for the van's flank, leans. They'd laughed. It had become a golden anecdote, too good to be true. That's one of the things that mean I'll never be able to kill myself, Nathan had said. You can't when you've got something like that, it's a talisman against despair.

The rear door swings open, revealing a dozen police with torches and two German Shepherds. The sirens revolve silently. All of them in the van think of television. *Casualty. The Bill.* It's like that, except you feel sick.

'Tell them I'm on the register for fuck's sake,' the man on the floor gasps. The boy takes his foot off the man's ankle. Cheryl moves, so that his hand slips from the small of her back.

'They know you're on the register, Eddie,' an officer says. 'Right. One at a time. Out. You first.'

In the car, handcuffed and flanked by two female constables, Cheryl can't imagine speaking again. They've taken her name and address and told her she's under arrest and that she doesn't have to say anything but anything she does say, etc., but after forcing out 'Cheryl Clark, 24 Roseberry Road, Exeter', her throat's seized up. Her body has become an irritant to her, she doesn't want it. Her mouth, silent now, feels like a sentient thing, her tongue science fiction, alien life. She clamps her jaws shut. The Lois memory had halted her not, as Nathan might have imagined, because of its talismanic virtue, but because nothing much had followed from it. Only frustration and a feeling of irrelevance. Standing with her foot raised over the man's face Cheryl had thought: in a short story written by someone this hadn't happened to, in a short story written by me before it *had* happened, this would be the moment when the memory of Lois saying When will you shave it back on? would be wheeled in to pull the protagonist back from violence, to help her hold on to her humanity as a way of honouring her daughter's memory. Or, alternatively, the memory's failure to do just that would let the protagonist's rage out once and for all. Then you'd have either penitence or a descent into madness. She'd thought all this with her foot raised and the jerking man's face like the tragedy mask underneath. It brought two intrusions. One was the familiar trivial disgust with art and the persistence of that part of her consciousness still bothered about it. (At other times, when she'd found metaphors or similes trying to insinuate themselves, she'd dealt with them by calling up a scaffold supplier for a quote, or her dentist for an appointment, or the bank for a balance statement.) The other was . . . What? She couldn't pin it down but something had deflated her. An intimation that no matter what she did there would be no peace. No resolution, nothing with which to answer what had happened. What had happened was, among many other things, a question: What will you do now? Or, as she more often phrased it: What do you say to *that*? The man on the floor wasn't the man who killed Lois, she knew; even if he had been, would killing him have answered the question with the finality it demanded?

She'd had a glimpse in that moment: there was no answer. There was an answer for your blood, to find the man who'd killed Lois, torture and execute him (that would answer blood and she'd do it without hesitation if she got the chance), but blood was only part of it. Beyond blood was all the rest, the agonising durability, the going on afterwards with Lois still dead and herself still alive. Beyond blood were years of approximate feeling and the laughable limits of language, what used to be ordinariness – what still *was* ordinariness to everyone else – insisting on readmission, on full pardon, on your concession that yes, you could once again put your make-up on and plan holidays and choose a washing powder, that you and the world had survived. That wouldn't be peace. Only your blood could be given peace. The rest of you would require constant distraction and sedation. Either that or you surrendered to madness. Or you built an apparatus, something to *do* with your time, something to keep at bay the question of whether you'd survived. Or – and *this* was the absolute horror – you tried to forgive . . . to forgive—

'Mrs Clark?'

Cheryl looks up. There's an officer at the open car window. Blond crew-cut and dashing blue eyes. Station heart-throb, Cheryl thinks. Knows it, too. Then she sees what's happened: they've realised who she is.

'Take the cuffs off,' the officer says.

'Sergeant?'

'Take them off. Mrs Clark, would you come with me, please?'

Cheryl drove back slowly, drained. Nathan, close, but with enough distance to think his own thoughts, remembered the way she'd been that night, when the police had brought her home. She acted as if nothing significant had happened. He'd stood there with his hands useless weights and his face thick with shame and thought that she was the one who was doing something, *something*, no matter what while he, that

184

evening, had washed the dishes and vacuumed the lounge and for no obvious reason he could think of re-alphabetised his books, which over the years had gone out of order. Luke and Gina knew enough to get out of the way. They'd missed so much school after Lois's death there was always the catching-up alibi to keep them in their rooms. Nathan himself had stayed off work for only three months, gone back for the term between Easter and the summer holidays. That had been, of course, the consensus prescription: best to keep busy, keep doing things. Until that night in August Cheryl had done nothing, except write to the publishers and tell them she was withdrawing the book. The Volunteer Bureau was keeping her job open with temps but it was becoming obvious to everyone she had no intention of going back. At a secret meeting with Nathan, George had begged (in tears, sometimes shaking as with rage) to be allowed to set up a monthly standing order to help them until Cheryl felt ready to work again. Nathan hadn't had the energy or the inclination to argue. (He had, however, seen that George hadn't until the very last moment known which tack to take with him, whether to bully or to beg. In the end, *at* the last moment, as it seemed to Nathan, George had opened his mouth to begin and his eyes had filled with genuine tears. Even at the time Nathan had been aware of George's alternative speech like a subsonic monologue: you fucking spineless, useless bastard. You should have been there. You should have . . .)

'I'm going to ask my dad for a job,' Cheryl had said to him the night after her arrest. He was sitting up in bed marking 3F's homework on causes of the First World War, thinking how bizarre it was that at least for a short time remote figures like the Archduke Franz Ferdinand entered the heads of millions of teenage girls and boys, became part of their mental bric-a-brac, alongside pop stars and foot-ballers. Lois hadn't got there. Hadn't been allowed to get there. (And what had he done about it? Nothing.) As Cheryl made her announcement in the bedroom doorway Nathan had been thinking that if they met in heaven, Lois and Ferdinand, she'd be one of the people who hadn't the faintest idea who he was. (And what the fuck had he done about it? Nothing.) He had no control over these thoughts; they came in spite of everything.

'A job doing what?' he said. They rarely went to bed at the same time. Cheryl stayed up late, smoking, making coffee, doing nothing. In or out of bed, neither of them slept much anyway.

'Whatever he does,' Cheryl said.

There hadn't been anything to say in reply. They were so many miles apart he'd wondered why she bothered telling him. Possibly just to hear herself say it, in the way she'd needed to hear herself say Yes when he asked her to marry him.

'Do you want anything?' she said, as he remained speech-less with the exercise book open on his lap. The question stunned him. For the last six months he'd barely existed to her. Now here she was asking him if he wanted anything. Presumably she meant what they used to mean: a cup of tea; a bowl of cornflakes.

'No, thanks,' he said.

She'd smiled at him, vaguely, then turned and gone back downstairs.

Cheryl parked the car in the garage and sat for a few moments in silence. Didn't matter how long you sat in silence, she thought, sooner or later you got up and did something, found yourself with words coming out of your mouth. Trick was to shape your life so that none of the words mattered. Trick these three years, anyway.

She took the keys out of the ignition and dropped them in her bag. Opened the driver door and swung her legs out. Then sat for a moment half in, half out of the car. She'd travelled a long way from her children. The thousand times she'd nearly gone back to them but at the last second felt the impulse die. It was as if she was waiting for something, though she didn't know what.

There were things to sort out in the house, the hired help, Frank's eyedrops. She got out of the Audi and softly closed the door.

There were still a few people at the wake but the ritual's momentum was petering out. The house had the feel of a half-dismantled fairground.

Nathan went upstairs to look for Luke. He was with Gina in her bedroom, him at the desk, her on the bed with her knees up under her chin. Matt, at Gina's scriptish request, had gone home. Think I might just need to be with my family for a while. Of course of course. You ring if there's anything, yeah? She'd felt him thinking that he didn't know whether he could go on with this, whether it was worth it. But there was the not having had her properly. She saw it all. It was as if she was watching a film. She didn't know how it would turn out, or how she wanted it to.

Luke sat at her desk, looking out of the window. Gina had realised he was lonely, that there'd been girls, most likely, but that for whatever reason (Lois, their life, everything, of course *everything*) he'd never been able to connect. When she imagined his life away from home she imagined a constant performance, an outer Luke people knew, and an inner one who sat still and watched, waiting for the next time it was safe to come out. She imagined her brother taking late-night walks, alone. It had occurred to her that he was an adult. Did she think of herself as one? It was the first time they'd been properly alone since he'd come home.

'What're you doing?' Luke said. Academically, he meant, having looked down at the notes on the desk.

'"Childe Roland to the Dark Tower Came",' Gina said.

'Never heard of it, what a surprise.'

'You don't know what you're missing.'

'Come on, you love it.'

'Yeah, I want to marry it.'

'What's it about?'

Gina rolled her eyes.

'Go on.'

'There's this guy, a knight, the last of a gallant band who set out years before to find the Dark Tower. All the others are dead or fucked up one way or another. Anyway, he wanders through this nightmare landscape, seeing one unpleasant thing after another – then just when he's about to give up hope, he finds it.'

'And?'

'And nothing. He blows his horn and goes: "Childe Roland to the Dark Tower came."'

'Sounds a cracker.'

'Yeah, well, it could be worse. We could've had John Betjeman.'

Luke looked down at the annotated page. Next to the last stanza Gina had written: End of quest he gets there and says I'm here – to whom? No one there. No meaning, but we have the poem. It was impenetrable to him. There'd been a point in their childhood when he'd left it to her, art, literature, since she had the grasp of and hunger for it. That as much as anything else had sent him off down the science fork. For a moment, he considered telling her about what was going on, all of it.

Tell her. Whatever it is, tell her. (The stealing, Nathan assumed.) It'll help.

Luke rehearsed, mentally. I'm having these turns, Gee.

What turns?

Funny turns. I get this feeling that everything I do, the smallest thing, lifting my finger, for example, isn't me doing it. Or rather I'm doing it because of everything else that's ever happened.

Yeah, well you're the scientist, that's the way it is according to you. Big bang, then toppling dominoes.

I know. But you're not supposed to *feel* it. Feeling it makes you feel . . .

What?

Nathan waited, thinking of the shift in Luke in the study just before Frank came in. He had to know. Even if there was nothing he could do.

But Luke had let it go. He was thinking of foreign countries again. The sound of Italian. Even thinking about foreign languages made everything seem less important. He wanted, Nathan could tell, to get up and go over to Gina on the bed. They used to use each other like furniture not so long ago, sprawled in front of the telly. Luke used to sit on the floor with his back against the couch; Gina would be on the couch, behind him, and would rest her feet on his shoulders, occasionally jigging them up and down. That was peace, among other things.

'I want to go away,' Luke said. Gina, chin on knees, raised her eyes. 'We've never really been anywhere, have we?'

'Cornwall, Dorset and Benidorm,' Gina said. 'No wonder we're so sophisticated.'

'Last year in Italy it was weird,' Luke said. 'I had these moments.' He'd been for a week with a group of friends into which he'd been drafted (he suspected) because they knew about and felt sorry for him. Someone's wealthy parents had a house on the coast an hour from Rome. 'Once when I was standing in the lane that led up to the villa. It was the middle of the afternoon, incredibly hot, and there wasn't anyone else there.'

Gina waited. She knew Luke wouldn't be able to explain it, whatever it was. Yet at the same time she had a very clear image of him standing alone in the lane in punishing sun, eyes squinting, deafened by cicadas. Pure. All the rubbish and false meanings of things gone and you left naked in all of it. You got the feeling that anything was possible and that nothing mattered much.

'I could've been anyone,' Luke said. 'D'you know what I mean?'

'Yeah.'

'That's not really it,' he said. 'I mean, it felt like I could become anything.'

'Yeah, I know.'

A pause.

'Do you?'

'Yeah.'

Another pause, slightly awkward.

'Anyway,' Luke said, 'I want to get away more.'

'Yeah, well, take me with you when you go, will you?'

Luke got up and went over to the bed. Sat, then lay on his

back alongside her, the edge of his hip touching her haunch. He laced his fingers behind his head. She stayed sitting up, hunched forward. He could see her vertebrae through the black blouse.

There was a knock on the door. Nathan felt it flash in both of them that they should move, that this was, by the smallest margin, questionable, but they didn't, and in any case Gina had called, 'Come in,' before they had a chance to rearrange themselves.

Lynn put her head round the door.

'Gran and Granddad are going home,' she said. 'D'you want to come down and say goodbye?'

Gina got up straight away. Luke uncurled himself, slowly.

Nathan stayed put after they'd gone. The room was sunlit and he felt tired. He wanted it to stop, now. Whatever it was. This, all of it, the neither-fish-nor-fowl state of being near to them and a whole death away. It occurred to him that he was purely anomalous, a cock-up. Everyone else died and *stopped*. There was no explanation. Nor anyone to record the anomaly.

Sorry, Lo. I think I might have made you up.

He couldn't convince himself either way. He'd had the energy, he supposed, to conjure his daughter out of the void. Fear gave energy. Anger gave it. Panic. Now? What did you get from loneliness? The opposite of energy, inertia.

It's beyond my control. The words of your own excuses come back wearing a new context. It *is* beyond my control. All of it.

It was an effort, but he got himself to move. Everything he'd remembered slowed him down. The moment at the leisure centre was the weight of a giant corpse resting on

him. Where's Lois? She'd had a book, *Where's Wally?*
Complex pictures crammed with detail in which the tiny
figure of Wally was hidden. You had to pick him out. Two
or three pictures where Lois couldn't find him. Refused to
believe he was actually there. Nathan used to sit with her in
his lap and the book in her lap. He'd feel her looking and not
finding, getting more and more irritated. He's *not there*,
Daddy. He is, Missy, I promise. Look up to the left, near the
yacht. Don't help me! Help was the cardinal sin. He knew,
but he couldn't stop himself. It was ridiculous, but he
couldn't bear her sitting there on his lap, suffering.

He moved towards the closed door and reached out, all
the phantom muscles all but spent.

Knew a split-second before, passing through the very last of
the irrigator mist, and this time the dread took hold as soon
as he settled.

Oh God. La-la land. Where Buriden's ass sat down and
starved.

Everything as before: the white bed with the corner
turned back in invitation; the door; the bare walls, ceiling
and floor; the solitary frosted bulb.

A moment of paralysis and then he thought: perhaps *this*
is Hell? Not the imprisonment, but the two perfectly balanced desires, to get into the bed and to go through the
door. Between them they generated a threat of impending
finality.

This was like the moments just before vomiting, when
you thought that not for one moment more could you stand
the feeling of sickness and that if you didn't vomit right this

second you'd die – none the less several such moments, all with the same unsupportable ultimatum. Except this sickness was dread, and you had to back away from it, back away from it, Christ the effort.

This time, Nathan knew, passing out through the wall behind him, would be the last time retreat was allowed.

Luke

All but a few of the peripherals (the young man?) had gone by the time Nathan came out. Gina sat in the dining-room window seat, Adrian at the table eating a cold sausage roll. Cheryl moved around issuing quiet instructions to the hired help, shadowed ineffectually by Lynn. Jake was on the couch with a big Scotch and his shoes off. They were more or less all at the stage where another assault on drinking was required if sobriety wasn't to be let in to do its damage. None of them was ready for *that*. Even Lynn had thrown down a couple of gin and tonics to stay loose. Frank was standing at the bottom of the drive with his hands in his pockets, doing nothing, but raising his head every time a car passed, as if he was expecting one in particular. Of the family, only Luke was missing.

Lois, what's wrong with your brother?

He couldn't break the habit. A great weight of scepticism (his own state notwithstanding) dragged against her being there, a great weight of loneliness pushed towards it. Maybe the thing was not to ask her, directly. Years ago he'd seen a film, *Damnation Alley*, a post-apocalyptic future in which a handful of people believed themselves the planet's last survivors. One of them went off on a motorbike to search for others who had made it through the holocaust. He was gone for days, but he returned, spotted through binoculars by one of the other camp members — and he had a girl with him, riding pillion. When he rode up, she turned out to be a shop mannequin.

Nathan found his son in the study, where he'd lit a fire in the hearth. The new house had all sorts of things they would have loved in the old life. Luke sat at the desk with the plate of food Frank had forced him to take, cold chicken, a pasta salad, plum tomatoes, a sad little heap of crisps, all untouched. He had the cherry-wood box in his hands.

Nathan felt the state the boy was in, something near hysteria, which manifested itself in an economy of movement and a look of beatific calm.

Luke was thinking of the evening Lois went missing, its quantum leap from normality into nightmare. He'd got home from five-a-side to find his mum on the phone to the police and Gina standing in the hall looking on with a strange forward tilt to her body he'd never seen before. Wrongness filled the house like gas. All the lights were on. The furniture was fraught and vivified. He'd gone through the motions — What's wrong? What is it? Well, maybe she's just — but he'd already made the leap himself. You made the leap straight away. It felt like you'd always known you'd have to. They told his mum to keep off the phone in case Lois rang. She'd had a mobile from George and Eleanor for her last birthday. (He and Gina standing there when she unwrapped it had played the expected role, tutting and shaking their heads and saying Decadence, terrible decadence, secretly amused because there was something funny about the idea of Lois, who wasn't socially skilful, having her own mobile. D'you want the number for the speaking clock, Lo? they'd teased. Directory enquiries? She'd phoned Claire, then Gayle, then Dominique, practised looking natural, not shouting down it.)

His mum had sat at the bottom of the stairs with her hands on the phone in her lap, rocking back and forth, willing it to ring. Still in his five-a-side gear he'd gone out to look. Running. The sweat had cooled on his skin. (His mum had wanted to go with him but they'd said stay by the phone. Gina'd put her coat on, too, but she would have slowed him down and in any case his mum said No, in the tone beyond argument.) He'd run miles, watched blocks of the city come and go, kept thinking he'd wake up or start to come out of it, the hallucination, the trip. His senses had surprised him: perception had ballooned and shrivelled by turns. How many hundreds of times had he seen this sort of thing on telly, or read it in the paper? Concern is growing for. Police tonight began. A full-scale search is now under way. The parents of. He thought he was in a film. You thought things like that. There was nothing it was beyond you to think. Why's it called a black hole? she'd asked. Because it looks like one, he'd said. But it isn't? No, it's a collapsed star, a dead sun, and it's so dense, its gravity's so powerful, that not even light can escape.

It's all right Luke. Don't be afraid. Whatever it is, you'll get through. Nathan sounded tired and slightly alien to himself, someone doing a near-perfect imitation.

Luke took the envelope from his rucksack pocket and

opened it. Inside it, folded, was a torn page from a magazine. The image was a young girl, no more than eight or nine years old, topless, in a pair of bikini bottoms. She was trying to get up off a couch the colour of dried blood, but was restrained by a large male hand and forearm (unnaturally large, even accounting for the girl being small), which was pressed against her left shoulder. She was off balance, smiling uglily, plainly under duress.

Someone had left it in his pigeonhole in Halls a year ago. He hadn't told anyone about it. It was as if he'd been waiting for something. It hadn't surprised him that someone had put it there. People were like that. The boy whose sister. They liked it, that it would hurt him.

He looked at it for a few moments, blinking, face emptied of expression. Then he refolded it, replaced it in the envelope and put it in the wooden box. Lighting a fresh cigarette, he got up and walked out of the room.

Nathan couldn't move. Something which would have been crippling sadness if not for the sudden pressure from all sides, the air-raid shelter's intelligent darkness and stink. I can keep you in this state for ever, every moment worse. Oh God. Not addressed to anyone, certainly not God. Or maybe addressed to his former self. You didn't do enough. Whatever you did, it wasn't enough. You weren't enough. He thought of Luke going through his future with a buried life, the giant cancer. Sooner or later. Oh Jesus, please not that, please not that. You know how it works. Fowler had talked too much one night, pissed, policeman's disease. Good coppers had gone. The fucking stinking contagion of it. Cheryl, years ago, stirring a batter mix had said turning and turning in the widening something. It *was* Hell, then, he'd been right the first time. The infinite gap between him and the living. Forced to watch. It's beyond my control. The intelligent pressure from all sides held him absolutely still, determined that he must be absolutely still to feel it properly. It's beyond your control. All the paternal nightmares down the years, bound and gagged while someone walked away with the kids. Cheryl used to wake him at arm's length. Nate, Nate, wake up, love, you're dreaming.

Still bent on staying to watch?

Fuck you. Fuck *you*.

A strand of anger left, after all. You could use it to haul yourself out. It was himself, he supposed, asking, or the dead's collective consciousness with like a jewel at its centre Lois. Dad, you're mucking it *up*.

He couldn't respond. He'd lost the ability to frame, to direct; who was he talking to? No one answered, anyway. What swelled and rang was the dimensionless distance between himself and the living. It would get bigger proportional to his need to close it. There were animal traps designed to constrict the more the creature struggled.

He found himself in the kitchen. The reflex to Cheryl. She had to know, be made to know. It hurt him with a new brutality, now, the force he had to bring to bear; this was what happened when you really tried to break through (*Dad, be careful*) but fuck it anyway there was a beauty in the absence of choice.

Cheryl. Nothing to scream with.

There was a lot of food left over. Cheryl was telling the helpers to wrap and take home whatever they could use. Little lights of pleasure came on in each of them, the automatic response to getting something for nothing; then a bit of guilt for the smallness of it next to someone dead, then, more or less, yeah well fuck it they're loaded anyway. They'd all have mixed feelings, later, eating the cold chicken, the black olives, the pasta salad. Some of the bites would give them the reality of their jawbones and from there the rest of their skeletons. It defied belief, the meat and machine of it. Or rather didn't defy it, quite. Put the telly on for Christ's sake.

Signals Nathan couldn't sort. Noises: the murderous fan blade, *whup, whup*; chittering here and there; somewhere the mewling of a radio between stations. Around or between all other sounds the seashell's meandering gasp and susurration. Life came off the bodies in incandescent flakes, held an orbit around them for a while, then began the drift away. It was as if he could see them shedding cells, millions by the moment. Sort of thing he'd very soon be unable to bear.

Getting away from it flung him to the door that led out of the kitchen into the back garden. Three bunches of keys hung on brass hooks next to the door. He just had time to recognise the cracked Ford fob of his own (thinned by the surrender of school keys down to one for the car, two for the new house and the old two from Roseberry Road) before its shrill signal cut through every other and opened a gap of pure silence into which – his explosive resistance meaningless to the weight of its pull – he fell.

Claire

One afternoon three weeks into the summer holidays Nathan finds himself alone in the Focus parked in a lay-by on the road between Exeter and Tiverton. It's oppressively warm and the light is agitated by the shiver of overhanging beech leaves. He's not sure how long he's been sitting here. The day's insistence – that something beyond imagining is available at its end – has been with him since this morning.

The lay-by's close enough to the traffic so that when anything heavy passes the Focus rocks, slightly. It saddens him that he's never spent the night on a boat. Moonlight flakes on the water, a small-hours pee over the side, a webbed acre of phosphorus. That would have been a memory. To his left, across the road, there's a dry-stone wall and beyond it rough pasture sloping down to the Exe. A dozen beige bullocks graze in the sun. The place names out there come loose from their meanings: Bamford Speke; Efford; Cheriton

Fitzpaine. There was a place-name project with the First Years, or Year Sevens, as they're now called. Who gives a fuck? they'd asked, in their many ways. Bamford Speke was Bumford Spunk. Efford F-off. Some homophobic stretch for Cheriton Fitzpaine. The sort of thing he would have taken home to Cheryl, who would have loved the nakedness of it, back in the days.

He opens the window to the reek of diesel, exhaust and hot tar. Electric windows. Adrian has thoughts about technology, the eco-toilet the world's going down; he's taken action, down the years. Every little. If not us, then. For evil to triumph. It's twenty-five years from the undergraduate slogans, and these days there's a Mercedes and a holiday cottage in Budleigh Salterton. The week before, when they were in the pub talking about the sale of Roseberry Road, Adrian had said: 'All estate agents are cunts. Not very nice, but there you are.' Fragments of the old maxims survive, touchstones to get things done, dirtily or otherwise. For evil to triumph it requires only.

Nathan takes his sunglasses off and puts them on the dash. He hasn't been avoiding thinking of the events of this morning, but since it's only just come to him he wonders what the hell he's been thinking about instead. Now, in any case, he is thinking about it: Adrian sitting naked on the edge of Nathan and Cheryl's bed, black-bloused Cheryl in the chair by the dressing table, both of them sitting forward with feet flat and knees apart, forearms along thighs, wrists as if broken and hands dead except that Cheryl's left holds a smouldering Silk Cut. Opening the door and seeing them, Nathan had thought of two gamblers who'd staked everything and lost, staring into the space where their visions of the future used to be. He'd felt sorry for them.

Adrian had looked up at him. Nathan had taken in not just the look – no words – but also the long shins, the flinty knees, the snuff-coloured pubes and shrivelled, glistening cock. He'd thought: She's fucked him. No question of it being he's fucked her. Cheryl owned it, the three of them knew. It was Cheryl's thing, the sort of thing she'd been licensed to do. Licence granted proportional to what you've suffered.

There had been a single moment of transparency in which their triangle's truths shone out, then Adrian's face had said: No amount of sorry is ever going to be but you can see why and no I can't imagine us surviving this except by becoming but we won't because *I* can't, not you, *you* can become anything. You've already had to.

He'd poured all this out without speaking, but too late, because in the transparent moment Nathan had seen Adrian's relief that now there was a good reason to stay away from them. Seeing Adrian sitting there trying to express despite the desertion of language the magnitude of his guilt, Nathan had known that his friend felt liberated at last from the husband and wife gravity, the couple's nucleus of horror. It had measured Adrian: he was no bigger than his relief at being excused further contact with them. Which had at first satisfied Nathan (he'd always taken it for granted that Adrian was morally or imaginatively bigger than him) then depressed him, because, whatever else, they'd had a long, true, rich friendship. Laughs. There had been a summer night, Nathan, Cheryl, Adrian and Saul, an artist, at one of the tables outside the Royal Festival Hall in London. They'd said: Let's draw each other; but everyone except Adrian had drawn Adrian, because of his cleft chin, of which much fun was always made. Saul had drawn a cartoon Adrian, an astute caricature, but both Nathan and Cheryl, neither of whom could draw at all, had attempted naturalistic drawings, in which Adrian's cleft had looked like some genital deformity on the bottom of his face. A group of teenagers at the next table, annoyed that this adult quartet was making more of an hysterical spectacle of itself than they were, began throwing insults and plastic glasses at them.

The memory – of how hard they'd been laughing, Cheryl having to get up and walk away holding her sides because she couldn't *look* at Adrian – flashed into Nathan's mind when Adrian looked up at him from the bed. (The only thing to do with good memories, Cheryl had once quoted from somewhere, is treasure them.) This memory and so many others would be spoiled now, not because of Adrian's betrayal, but because of his relief at being disencumbered of their friendship.

Nathan sticks his head out of the window and looks up through the flashing beech leaves. A gap in the foliage reveals a high blue sky, implausible for England, inched across by a solitary wisp of cloud. The blue of God, that used to be, into which as a child he could dissolve. Now the blue swarms if he looks too long, yields dots and swimming strands, says physics, particles, science, nothing personal. Cheryl, years ago, had read them a poem about the sun. The sun, Luke had said, is a gaseous body with a core of thermonuclear reactions at 15 million degrees C. It'll be gone in about five billion years. They'd all laughed.

Some of the car's heat escapes, releasing him. He gets out. He wants to stretch but can't, synapses committed to some other deal. The sun fits the back of his head like a skullcap.

Cheryl had smiled at him in the wake of the transparent

moment. Not maliciously, but because she saw for the first time that like her he was past the old ways of thinking and feeling. For a second or two their collusion had returned – both of them thinking of the moment they'd been told Lois was dead. (It came round from time to time as an acknowledged obligation between the two of them, to try to recreate that moment.) Nathan's not sure now, but thinks he might have smiled back.

Apart from him the lay-by's empty. There's an overflowing litter bin halfway along, a ragged arc of rubber from a blown-out truck tyre; near his foot a desiccant yellow condom and heap of fag-ends from an emptied ashtray. Traffic passes, lorries rattlecrashing, cars flinging light, two speedbikes with kids' *meowms*. The beech shade salves his face and hands. He thinks of Gina, years ago, found on a hot day with her limbs wrapped round the porcelain stand of the bathroom sink, stripped down to her knickers and vest. It's nice and cool, Daddy. That was childhood, the dictates of the senses, all sorts of things doable before the categories and parameters tightened up. Things tightened up, then loosened when the police came. Certain words unravelled them. I'm sorry to have to tell you. All the objects in the living room had wobbled free, then. A Kant enthusiast pissed at a dinner party had gone on about things having for all we knew a whole range of properties we couldn't with five senses space and time know about, a thing-in-itselfness which must for ever elude us. When the police came and said I'm sorry to have to tell you, the objects in the room had wobbled free and shown themselves as they were, even the chunk of street and sky outside the window, all absolutely alive and indifferent. At that moment life had been revealed as a human conspiracy (from which only the police were exempt) to prevent the thing-in-itselfness of everything from showing.

He stands with his hands by his sides, wanting to stretch but still unable to. The land around feels big and solid. The death of the planet used to bother him, vaguely, but now the notion of the world as a finite and terminally diseased object leaves him indifferent, as long as Gina's and Luke's lives are okay. Where was it written – *believably* written – that the planet should last for ever? He supposes, trying again to unlock his scapulae and failing, that he shouldn't be having these thoughts. None the less. He yawns, and his eyes fill with water.

Adrian had got up, snatched at his clothes, bundled them in front of his groin and hurried from the bedroom. The room's attentiveness peaked as he passed Nathan. He slowed, as if to give Nathan the opportunity to lash out. Nathan almost did; not because he wanted to do violence to Adrian, but because the specific violence he'd wanted to do for such a long time had been denied him. It was still in there, available. Cheryl, seeing this, didn't exactly raise her eyebrows, but there was a flicker of curiosity. Nathan smelled her cunt on Adrian's face. Had it been an anti-climax? Years of masturbation (confessed by Adrian to Nathan one night as the two of them staggered home, pissed), then the real thing. Didn't the concrete details always fall short?

But that thought had led (as did the majority of thoughts) to Lois. To someone else's fantasy. To a different set of concrete details. These had been waiting for him for three years. No question of outlasting them. Their patience was infinite. Once they'd been admitted into the world they were ineradicable. And they waited. You could make a thousand cups of tea, mark a thousand essays on the industrial revolution, pull up a thousand weeds in the garden, a thousand, ten thousand, a million postponements: these concrete details weren't going anywhere. Early this morning, before going out to the dig, he had set the video to record a programme about the Orkneys; just the sort of innocent activity those concrete details could hijack – and they had. Like love they could find their way into anything. They could appropriate anything and turn it into code for their reminder: We're still waiting. When are you coming to us?

The heat weighs on him. His body feels tender, as if the glands in his armpits and groin are up. He takes a few steps away from the car towards the trees. He's left the driver's door open, which to him has the look of an obscenity, but there's no going back to close it. Four or five paces in under the beeches, he stops. This is that kind of time where you stop and wait until you know what next. Recently there have been chunks of time like this, about which he's kept quiet. Two hours in the garden shed frozen by a pulled-out drawer of screws and rawl plugs. Half a Sunday morning lying on the bathroom floor, liberated eventually by Gina knocking and saying, Dad? (She suspected breakdown; he could hear it.) Dad, I need to go.

For a minute or two Nathan and Cheryl had listened to the sounds of Adrian hurrying his clothes on in the room next door, an unfurnished room, as it happened, bare but for a few boxes of Cheryl's surplus clothes and shoes. They heard each leg go into the jeans, then the tinkle of the belt buckle and cheery *zzupp* of the flies. Followed by silence:

Adrian cogitating, fighting his impulse to make a clean get-away. He was so obviously trying to think of something to say that the process might as well have been accompanied by mechanical noise. *Whrr-clunk-pssst-wah.* Cheryl, Nathan could tell, was close to laughing. He was close to it himself. Then it passed. Adrian thumped down the stairs, across the hall and out of the front door, the two-syllable closing of which – *ta-dah* – left them suddenly alone with each other.

They were familiar with what happened next. A demand for words made itself felt like a spirit in the room, and each second they resisted extended their feeling of miraculous endurance. They'd got used to it since Lois's death, the addictive discomfort of the ability to go on not saying anything in these moments that insisted they say something. It was like a staring contest – or the hilarious footage they'd seen on television years ago of two men competing against each other at trying to stay balanced on bicycles with as little forward motion as possible. (They'd been watching with the kids. *The Guinness Book of Records.* Gina had gone into hysterics. Luke, who had no sense of the absurd, had had to force laughter, suffering inside. Later that night, after sex, Nathan had been able to tell Cheryl was thinking about this discrepancy between her and her son. She was ashamed, he knew, of liking Gina and Lois better than Luke. He knew because he liked them better himself. *He* was ashamed of it.) He'd remembered it this morning, standing opposite Cheryl in the sun-shafted bedroom, and had thought for the umpteenth time how much worse the guilt would have been if it had been Luke instead of Lois. *You didn't love him as much*, the voices would have said, and they would have been right. It was a grotesque lie, that you loved all your children equally. If Sophie's choice came calling you'd make it, whatever sanity it would cost in the end.

Satisfying, having these little neat thoughts just now, coming to the end points of things. It gives him a feeling of righteous, comfortable mischief.

'How come you're back?' Cheryl had said, at last, when their not speaking had given the silence a high-pitched whine.

'We were waiting to see if Urquhart was going to put up any more money. He isn't.'

'So what happens now?'

This was the other thing available under the demand for language: irrelevance. They'd be able to keep it up for a very short while. Then the spirit, initially fooled, would wise up.

'Nothing,' he said. 'There's no more money. The dig stops. Urquhart's had new information on a possible site in Cornwall. He's fickle.'

That was the irrelevance allowance spent. The room warmed and cooled, brightened and dulled, with the passing of clouds. Nathan opened his nostrils, smelled Cheryl and sex, but with the base notes different. It recreated her slightly, the way a tan or new hairstyle might. For an instant he saw her from outside familiarity, a woman who'd grown into her broad bones with something a long way from the conventions of beauty. No consultation of the notional ideal would lead you to Cheryl's appeal; only age or experience enough to align yourself in the right way to see what she had, a ghost of Saxon hardness, green eyes dead, available for your own projection, whatever it was (helplessness, power, love, cruelty), ultimately the thing so few men or women had: terminal mystery. What she had was that she was a finality. There was no going beyond or into her, only off in another direction, invariably retreat. Whoever you loved or fucked afterwards, you'd remember her, the occult one who'd made you turn back to the familiar, even the familiar pains and neuroses, the one who was in the end, fundamentally mysterious, and for whom you were, by definition, not enough.

'What are the options?' Nathan said.

Cheryl shrugged. She reached for the Silk Cut on the dressing table, chain-lit a fresh cigarette, stubbed out the old one.

'How do you feel?' she said. Then 'Sorry. Didn't mean that.'

They'd agreed three years ago never to ask each other how they felt.

'Very alive,' Nathan said.

'Do you want to know anything?' Cheryl asked. 'How we did it? What he was like?'

He considered for a moment. She wasn't goading. The question was genuine. It was clear from her tone there had been no surprises. Cheryl's (correct) assumption was that Nathan had imagined Adrian fucking her in the past; therefore did he want the facts to compare it with? A succession of tableaux passed through Nathan's mind, Cheryl and Adrian in various positions. In each Adrian's eyes were closed. Cheryl's were open, revealing only that her mind was elsewhere − which was why Adrian's were closed. Nathan had experienced it himself over the last three years. Cheryl's body was a machine furiously gathering data and sending it far, far away to wherever her mind had gone. Worse, however, had been those times when she'd brought her mind back during sex, when, armed with everything that had happened to them, she'd *looked* at him.

'Do you think we should separate?' Nathan said.

Cheryl looked at the bed, then out of the window, then at him. 'Anyone watching would think so,' she said. 'It depends who we're living for.'

It occurred to Nathan that she did these things because they forced them together. Most of the time it was as if they were both floating separately in a huge, empty room, the only company for each other but incapable of contact or communication.

Taking the cigarette and ashtray Cheryl got up and crossed the room – strong white thighs sun-striped for a second – to the bed. She lay down on her back.

'Why now?' Nathan said.

'Who knows? It's been building up.'

He felt sad for her, but also as if she'd closed a new door against him. Sad for himself, too, and for Gina and Luke, who, at these moments, he sometimes forgot about. Cheryl at full strength retained the power to claim all his available mental space. He went over and lay down next to her. An anachronistic version of himself protested, demanded things, jealousy, anger, but it was a tinny racket, miles away. On the other hand he couldn't see a way forward. He moved down the bed and laid his head just above her pubis. At one time she would have begun playing with his hair. He put his hand over her cunt, cupping it. Softness and heat, the way the kids' faces felt running a temperature. He didn't know what he was doing, forgiving her, he supposed, but with a feeling of redundancy. Her limbs remained still. He could feel coming off her how much was left of her curiosity about life. Not much, the faintest electrical charge. She was tired of carrying her flesh and blood around. She'd gone heavy with the boredom of it. He had no idea where she was going or what would be involved. He wanted to come close to her, just once before they disappeared from each other completely.

The open car door nags him, so he goes back to the lay-by and shuts it. A shuddering lorry carrying scrap – he sees a washing machine, a doorless fridge – crawls past. Nathan and the driver, a dark-eyebrowed man with only his face's deepest lines untouched by tan, look at each other. In potentia there's a nod or a roll-on-Friday look, shorthand for shared suffering (the job, the clock, the wife) and the thankless task of being a man. There's a moment in which both of them see the opportunity for this look (and see each other seeing), but it passes without the look being exchanged. In fact, at the very last the driver turns away with a frown, as if he's seen something irritating or offensive.

There's a lull in the lorry's wake. No traffic, but the land's reassertion of itself, hot, dry, alive. Crickets rasp at a volume Nathan associates only with the nighttime scenes of jungle films. He stands locked, listening, then something in the Focus's cooling engine *tonks*, freeing him. He moves back into the beech wood.

It's cooler in here. Nettles, docks, brambles and wild blackberries, but also bald and root-broken patches of dry earth. No paths, but he's been here before. Further in, he'll find two or three burn scars from tramps' or teenagers' fires. There's litter everywhere, some of it blown from the lay-by's bin but most dumped deliberately. They're always inhabited and used, he knows, these uninhabited unused places. People need them. Like public toilets they're sites for the publicly unseeable and unsayable. Until Lois's death he'd never considered the unvarying violence of toilet cubicle graffiti. Here's some space, write whatever you want in absolute anonymity. Fuck cunts. Kill pakis. Split her arse. Over the last three years he's avoided them. But he's been here more than once. How many times he wouldn't be able to say.

Tin cans, soiled carrier bags, old newspapers, dogshit, a footprinted sheet from a bank statement, the skeleton of a pram. There's a smell of burned oil and rotting food. Something else, too, he thinks. Unwholesome. Further in.

He and Cheryl had lain in silence for what seemed a long time. Then, feeling her beginning to want to move out from under him, he had lifted his head and looked at her. Her eyes were open. She looked back at him. She hadn't, he could see, expected him to react like this, and the surprise had woken a flicker of her interest. Only things that confounded her expectations pricked her interest. Before Lois's death one expectation had been that she wouldn't live through a child's death, but here she was. That, her surviving self, had commanded her interest for three years.

Suddenly, it became painful to look at each other. Their shared past rose up, shocking both of them. It was as if both their former selves, imprisoned and forgotten for so long, had broken out and screamed at them to recognise each other. They both looked away. Cheryl made a slight move-ment – the beginning of getting off the bed – but Nathan put his head on her midriff again and his hand back between her legs. This was a new variant of those moments demand-ing speech: they weren't resisting, now; they just couldn't think of anything to say. Nathan dreaded that out of sheer panic Cheryl would say something ugly: I swallowed his come, stuck my tongue up his arse. He could feel panic driving her to it. Their former selves had commanded them to remember how good they'd been together at their best, which made the ensuing silence raw. Both of them were thinking they shouldn't have let themselves get close like this, lying in the familiar position. Any second, Nathan thought, she'll have to say something, shove something in the way of it.

But they withstood it and lay motionless, not knowing what to think. With a minimum of movement Cheryl stubbed the cigarette out and transferred the ashtray to the bedside table. Nathan kept his head and hand where they were, feeling her stomach muscles moving under their wrap of fat. (The kids had loosened her body, given it accents of pathos from which his sexual self stepped aside to make room for love.) He could tell she didn't know what to do next. A part of her, the dominant part, was insisting on the absurdity of the two of them lying there like teenagers on a Saturday afternoon, and on the further absurdity of her husband's fingers between her legs wet with another man's come. With the slightest effort (Nathan imagined the no-nonsense voice in her head) she could reduce this to something crude, her husband's complete emasculation, his abdication from dignity, a risible impersonation of Jesus turning the other cheek.

Yet still neither of them said anything. Knowing that in perhaps seconds this balance would be lost, Nathan gently but unambiguously applied a gentle pressure between her legs. They'd started like this countless times. In their old life Cheryl might have said: I hope you're not intimating a desire for any of those saucy antics, mister? He loved her for it, the way she said it. Excuse me, but that's my secret place you've got your hand on *if* you don't mind.

He waited. No response – but not, he thought, definitively. He waited, then moved his middle finger against her again.

This time Cheryl moved slightly in reply. He thought: It's nothing, just an extension of the perversion, immediately after Adrian. Then either the thought passed or he forced himself beyond it. He moved his hand again. Response. Again. Response – by which time he knew success would depend on both of them losing the bulk of consciousness; if either of them stopped, if a button snagged or the phone rang, if they were forced by any detail to remember that they were making choices, that time was still passing, the whole thing would collapse. Their identities would come back and cling, Nathan and Cheryl Clark, whose daughter.

He moved on top of her, kissed her mouth, felt her hands working quick and dexterous at his belt and flies. Her eyes closed, which stabbed him with memory; it used to unnerve him, when they were young, the look of transport or elsewhereness on her face when she made love. He used to want to bring her back, to him, to the level where they were just fucking, nothing transcendent. Her face like that, eyes closed, a frown (as if, wherever she'd gone, she didn't quite understand where she was or how she'd got there) had been terrifying in its vulnerability. It had made him feel tawdry, as if he was letting her down by not going with her, by not being able to. (It's all right, she'd said to him once, jokingly, afterwards. I know it's just a good fuck. It had been meant to reassure him but it had made him feel worse. He'd felt *sorry* for her, that she got so much from it. Sorry for himself, too, because he found the look a slight turn-off.) But now, Zennishly balanced between desperation and hope, he saw her closed eyes and faint frown and felt a rush of loyalty. He kissed her open mouth again, feeling the air on his bare buttocks and thighs as she shoved the waist of his jeans down.

A navigation with no margin for error, every movement carrying the potential to reduce them to perverseness. This danger flared, at moments, his cock's first nudge at her cunt still slick with Adrian's come – her eyes flashed open, worried she was going to see him enjoying that, *just* that, wife fucked by other man, sloppy seconds. Nathan had to turn his face away, because there were moments – this was one of them – when he didn't know *what* he was enjoying, when he knew he couldn't stand her looking at him and asking.

But then he was inside her and overwhelmed, shocked by the feeling of newness and familiarity. So far the defences against the wrong kind of consciousness were holding. He daren't think, but couldn't not think, felt dangerous thoughts begin to spiral up; so he concentrated instead on the mechanics, on getting the rhythm right, on (a flicker of genuine joy) fucking his wife as well as he possibly could.

For a while it worked. Signals burgeoned in and around her – hold, there, kiss, wait – and he attended to them. The world receded. There was room, it could be done. Each touch was a light coming on in the darkness. They were doing it.

Then all the lights were on and it had to become something else. Cheryl, legs wrapped round him, opened her eyes and looked at him. He knew what she was asking. It was what one of them always asked: Can you think of it and still go on?

In the time it took for him to see that this was what she

was thinking, she went away from him. Their bodies kept moving, him into her, her up to meet him, but she was losing the fight. Her face crumpled once – righted itself – held – crumpled – then recovered again. Time and consciousness had bullied their way back in. They were themselves, Nathan and Cheryl.

Cheryl turned her face to the side. Her eyes closed, but this time the closing was the beginning, Nathan knew, of a contortion, an expression that would take possession for a second or two, seem to presage a screaming fit or psychic implosion, then abandon her, leaving the look of vacuity.

He put his arms round her, pulled her close. But she'd gone. Or rather returned, fully. All consciousness, all memory, all concrete details. He felt a last flicker of the hope, then it went out.

'Get off,' she said.

He held her tighter.

'Get off me.'

He's moved further into the wood now. The unwholesome smell he caught earlier flirts with him. He feels hot in the head, but also increasingly tender on the surface of his skin. Hyperventilation over-oxygenates the blood, gives your extremities the feeling of being about to burst. He supposes this is what he's experiencing, being long since done with the supernatural. The last time he felt anything like this was in childhood, with the onset of fever. He'd thought the Devil was trying to enter and take possession of him. Well, his father had said, mischievously, he *might* be. Have you said your prayers? Then an admonitory thump from Nathan's mother, and his father laughing, and himself feeling that between them his mother and father could see the Devil off without much trouble, should he come sniffing around.

By the black scar of a fire he comes across two separate pages from a porn magazine, once sodden, now dry, lying at an angle to one another like flags in semaphore. (Who knows what's become of the rest of the magazine? That's the way of it with these places: one perfectly good shoe; an untouched pack of cigarettes; two pages of a magazine. Physical non sequiturs.) One page shows a close-up of a young white girl sucking a huge black cock, the other displays illustrated ads for sex phone lines. The colours of this page are aggressively optimistic, sky blue, sunflower yellow, electric pink, mint green; they connote sweets, treats, the circus, comics, all the verve and adventure of healthy childhood. Barely Legal Teens. Big Dicks Small Holes. Into Boffin' Tiny Twats? Fuck Her Arse Then Come On My Face. Whip My Little Sister While I Suck Your Cock. Like the place names of earlier the words drift loose from their meanings as he reads, until it feels like he's pronouncing a foreign language phonetically. Then the words resettle into English and it occurs to him that he should have some feelings about the paedophilic insistence. Barely Legal. Tiny Twats. 'Is it a coincidence,' Adrian had asked in an editorial (before Lois's death), 'that the alleged increase in paedophilia in the West coincides with the unprecedented presentation of children as objects of sexual desire in the media?' Over the last three years Nathan's seen the same message everywhere: children are fuckable. He's felt everything on the spectrum from rage to despair. A GAP poster of a ringletted six-year-old in a bikini wearing eye make-up and lip gloss. This is the high street. His mind had nearly gone. Now, though, he feels a curious indifference, as if he's being asked to bother about politics on a hypothetical planet. A handful of times when Luke or Gina or Lois as kids sat on his lap at the wrong angle or moment, he'd felt his dumb cock begin to stir, but he'd known enough of himself to write it off, just the body's hiccupping egalitarian idiocy. He's wondered since if he should have reassured himself so readily. But it *was* nothing. The trail of self-interrogation always petered out, went cold. The flesh was a fool, that was all. Perverse, to boot. In any case it seems irrelevant, now. He's a long way from all that. The questions and worries of those times have the sad and distant look of faded toys in an old shop window. He registers the lightness this image brings, then is distracted by the feeling of his blood expanding again, not just in his fingers and toes but in calves and forearms, too. It is, he reminds himself, the effect of hyperventilation. If there's a paper bag around . . . You put the open end of the bag over your mouth and breathe through the paper. Less oxygen in the blood, the tingling stops, the feeling of being about to burst goes away.

Years ago, when he and Adrian were teenagers, there had been a girl called Dawn, their age, but unnaturally small. All in proportion, but everything tiny. Unreconstructed Adrian had said that sex with her would be handy. You could stick her on the end of your cock and at the same time 'walk about and do small jobs around the house'. They'd both become (allegedly jokingly) fixated on the idea, and had actually courted her, each pretending to the other that it wasn't serious. Dawn being uninterested in either of them, nothing had come of it. But he and Adrian hadn't let each other forget it (it was one of several politically incorrect indulgences), until Lois's death. Since then Adrian's never mentioned it. But Nathan's often thought of it – and he thinks of it now. There's a little flame of affection (for himself and Adrian at a time before anything had happened to either of them) but with a vast space around it. There are a lot of things like this, little flames or lights, but with infinite, freezing emptiness around them.

He moves away from the dead fire site, deeper into the wood. The litter thins but becomes more bizarre: a plastic draining rack; a lady's hat; a toy arrow with a rubber sucker instead of a point. The sound of the road recedes. There are blue and pink flowers dotted here and there, fairyish presences in the murk.

Suddenly, two boys come crashing through the undergrowth. Hard to tell how old, twelve or thirteen maybe. Muddy, baggy jeans, a Manchester United top, a maroon baseball jacket with white trim. They're absorbed in themselves. In the heat and undisturbed privacy their spirits have mingled. They don't see him at first. Then they do, and stop.

They're young enough to have to master their reflex, which is, on the appearance of an adult male, fear, meaning guilt. But they do master it, in a second, and their faces so recently thick with the afternoon's dream adjust to express cockiness, cynicism, superiority, scorn. It's taken only a moment for them to assess him, the likelihood of authority, his potential speed and strength. They're not worried. They'll keep this distance and outrun him if necessary.

'What is it?' Nathan says. He's not sure what he's asking them. He had felt, before opening his mouth, his teacherly identity rush to the surface (he deals with boys like this every day) then just as quickly evaporate.

There's a pause, in which the ambiguity of his question throws them. It's a trick. Is it?

Then the smaller of the two, blond and bony with a swipe of smut on his cheek, lifts his head, opens his throat and goes Ooouuuwah! Ooouwah! – a mock jungle noise – and gives the other's shoulder a gentle shove, and almost immediately they're off, giggling, in no particular hurry, away from him. He's been dealt with. Yeah, we know you're there. We heard you. We're ignoring you. You're not dangerous. You're not going to do anything. Ooouuuwah!

He waits until they've disappeared, then moves on down the way they came. They've reminded him of his last day at work before the summer holidays, the conversation with Lomax, the Head. He, Nathan, had been incredulous then, and remembering it he's incredulous now.

'Nathan, what are you doing here?' Lomax had said, and all the events of that morning had begun to reshuffle themselves. Nathan had known that if they lined up in a certain way, he'd feel bad. He'd begun to feel bad anyway, sitting in the chair summoned pupils sat in, wishing they hadn't done it, whatever it was.

'Well, this is going to sound bizarre,' he'd said. 'But there's someone taking registration in 4C.'

Sometimes Cheryl talked rubbish in her sleep. She'd wake him up with a random utterance: 'What are we going to do about the fridge?' For fun, he'd engage her in what he always hoped would be a long conversation, but it always broke down two or three exchanges in, as Cheryl came properly awake. She'd be sheepish and exasperated: I've been talking rubbish, haven't I? Sorry, love, I'm afraid you have. She said there was invariably a point in the conversation when she began to realise something wasn't quite right. With Lomax, Nathan had begun to have that feeling as soon as his first words were out.

'Didn't know you loved the place so much. Cheryl making you do the housework, is she?'

'You don't understand: there's someone in my class taking registration. Another teacher.'

Lomax had looked down at his desk for a few moments, then back up at Nathan. He was in his fifties, with a plump, ruddy face and greying blond hair in a schoolboyish side parting. Bi-focals, too much aftershave. (Compulsive masturbator, Cheryl had said, fixing an unpleasant image in Nathan's mind.) The look down at the desk had been to decide whether or not to come straight to the point. Underneath his bewilderment, Nathan had respected Lomax's courage in letting him have it straight.

'Nathan, you don't work here any more.'

A long silence. Lomax picked up a silver ballpoint and clicked it a couple of times, slowly. Nathan couldn't speak. Finally could. 'Did you sack me?'

'Good God, no. You've been one of the best teachers this school's ever had.'

They weren't saying anything about it, the central thing, that Nathan didn't remember any of this happening.

'It was just that you and I agreed, in the light of . . . You were under a great deal of pressure. It was honourable. You told me you didn't need the money because your wife's company was doing so well, and so we agreed you'd resign.'

'What did I do?'

'Nothing, nothing, Christ.'

Nathan had looked him in the eye.

'There were a couple of reports that you'd talked to pupils about the events . . . the events of three years ago and they were upset, a bit upset and apparently told the parents.'

Nathan had sat, frowning, experiencing déjà vu, simultaneously believing and disbelieving everything.

Eventually, he'd said, experimentally: 'This isn't the first time, is it?'

A pause, Lomax again debating with himself, again concluding be cruel to be kind.

'No. Sorry, Nathan, it isn't. It's the third. Look, why don't you let me give Cheryl a call?'

After twenty paces he finds the source of the smell, as he's known he would. Flies lift in a swirl with their sound of irritation. He walks through them, moving his hand gently about his head. The trees are close here. A shout wouldn't travel (as in his mother's talc-scented wardrobe, forty years ago, out of curiosity). It's stifling. His sensations contradict one another: he still feels fat-blooded in hands, feet and face; but simultaneously there's a suspicion of effervescence, as if by degrees he's fizzing off into the atmosphere. He thinks, absurdly, of Alka-Seltzer, imagines his head as a shrinking froth. It's not unpleasant, just an acceptable inevitability.

Hard to tell how long the dog's been dead. There are two explanations: either it was hit by a car, left, and dragged its way in here, or someone's brought it to this place and done this to it. Nathan thinks it's a bit of both. The back half of the animal (a black mongrel, collarless, though there's a stiffened indentation where the collar used to be) looks broken. It's lying on its side, eyes half open, slit from diaphragm to loins. The spilled-out organs have turned tough and meaty, and are busy with maggots. A tangle of viscera has been yanked out. The smell is so rare that for a split second Nathan has nowhere to place it, no response for it. Then nausea. He thinks of the two boys;

the dead animal would have been irresistible. That age, you can't do nothing. You've got to do something to something like that. The viscera would have been pulled out (awkwardly, with that stick lying nearby) because it could be. When you could do a thing like that, you did it. He remembers being their age.

They've put a cigarette in its mouth, sticking out between two yellowing teeth, and tied a Tesco carrier bag pirate-hanky-style round its head. Another page of porn (from the same magazine, perhaps) showing a deep penetration in close-up, lies by the muzzle, and, an odd touch, a battered playing card – the joker – has been slotted between two pads of its left paw. The half-closed eyes, the rictus and gang-sterishly gripped cigarette give the animal a degenerate look, as if its excesses have killed it – but what a way to go. Nathan's not sure how much the boys will have known the effect they were after. Probably it had felt spontaneous and random.

He asks himself if he knew about the dog. If he did, he's been here more recently than he thought. He can't remember——

Nathan fought his way to the edge of the opening the keys' signal had made. He could see out of it, back into the kitchen, where the washer-ups were putting their coats on. Cheryl stood leaning against the cupboard with one arm wrapped round her waist and the other holding a drink and a cigarette. She looked very tired. Nathan wanted to get out and go to her. The effort took him to the limit of whatever version of his strength this was. There was one moment when it seemed he'd matched the force dragging him back with his own pushing him up and out. But then, without warning and as if it had been up until now playing with him, the gravity from below doubled, plucked him from the lip and sucked him down at sickening speed——

He pulls up outside their old house, a mid-terrace on Roseberry Road for which he still has keys. He's come here a few times since moving, though he's kept it from Cheryl, who in the old life would have said sentimentality and shaken her head. There's always the possibility the agent will be showing it, but so far that hasn't happened. It's not sentimentality. He doesn't know what it is. He likes the empty rooms with the light coming in. It gives him the feeling of being out of time. The last time he came, he was sitting on the bare floorboards in what used to be his and Cheryl's bedroom when it had started raining, gently, with a very quiet sigh into what had until then felt like pure silence. He'd had the feeling of being privy to a rare and secret utterance. Which again you couldn't tell Cheryl, the Cheryl after Lois's death. Mostly, though, when he's come back here, he's just lain down and let himself drift. He's discovered a vast world of meaningless content into which his mind can dissolve. You come back to the Roseberry Road house, lie down on the floor in one of the upstairs rooms with your face turned so that you can look out of the window into the sky, and within no time at all you're in that state where things come and go, harmlessly, little bits of telly commercials, memories, songs, pictures, dreams, the anaesthesia of rubbish. You bring the blanket from the car; in fact, there's a battered sleeping bag that got left behind in the closet under the stairs. You come here and it's like peace.

But today it's not working. There's an oblong of sun in

what used to be Gina's bedroom, but he finds he can't settle in it, or anywhere else. Instead he moves aimlessly through the rooms, opening cupboards and drawers, making a pointless mental list of the oddments they've left behind: a savaged red toothbrush; a wobbly Stanley knife; a cushion; a vegetable rack; an unused pack of Christmas cards; a yellow kagoul——

Presumably because it could the signal let him go for a moment. He kicked for the surface in a confusion of blood-coloured bubbles and a sound like someone shouting underwater. Then he was free. Briefly, the outlines of things blazed with light, stretched, blistered and threatened to burst; then settled, Nathan stunned by the suddenness with which the pain of transition left him.

Cheryl stood on one side of the kitchen's central island, the young man on the other.

'To be honest with you I was in two minds about coming,' the young man said. Nothing surprised Nathan now. That he could see, for example, that the young man had seriously miscalculated his drinking and was in danger of letting something wrong out. The smiling and frowning by turns gave it away, and the formerly chilling aura now thinned to something merely . . . what? Tepid? Sour? 'You know I thought – well, she did, too – that it'd be sort of . . .' Whatever the thought his vocabulary disappointed it, let it fail into an over-articulated shrugging of the shoulders and wrinkling of the nose.

Nathan felt it opening up for him again. Something wrong with the light.

'I wanted you here,' Cheryl said.

No time. Please just give me a minute. Cheryl had drunk

since coming back from the beach, too. The slightly deeper version of her voice, all the utterances clipped at either end by impatience.

'You were the last people to see him alive.'

The young man was nodding, nodding, without an inkling, Nathan thought (slipping back, feeling the grip go), of the destructiveness she had at her disposal, what she could do if she let the drink release her. He's stupid, Nathan thought. Stupid. Last people to see—

It was no good. It opened up behind him again (the language of orientation forced itself knowing it wasn't any use), gave him a blast of pain down the centre of his phantom self before plucking him from the edge and hurling——

Nathan sits in the Focus opposite the newsagent's on Union Road. He's bought paracetamol and a strawberry-flavoured Solero ice lolly, but the painkillers lie unopened on the passenger seat. He should go home, he knows. He'll go. Finish the ice lolly then go. Ignition, start, forward, some turns, lights, the bend, gateposts, drive. Switch off. His feet on the gravel, five steps to the front door. Key, the oiled latch, the hall's parquet and unopened post and shade. The door shut behind him and then the unfamiliar house's big spaces smelling of new paint. He'll draw the curtains and lie down. No one'll be there. Cheryl will have gone into the office this morning, no reason not to. Gina'll be out with Matt. Except she might be in with Matt. Why wouldn't she be? He'll have to think about that, the two of them, fucking. He'll have to get round to thinking about that, in case it's important. In case it makes any difference.

'Hello, Mr Clark.'

Nathan looks up. It's Claire, going on fifteen now, but still with the black oboe case, which makes her look like a little doctor.

'Hi, Claire, how are you?'

He's surprised he's managed to respond. Through the day privacy's thickened around him leaving him as if dressed in a padded suit. But someone says hello and you say hi straight away, easy as that.

'Fine, thanks.'

She's on the opposite pavement, regretting having said hello. She's not up to a conversation with him. She'd wanted to walk past, then felt ashamed because he'd always been nice to her and he looked miserable and what would it cost her to say hello? She's one for doing the right thing, he remembers. Over the three years he's got used to the awkwardness people feel around him. He's learned to pretend he can't see it, to operate as if he doesn't know what everyone's thinking: Jesus Christ how do you get past that? Your daughter. Your *daughter*. Poor bastard. Complacent compassion. That was as good as it got. Elsewhere on the scale was prurience. How did it feel? Semen in the vagina and anus, multiple contusions, three broken ribs, a broken nose, death by strangulation. How did it *feel* having the information delivered? All words you'd heard before, but strung together and tightened around your daughter's body like so much barbed wire. A man did this and you weren't there. A billion things made it possible, but one of them, the only one that mattered, was your not being there. You stood in one relation to her (half a mile away, at home with your feet up, reading the *Guardian* review section), he stood in another. He. Him. Now there was only one Him. How did that feel?

There have been these mental swoops and glides recently. Anything can set them off.

'What you up to these days?'

Claire shrugs, smiles. What else would she do? What can she possibly have been up to that would make any difference to him? She lifts the oboe case. 'Been for my lesson.'

Nathan smiles. Going on fifteen but still playing the oboe. She's like that, he remembers: no fads. Starts things and goes on with them. Most likely still doing ballet as well. He remembers thinking how lightly she seemed to have received the impress of her times, Lois's impatience with her because she wasn't *au fait* with the requisite pop stars and celebrities. Lois had befriended her in the first place out of pity, because she was a sort of anachronism at school, where even the teachers called her Granny. Claire's weird, Lois had said. She knows all these *names* of things like flowers and birds. And she's only got two CDs. Gina, a teenager herself at the time and flexing newly developed muscles of judgement, had said: Claire's like a little nineteenth-century medium. We should watch her nostrils for ectoplasm. He'd laughed; they all had, even Lois, who didn't know what ectoplasm was, Cheryl smug because Gina was the smart-arse she'd been herself at that age.

'How's the digging going?' Claire says. This is a relief for her, he sees. She's found something to ask him. Sophisticatedly, too, 'the digging' managing to suggest a harmless (and pointless) eccentricity. She's telling him she's grown up quite a bit since he last saw her. Not his equal, but brave enough to imply inverted commas round amateur archaeology. He likes her for it, indeed feels a powerful surge of love for her, that she's just where she is, not quite confident, testing her range, terrified of a gaffe; but trying, feeling her way. It makes him feel that actually they share the same view of the digging – silly and doomed – but that it's his only indulgence and that she's right to humour him in it. Then he remembers that Urquhart's pulled the plug. No money. No dig. It's over. It feels like the first time he's really taken it in.

'We've packed in,' he says. 'The bloke who was funding it's pulled out. Have to find something else to do all summer.'

Not a good thing to have said. It makes the summer a big open space with nothing to do but remember. She won't know what to say. She's already shifted the oboe case from her right hand to her left.

'Where you off, anyway?' he says.

'Home,' Claire says.

'I'll run you if you like.'

'Oh, no, it's okay.'

'Go on, it's no bother. I'm going right past your house. Unless you've moved, too.'

'No, we're still there.'

'Go on, then, jump in.'

Pointlessly, Claire looks up and down Union Road, as if she's about to do something clandestine. Nathan sees in her tight shoulders how much she doesn't want the lift, not because she thinks he's dangerous, but because what happened has made him terrifying. She'll have to talk to him for five minutes in the car. That's what she's scared of, having to have a conversation with him as if what happened to Lois hadn't happened. He sees all this and feels sorry for her, but to unoffer the lift now will be worse, an admission that he knows what's going on in her head. For a moment, he sees the bit of Claire that hasn't grown up (the bit that doesn't hold with all this *social skills* nonsense) readying her to turn and sprint away without another word. It's a comforting image, sunlit Claire with her little black case, running away from him, getting smaller. He believes the girl's got limitless energy, once she gets going.

But she's going on fifteen. She won't do things like that any more. Maybe he should just start the car and drive off? Say nothing. At least then she'll have somewhere to put it: Mr Clark's having some sort of breakdown. Because of Lois. Poor chap.

It's only a few seconds looking at each other across the road, but for Nathan it's another bubble of non-time, the wobbling *things-in-themselves*ness of things coming to the surface and slipping the words meant to hold them. Trees. Grey. Hot. Details throb: the newsagent's window; the redbrick wall and pink rhododendrons of a neighbouring semi; the lights at the Pennsylvania Road junction turning from red to green. There's a busy and indifferent life to it all inspiring in him mild revulsion and excitement. *Because the Holy Ghost over the bent world broods* . . . something. He can't remember. That's Cheryl's thing, the quotes. He's dates, she's quotes, and all her Catholic ones are delivered ironically, as if their absurdity is patent. *Broods with . . . warm breast and with ah! bright wings.* Claire's in bleaching sunlight. She doesn't have a hairstyle, just shoulder-length fair hair, slightly wavy. Her whole appearance is archetypal. They sent a probe out into space, didn't they, with things like Shakespeare and Mozart on it, and pictures of male and female – the human species – Hello! Claire would represent Girl. He'd never thought of it at the time but now he wonders if they'd put anything about all the other things people did, apart from the Shakespeare and Mozart.

'Okay,' Claire says. 'Thanks.'

There's no traffic. This is one of those summer road lulls in which traffic is inconceivable. Something else might appear: an elephant bearing a maharaja; a dozen shy horses; anything but cars.

Nathan leans over and unlocks the passenger door. She's a bony girl, and ugly getting in, knocking the case against the glove box, then the gear stick, Sorry – oh God sorry, him laughing, Don't worry don't worry, it's nothing.

He's glad to have finished the ice lolly, otherwise the question of whether to offer her a bite and all the monstrosity that would connote. He shudders slightly, slotting the lolly stick into the doorwell among maps and parking change, but then realises that the fat-fingeredness, the thick-bloodedness of earlier isn't quite done with him. He wonders if he's going to be able to manage the car, since he feels like he's wearing wasp-filled gloves. He laughs quietly, then realises seeing her tightening up that he shouldn't have. Think of a rationale for the laugh. But he can't. The problem is he's not sure in his current state what's inside and what's out. He'd thought that was an inner laugh.

'I've been feeling funny all day,' he says. 'I've had the most unbelievable pins and needles in my hands and feet. God knows why.'

'Pins and needles?'

'Yeah. Weird. I think I'm allergic to being on holiday.'

Oh. Right. A joke. She laughs, once, with a little snort through her nose. He rolls his eyes to confirm it. Starts the car, indicates, pulls out onto Union Road. She relaxes, slightly. Now it's begun, a finite period of agony, she's resigned to getting herself through it. But there are unhelpful memories of having been tickled (almost to the point of wetting herself) by him back in the days of Lois. And a series of delirious afternoons one summer when the Clarks had had a paddling pool in their back garden. Had she ever sat on his knee? She thinks so. That whole summer was drugged. Their skins tasted of chlorine and the pool's rubber. The edges of herself had blurred. She'd felt an arousing disloyalty to her mum and dad, being more at the Clarks' than at home. She remembers her and Lois sticking their fingers into each other's bottom, hysterical. Doing that and things like touching tongues on and off for a few days at moments in secret then mutually backing away, laughing. She's still young enough to be alarmed by the memory. If he looks he'll see her blushing. But he's not looking, thank God. Semen in – she stops that; no she doesn't – the vagina and anus where I put my finger so I'm sort of connected to him don't think of it they haven't caught him. Dad said if it was his daughter he'd kill the bastard himself. Said he'd torture the bastard slowly to death. His mouth goes ugly when he swears.

Claire's face, Nathan thinks, has the tawny and angular look of any of those animals killed by big cats in wildlife programmes. He does briefly imagine her clamped in the paws and jaws of a lion, bleeding, but with that abstracted look, as if nothing of any significance is happening.

In the meantime he's driven the wrong way, straight past the lefts which would have taken him towards her house, and now he's passing black-and-white Friesians in the field bordering Prince of Wales Road, heading west.

'Okay,' he says, pulling over. 'Brain's gone to mush in the heat. This is what happens to me when I stop digging.'

She doesn't know what to make of this, except nothing good, and is noticeably rigid as he steers the Focus through a U-turn and heads back the way they've come. Never mind, she tells herself. It's not going to be more than five minutes. Five minutes, then you're home.

Detective Sergeant Fowler had said, Look, this is an opportunist. The opportunists don't plan, and because they don't plan they get caught. None the less, Nathan thinks, they haven't caught him. Don't say it, Cheryl had said. What? he'd asked. The word 'him', she'd said. Just don't say it around me. He. Him. His.

'Did you ever go to the place?' he finds he's said to Claire. They're at the Old Tiverton Road roundabout. She's been thinking: Old Tivvy Road, then left on Iddesleigh, right onto Mount Pleasant, left onto Elmside and right again onto Thurlow. Home.

'Sorry?'

'Where they found Lois.'

The name's like a flash of light off the windscreen. Her salivary glands discharge. She's not afraid, only desperate not to have to talk to him.

'No,' she says. She doesn't have the authority to change the subject. Instead she presses her ankles against the oboe case between them. You look like a duck when you blow into that, Lois had said of her and the oboe, not evilly, just honestly. Claire had laughed. It had been that sort of friendship, where they could say things like that. Lois wasn't cruel. She didn't have the streak that Gina had, and her mother, Cheryl. Opposing sides had formed during that paddling-pool summer, her and Lois and Mr Clark on the one, Cheryl and Gina on the other. (Luke had been away, camping.) The opposition had been played out in everything. Swingball, in particular. Claire was used to the unsatisfactory allowance of being let to win by grown-ups. Not Cheryl. Swingball, her eyes had flashed.

'Sorry, sorry,' Nathan hears himself saying. 'That's what my wife will tell you is a non sequitur. Do you know what that is?' He looks at her. She shakes her head. 'It's when you say something that has absolutely nothing to do with what's gone before.' Signals are reaching him that he's way off. Frightening her. It's as if he's hanging at a cold depth in the sea, looking down into a further, unimaginable depth, out of which these signals of how much he's frightening her are trying to reach him. They're like those luminous science-fictionish creatures that live where no light reaches. Fascinating.

He hadn't been there when they'd found Lois's body on the eighth day. He, Cheryl, Luke and Gina had been on their way back from the second of their televised appeals. (The press room had been full of camera flashes and the gangling of tripods. He remembered the irritated concentration on the faces of the photographers and sound crews, had a glimpse of how Lois's disappearance translated into problems of shutter speed and balance, aperture and compression.) They made only two appeals, only had the opportunity to make two, because three days later they found her body. Months afterwards, alone at home, Nathan had found himself watching an American documentary, which revealed that one of the reasons police encouraged televised appeals in cases of suspected murder was that if the murderer was a member of the family there was a good chance the strain of guilt would show in front of the cameras. Journalists were briefed by the police on how direct their questions might be. The stronger the suspicion, the more confrontational the approach. In some cases, the documentary claimed, journalists were encouraged simply to ask a suspect (generally the father or husband) outright whether he had killed and concealed the body of his child or wife. The reaction, caught on film, would be studied by an expert later. Nathan had sat and watched the programme to its climactic conclusion, a case in which a father had raped, murdered, cut into pieces and buried his fifteen-year-old daughter. (The crime was uncovered by a sniffer dog famous for its ability to detect minute traces of blood – which it had, between two kitchen units in a room that had been scrubbed and bleached several times by the culprit.) Each family member had spoken in turn, the father last. He'd begun calmly, with the reassurance that nothing bad, absolutely *nothing bad* would happen to his daughter if she came home, that she would be welcomed with nothing but love and relief, that she was not, in any way, in trouble. Then, when he said her name – Janine – his face had contorted with what could have been horror or grief. Tears; he'd been unable to speak. The cameras had flashed, clicked, whirred, as if sharing sensational gossip. Then he'd recovered himself and finished the appeal. The documentary's narrator had dwelt at length on the father/murderer's incredible 'performance'. But to Nathan there was no doubt that the moment of horror had been genuine. It was the moment at which, through a hole in the wall of delusion and denial, the father had caught a glimpse of reality and truth: that he had raped, murdered, cut into pieces and buried his own daughter. Saying her name – Janine – had opened it. For a few seconds he'd seen everything. Then the hole had closed, leaving the wall of delusion and denial intact once more. Considering the father's eventual arrest, Nathan had found himself envious. That you'd done such a thing yourself meant you'd gone. That was the end of yourself. You hanged yourself in prison. That was – he repeated the phrase to himself often – the end of yourself. You'd done the thing that made going on as yourself impossible. You either killed yourself or left your identity behind, resolved yourself into monstrosity, killed as many as you could before they caught you. Either way you'd be free of who you'd been. Either way you refused to accommodate both the past and what had destroyed it.

His own position was worse. Someone *else* did this to your daughter. You must remain in the old world and remain yourself – otherwise how could you remember her and how could you catch him? He'd left her body like a remark or an invitation to which you couldn't reply. Unless you found him yourself. Unless.

We're not dealing with a member of the human species, Fowler had said. Nathan had thought of all the times he'd heard other people say things like that. Hangin's too good for 'em. Somebody should do the same to them. Torture the bastards, make 'em suffer. In childhood you were tit-for-tat, that was the natural thing. Then you talked yourself out of it. Perfected the fucking liberal sigh. When Fowler had said what he'd said, Nathan realised how much he'd needed to hear it. It filled him for a moment with a sort of blood-joy, that he could find this animal and kill it.

At the same instant that Claire says 'Mr Clark?' a car behind them beeps protractedly, startling both of them. Nathan has no idea how long they've been waiting at the junction, but there's a feel in the car of Claire having been on the verge of flinging her door open and bolting. He hurries into first, indicates right, and goes too fast round the roundabout.

'Sorry about that.'

'Are you okay?'

He gives her a look of being exasperated with himself. 'Might've eaten that ice lolly too fast,' he says. This time there's some lag between his remark and her smile. It hasn't occurred to him before, but he supposes now that kids *do* go there, where the body was found. That's what the two boys were doing there before. He imagines the whispers, the bravado. Then they'd found the dog and had to make something out of it. A thing lying there like that, you had to make something out of it.

He pulls up outside the Roseberry Road house, three streets away from Claire's home on Thurlow Road.

'Thanks,' Claire says. 'Say hello to—'

'Hang on a minute Claire, would you?'

'Pardon?'

'I've got something for you. Something of Lois's.'

There are these little movements of his will today, things that run out suddenly and pool or shape themselves into a conclusion like having something for Claire, something of Lois's. He's watching himself, but with most of his consciousness scattered elsewhere. Couldn't say where; just out there, sprinkled on the tarmac, the air, the house fronts, the street's margin of shade.

'Something of Lois's?'

He's switched the engine off. She's got her door open and one foot out on the pavement. Nathan can feel the pull on her of everywhere that isn't here. She's old enough to have started working it out, the possibility, the potentiality. She'll have seen films, most likely. The detective who gets inside the mind of his serial killer and can't get out. The policeman's disease. It's coming off her to him like the first whiff of what will soon be a powerful smell. It's so obvious that he almost says, it's okay, Claire, I'm not going to do anything to you. You're perfectly safe with me. I'm not that man.

'Come on,' he says, and gets out of the car. He turns his back on her and walks up the short front path to the door.

She's unsteadily balanced. She hasn't seen the films (she avoids them), but she's absorbed the convention from somewhere that the more terrible things you've seen, the more terrible things you're capable of. Or rather not absorbed, but half grasped. These aren't the things she dwells on, since Lois. But there's abuse, isn't there? People abused as children grew up to be abusers themselves. Everyone knew that – and what was that if not a kind of contagion? If something happens to you, you can't say you can't imagine it. The more that happens to you, the less there is you can't imagine. And when you can imagine something, you can . . . Well, when you can imagine something it's like knowing the vampire can't come in unless you ask him. Just knowing is asking, isn't it? Once, that paddling-pool summer, in the bathroom, Lois had fished a pair of her dad's underpants out of the linen basket and in a moment when she, Claire, wasn't on guard had pulled them over her, Claire's, head. Again the two of them had been in hysterics; even as the victim Claire surrendered to the exquisite horror and profanity and unbearableness of it. But Lois had said, That's like you're kissing my dad's willy, and the words had combined with the smell of the underwear (salty, with a flash of sour) and forced the image onto her so that ever after she'd felt as if she'd done it – or that, if she was ever made to do it, she'd have forfeited her right to resist.

She vacillates between all this on the one hand and on the other the thought that she's being ridiculous. This is broad daylight and she's practically outside her own house and there three doors down are two thick-bodied women sitting in fold-out chairs smoking and ignoring their two small children who are scuffing around with toy cars in the dry flower beds.

'Tell you what, Claire,' Nathan says. 'You wait in the car if you feel funny.' He smiles at her, sadly, when he says this. He looks absolutely exhausted, as if a thousand years of sleep wouldn't be enough. He knows what she's thinking, she believes. He knows and is helping her out. If it was her dad he'd say, How *dare* you? How dare you think for *one second* that I'd . . .? But Nathan's always been kind to her. She's always thought of him in the same way. Gentle. Harmless. Brainy. Now, seeing him enter the empty house, she feels she's let him down. The way he turns and disappears into the shadow of the hall, he might collapse in five paces, the last bit of fuel gone. Just conk out.

But there's the thing about having something of Lois's, which can't be true. What thing of Lois's? Besides, the house is empty. Did you ever go there? he'd asked. The place where they found Lois? Suddenly, she wonders if this is the anniversary of Lois's death. No, that was winter, stupid. Maybe he's . . .

Now she's worried. There's nothing to stop her staying where she is. But the thought that he's somehow in danger begins to gnaw. What if he's really not well? What if she leaves, and he collapses in the empty house? Who would know he was there? And she'd have to say, Well, I just left him. I felt funny. I felt that because his daughter had been raped and murdered he might do the same to me.

Nathan moves in small steps down the hall to the back

room. Ten years ago they knocked through into the kitchen so they could have a dining table where all five of them could eat together. Because we want to be like the Waltons, stupid, Cheryl had said, when Luke had asked, Why are we doing all this and how long is everything going to be covered in dust? Where had the money come from? They must have saved, Nathan supposes. What a lot of life there was to remember, how things happened, where they went, how they ended. They'd come back here from the televised appeal, sat in this room. Cups of tea. Cups of tea were the matchstick supports holding off collapse. DS Fowler had gone out and left them with two officers and a woman from the counselling unit. In front of the cameras Nathan had hardly been able to speak. Keep saying her name, they'd said. If someone's holding her we have to keep reminding him she's a *person*. But every time he said 'Lois' it was as if someone had whacked him across the throat with a stick. If someone's holding her. He'd had a vision of her with someone's arms wrapped tight round her waist from behind, lifting her off the ground, her struggling to get out from the hold, legs bicycling. He hadn't wanted to give him her name. He already had too much. Giving him her name would be everything. There'd be nothing between her and him then. But of course he already had her name, if he was holding her. Her name, her address, the names of her mother, father, brother, sister. It was all over the newspapers.

They'd sat in this room. The phone was a black god, a little Jehovah to whom they craved and dreaded being summoned. Time had passed, every fraction of which carried its quota of agony. He and Cheryl had been driven to put their arms round each other by the unbearable quality of time; but they'd recoiled. The comfort was so small that to take it only confirmed the scale of what they were taking comfort *from*, its annihilating dimensions, its irreducibility. Every minute, Nathan had thought: Not another minute, not one more, please, please God, please God not one more minute. But the minutes had come, hard and bright as diamonds, one after another.

Claire steps into the hall. It smells of floorboards and earth. She's very conscious of her body, the particular size and shape it's arrived at after fourteen and a half years. Her life, she thinks, can be divided on either side of her gran's garden. She used to sit with the old woman on the back step of the little house in Pinhoe, learning the names of the trees and plants there. In the sun, there was no peace like it. Her gran's knowledge sprawled, weirdly. Hawthorn bloom and elder flowers/Will fill a house with evil powers. Peonies cure epilepsy. Go out into the garden at midnight and pick twelve sage leaves on the stroke of twelve: you'll see your future husband. The two of them had sat soaking up the sun and from that centre the world had seemed to spread outwards under a web of magical order. Whatever was out there, there was something to be known about it that would make it manageable. That was one half of her life. She can't remember exactly when she crossed over into the other half. Her gran had died a few years back, but that wasn't it. The other half of her life was lived in a different world, one in which no matter what you thought you knew you didn't know anything. Anything at any moment could change and become something else. Standing in the hall of the Clarks' old house watching Nathan, who himself stands with his arms slightly lifted from his sides, as if he's balancing on a narrow beam, she thinks: It's since Lois died.

That's when the other half, when . . . The world's so *old*.
You never think of how old it is, how people's families go
back to Romans and Vikings and before that when the
countries were all one land mass before America split off
and before that to hairy people with spears and before that
what? Monkeys? The other half of her life is lived in a
world which feels like it's making itself up as it goes along,
putting out shoots in strange directions on a whim, just to
see what happens. There's nothing to know, only things to
observe.

Nathan turns and sees Claire standing in the hall, lit by the
afternoon light coming from the living-room doorway. She
has the golden hair of Ladybird book children, blue eyes
with the look of being made to water by the cold. It's
another of his mythic images of her, he realises, the girl
standing on a hard hill in sharp air, eyes streaming from the
blowing cold, golden hair with a spring blue sky above. It's
the blue and gold of those early Renaissance paintings,
which used to have such an effect on him.

'I think I'd best be off,' Claire says. 'My mum'll be getting
worried.'

'Yes,' he says. 'Of course.'

There's to be no mention of the thing of Lois's he's supposed to have for her. On the other hand, he's confused. *Isn't*
there something? He puts his hand in his pocket with a feeling of déjà vu, and there's the Hermes stone. It's the
morning and he's in the reconstructed Lois room and he's
going in the drawer and taking it out and putting it in his
pocket. So now it's here. He remembers.

'Are you all right?' Claire says. 'You don't look . . .'

I'm sorry to have to tell you. Consciousness had persisted. Even as Fowler had delivered the information a small

part of Nathan was reserved for asking himself: How is it that you don't die? How is it that you can stand there, bearing this? There was no answer. In those first moments when Fowler brought the news Nathan had realised he'd lived his whole life on the understanding that certain things wouldn't have to be borne, that some experience would break the world or your mind, excusing you from having to endure it. But here were the moments, here were the words. We've found the body of a young girl fitting Lois's description in a woods area just off the A396. Here was the event to break the mind or the world – but here, too, were the enduring details: a *TV Times* on the living-room floor, *Coronation Street's* Deirdre and Ken on the cover; Cheryl on her knees in the doorway, Gina with her arm round her; Luke standing holding an empty coffee mug. Certainly there had been the *things-in-themselves*ness of things, objects slipping their labels and meanings, but the truth was it had only been a moment. These years he'd used that moment to cover up the worse horror, which was that the world and himself had remained and endured the rape and murder of his youngest child. He'd known, then, that there couldn't be a God, not because his daughter was dead, but because his daughter was dead and he could (and did) in the moment of hearing the news identify the characters on the cover of a *TV Times*. The moment equalized every-thing. No one thing was any more important than any other.

'It was this,' Nathan says, holding the stone up for Claire to see. 'But it's probably best if I hang on to it. It's not really mine to give, anyway. I'd have to discuss it with Cheryl.'

'I couldn't take that,' Claire says. 'There's no way I could take that.'

'No, I know.'

'Was it *here*?' Claire says, before she can stop herself.

'No.' He looks down at the bare floor, then back up at her. 'No, it was in my pocket.'

Silence. The unasked question of what, then, they're doing in the house. Which, at last, lets him know he's arrived at the edge of himself. He hasn't planned this. But for three years he's buried the light of that day's truth under routine. From the day of Lois's death he's been granted a three-year allowance of ordinariness; the habits of work and love and thought have been running on a finite fuel. Now the fuel's gone. If the dig hadn't been stopped, if Cheryl hadn't . . . if even the dog . . . But it wouldn't have made much difference. Another day, a week, a month. Sooner or later this is where he'd be, facing the paradox: if it's bearable, he can't bear it. And it is, apparently, bearable. Therefore he can't bear it. Something must be done so that he stops enduring. He's been waiting three years for someone or something else to do it for him. In her own way Cheryl's tried, for herself, but she must have thought it would affect him, too. He feels a last stirring of love for Cheryl. He sees how lucky he's been in her, her strength and humour and intelligence, the fabulous wealth of her sex. What a sad thing that he won't have the chance to say goodbye – then like all the other little flames of light this goes out.

Claire doesn't want what she's seeing to be what she's seeing. He's crying. Or rather, tears are rolling down his face without any other sign of emotion. He remains still, looking, she thinks, at her shins. She's never seen a man cry in real life. It's terrible. She thinks of wars, the trenches, for the first time it dawns on her that all the horrors of history really happened. Men, channels of bloody water, corpses. Men.

Nathan had asked to see the photographs of the body as it had been found. No, Fowler had said. What's the point in putting yourself through that? Nathan didn't know. There was just an ungainsayable imperative. It wasn't until, after much argument with Fowler, he was allowed to see the photographs that he thought he understood: because otherwise the man who had done this would have succeeded in taking her into a place so terrible even her father wouldn't follow.

Fowler gave him an A4 manila folder and left him alone in an interview room. They made people talk in here, scrutinised alibis, spread them out, poked, prodded, found their weak points. Nathan felt the room's residue, all the degrees of capitulation, the increments of admission. When they got him, whoever he was (he had to think when, not if), he'd be brought into a room like this.

It's only recently Claire's mum and dad have eased off a bit on letting her move about unaccompanied. Now she thinks, I'll have to not tell them about this or else they'll get paranoid again. She can sense a time not far ahead when the balance of power between her and her parents will have shifted, irreversibly, a time when she'll be worrying about them. It still astonishes her that she's begun keeping things from them, *for their own good*, as she tells herself. This was what happened as you got older, the world sidled up to you and said, *You know me better than they do.* You thought about the things they said and the telly they watched and all the things you knew that they didn't and you were forced to agree. Presumably the world just went on like that, transferring its real self repeatedly to the youngest generation.

If a tree falls in the forest and no one's there to see or hear it, has it really happened? Nathan had taken that one home to his dad.

'God,' his dad had said. 'God knows it happened. There's never no one there because God's always there.'

Nathan had caught him after the second whisky before Sunday lunch, Frank precariously balanced; the second White Horse invariably put him into a state from which could follow either the certainty and benevolence of God, or radical religious doubt. He prowled, psychically, from his armchair, looking for something to latch onto and get fired up about. If Frank had been a man who hit his kids it would've been a risky game for Nathan. As it was, Nathan knew the worst he'd get was incredulity.

'D'you know what "omniscient" means?' his dad had said.

'No.'

'It means God knows *everything, all the time.*'

It used to irritate his mother that they had these conversations after the second peg. Something disrespectful about them, she felt, even when father and son were in agreement about how amazing God actually was, when you thought about it. They always seemed to her to be on the verge of hysterical laughter, as if God were the biggest joke ever. She didn't know why she thought that, there was just something dirty about the way they went on about it.

Nathan stands with his arms raised slightly from his sides, the Hermes stone in his left hand, his finger through the smooth hole in its middle. He's not sure of his balance. There'll be things to do, and he thinks for a moment he should ask Claire to stay and help him. But no, of course not. Stupid.

'I'd better get going, I think,' Claire says, again, but still doesn't move.

He'd been describing himself as an atheist for years, certainly since university, but it wasn't until he saw the photographs of Lois's body that he realised he'd been kidding himself. Until that point God had remained as a grudgingly allowed morally disinterested reckoner, someone who totalled up the numbers, netted all the details, knew everything, all the time, the infallible repository of history. But alone in the interview room Nathan had looked at the first of the photographs and the numbers and details had gone whizzing away through a storm of chaos into nothingness. No one was reckoning, keeping tabs; this wasn't a story someone was following to see how it turned out. This wasn't any kind of story. Why do kids like stories? Because there's a beginning, a middle and an end, Cheryl had said. Partly exposed through the dark loam of her shallow grave, Lois's pale hip and knee. His lungs had filled and stuck. There was the body and there was love. The body was finite. Love was expected to bear the finiteness of the body. His father had had an allotment and it had been strange the tenderness Nathan had felt taking winter vegetables from the ground. Which memory was unwanted, the feel of soil against skin and the soft tearing of the roots, the pale tubers and the dark earth. All memories were unwanted, memories of Lois most of all because if they came they'd have to be made to fit with what was in the photographs. The persistence of connection and the whizzing away of all the numbers into nothingness. These were the two things. Opposites. That was life's question: can you bear the opposites?

When, Nathan wonders, did he think that? Suddenly he

has a memory of the faces of 4C turned to him, uncharacteristically attentive, indeed silent, rapt. There'd been a couple of reports that you'd talked to pupils about the events, Lomax had said. It filters through to him that there are, presumably, other chunks like this he doesn't remember. If he goes back into the world there'll be other Lomaxes, other conversations like the one in his office. Why don't you let me give Cheryl a call?

Claire's been holding a lot back and now it comes forward. There had been the thought that she should go with Lois but the truth was she'd been mesmerised; Gayle and Nick on one side, Dominique and Nee on the other, both pairs of mouths and heads moving as if mechanised. It had looked as if each couple had been given a quota of snogging to be got through, so there they were, getting through it. Meanwhile Rob sat and talked, endlessly, only very occasionally looking at her – but on those occasions the surge of nakedness she felt made her scalp tingle. She hadn't wanted to kiss him, but there was no way she could tear herself away, either. It was fascinating, that they'd met these boys by accident, that they could, unimpeded, walk the five minutes from the leisure centre to the bus shelter, that cars passed, saw them, went on their way. It had been like entering a foreign country in which suddenly your choices and actions were legitimate currency, just as good as your mum and dad's. The first two weeks she'd kept expecting some force of authority to appear and put a stop to it. But no such force had materialised. By the third week she'd been giddy on it, the freedom. When Lois had said she was going back for her stone Claire had felt the certainty that she ought but wasn't going to go with her as a sensation of warmth and heaviness in her body.

The thing she's been holding back is the thing she always has to hold back and which always at some point breaks through. If I'd gone back with her she'd still be alive.

Certain points on her body — shoulders, wrists, nipples — stir and come awake as she watches Nathan take a few uncertain steps towards her. That's what *he's* thinking, she believes, that if I'd gone with her. It was the big thing between them and all this time in the car and in the house they'd managed to say nothing about it. Everyone, all the time, managed to say nothing about it.

She should go, she's sure of that, but similarly sure she can't. She's fascinated in the way she was that night. He walks towards her as if on unevenly spaced stepping stones. He's stopped crying but his face has been pummelled by it, eyes small, cheeks baggy, mouth half open. She's already said, twice, that she should go, but here she still is. A circle she can't step out of. Extraordinary, the way he moves. She can't really tell if he's looking at her.

A cloud shifts and the sunlight flares from the living-room doorway, sharpening her. The wisps of hair form a silvery halo and the blue eyes bring in cold spring skies. He feels thick in his blood and skin and his hands torment him with sensitivity. He has this image of the planet's slow swirl shedding everyone's thoughts and actions and feelings in a spiral that can't keep its shape for long. Immediately round the earth there's a Milky Wayish pattern of glittering debris — our recent history — but further out the flung spars dissolve and drift in all directions, the difference of a few degrees in each trajectory eventually becoming unimaginable distances, until no one fragment connects with another. They go nowhere except away from each other.

As he comes within range and puts his hands on her

shoulders Claire feels as if all the accidents and choices in her life have been secretly leading to this moment. She hasn't known; it's been a conspiracy, but she recognises it here with a combination of horror, resignation and a strange relief because at least now it's out in the open that she's powerless. As she thinks this an alarm goes off in her bones and adrenalin floods her. Suddenly just the opposite seems true, that she can do anything, jump out from under his hands, flip backwards, fly away. She thinks of him saying, Stay in the car if you feel funny, which of course meant everything to do with Lois and a man and a girl and all the years of don't talk to strangers. It meant that they, Mr Clark and her, shared an understanding, inhabited the same world. They still do. She looks up at his face and the intensity of the connection between them almost makes her laugh. Then the adrenalin explodes a second time and she thinks how bizarre that she'll never see her mum and dad again, nor eat tea and toast in the evening by the gas fire. Images – leaves in sunlight, her ancient tricycle, her dad shaving – hurry into and out of her mind, then she halts the process by thinking This is what they must mean about your life flashing before your eyes, and again is left convinced that she can jump up and take flight, that he'll be standing there with space where her shoulders were.

She's so much alive Nathan imagines his hands bursting into flame. There's the belief that in consuming the life of your victim you acquire his or her power. He can feel it, not just the imaginative logic of it but the physical reality, which exerts a sensuous gravity on him, as if the act as yet in the future is reaching into his present flesh and blood and hurrying him towards it. He has a glimpse of how it'll be, like taking a huge drink, the warmth spreading from core to extremities, or extremities to core. He took her life, they'll say, and they'll be right. All the details of her, her unique total, will pass in those moments from her to him; he'll be enriched by her precise quantity. Satiated, then quickly hungry, infected by the knowledge that there's only one certainty for the future: that because he can bear having done it he'll have to do it again. As soon as he understands this it seems certain not that he'll kill her – that's neither here nor there – but that there are several ways of deciding not to go on. One way of not going on was to look for Lois. Another was to look for the man who killed her.

'You'd better be getting home, hadn't you?' he says, removing his hands from her shoulders.

She nods.

He feels cold despite the heat. Tiredness throbs in his arms and legs. She keeps looking at him, then away.

Eventually, she turns and walks out of the house, looking back only once from the front step.

After a few moments, he goes down the hall, closes the door, then comes back into the empty kitchen——

Nathan tore himself out, deafened by a stretched scream then suddenly encased in silence. No control. One moment he was flung out of the house, jumped by all the garden's phantom smells and colours, the next he was swung back in, hurled through the mist and a jumble of the house's spaces. Rooms, or parts of them, came and went. Sounds – voices, a door closing, ice cubes in a glass – returned, compressed and expanded at random. There had been childhood fevers like this, tumbling through the old house in Polsloe, walls jabbering their histories, window views upside down, people not seeing him.

Orientation returned in sharp-edged slabs, dropped as if from a height. He found himself back-pedalling at speed from the kitchen doorway, down the long hall, at the end of which was Cheryl's voice and someone else's. He tried to turn but couldn't. Increasing panic the closer he got. There was some simple element of the turning-round manoeuvre still missing. It was right there on the edge of himself but he couldn't for the life of him—

Then he could, and had just time to see the blonde woman receive her black patent-leather handbag from Cheryl before he collided with her and a signal that whipped out and took him before he'd——

Mrs Lloyd

'It's on at one three five nine fifty,' the estate agent says, as she follows him down the hall and into the living room. 'I can tell you that they did turn down an offer of one two five about a month ago, so you might want to bear that in mind.'

She doesn't like him, but he's not as bad as the bloke yesterday who over-used her name. As you can see, Carol, this is a brand-new kitchen. Carol, I'm going to let you just have a poke around on your own while I make this call, yeah? These are the two latest things, over-using the name and not breathing down the neck. She's only been looking a week and already knows all the versions. It's still titillating to be just where she is, to have buying-power. The pleasure of buying-power never gets old. D'you mind if I ask what you do for a living? It's the women who ask, the young career girls. Can't help it, since she's where they want to be. Waxing, threading, facials, full-body exfoliation, manicures, pedicures, electrolysis, red-vein and skin-tag removal, non-surgical facelifts, body-scrubs, ear and body piercing, semi-permanent make-up, aromatherapy, Indian head massage, shiatsu, reflexology and a range of weight-loss therapies. Oh yeah, and hairdressing. She's tempted to reel the lot off, but in the end always just says, I run The Business, the beauty therapy centre on Fore Street. The women all know it. They've either been in or wanted to. They don't all know there are now eight The Business branches in the South West, but there are plenty of giveaways that she's more than a salon manager. Not just the gear and the two serious rocks, it never is just that; it's the way she moves through space, no apology, a radius of entitlement, the glow not only of having money but of having made it herself. The old moneyed are vaguer, not really seeing you. Women like her are always seeing you. The satisfaction for women like her is in the perpetual measurement of the earned distance between you.

She knows all that, she's used to it, doesn't mind, enjoys it, even. As she can in the right mood enjoy the blokes not knowing how to be with her. The default male reaction to an upper-class woman is contempt, get her on her hoity-toity back and show her she's just another cunt as far as they're concerned. Slightly different with a woman who's got her hands dirty making her own money. There's a disgusted, sheepish, grudging admission that they speak the same language, though sooner or later she knows it'll resolve into one sort of contempt or another. It always does, eventually. Men always do. At least the ones who aren't plain terrified of her, like this twit.

'Now obviously they've knocked these two rooms

through to make the sitting-room-kitchen-diner. Not a big job to put the wall back in if you want.'

He hasn't asked her outright if it's a buy to let, but he's made the assumption. This is the heart of the student quarter. Obvious from her current address that she isn't thinking of this as a place to live in. Hence the wall-replacement remark. You get another room, you get another rent-paying student. Screwing students is okay with him, he wants her to know, especially Exeter's toff wankers. Yes, she's sure he's pegged her for a putative landlady, a Thatcher entrepreneur who managed not to go tits up in the Nineties and who knows in the end you can't beat real estate for peace of mind. A twit as a man, she thinks, but as an estate agent he knows his punters.

He trips going up the stairs ahead of her and she feels sorry for him. He's got a womanish arse and blond hairs on the backs of his hands. She knows it takes all types but he'll be few women's cup of tea. She really does feel sorry for him. She feels sorry for men, eventually, sympathy she thinks of both as a weakness and as the remnant of something precious the last thirty years have eroded. She remembers coming out of school at fifteen with no qualifications but the bone-deep certainty that you had to get money and that it was no one else's responsibility to give it to you. She'd gone into Chop and Change one day and told her Aunty Bernice that she wanted to learn how to cut hair.

'I won't lie to you,' he says, opening another door. 'Fourth bedroom's basically a glorified cupboard. But, you know . . .'

She's thinking, okay, get rid of the carpets, strip the floors, paint the whole thing white. Four futons from the wholesale place out at Marsh Barton. Double glazing's new. Kitchen's fine. Four upstairs, put the wall back in downstairs gives you another two. Fifty a week for those and thirty-five for the glorified cupboard. She takes a black leather Filofax out and jots down the figures. That's two eighty-five a week's about eleven hundred a month—

It's a terrible, ugly sound when he screams. He leaps backwards and stamps on her foot. She takes in that surprising pain but also his shriek like a ten-year-old girl. It's horrifying on its own, exposes him to her, obscenely. Somehow she's alongside him, gripping his arm. (She takes that in, too, that you grab people, as if that'll help.) The bathroom door completes its opening arc.

'Fuck *me*. Jesus Christ.'

'Oh my God.'

'Jesus Christ.'

'Oh my God.'

For a moment they freeze.

'Is he dead?'

She moves past him, into the bathroom, Filofax clutched. The tub's three-quarters full, tinctured with blood. There's a brown Stanley knife handle on the rim, next to it, the removed blade, with a trail of blood attached like a pennant. Behind her, he's fumbling with his mobile, going Fuck, fuck, fuck . . .

He dials nine nine nine. Stares wide-eyed while the mobile does its thing.

'It's the guy.'

'What?'

'The guy, the guy, the fucking *vendor*.'

She doesn't know what he means – thinks ice-cream vendor – then remembers the context: the vendor. The person selling the house.

The naked man in the bath looks troubled. You'd expect

it to erase expressions like that, but apparently not. The water's still and translucent. It might be weak strawberry jelly he's been set in. Bits of him break the surface: kneecaps, toes, belly. The little penis sways like an underwater tuber. She's never seen a dead person before, assuming he *is* dead. She wondered why he bothered undressing, except maybe there was an instinct to go out naked the way you came in. She's surprised how sad it makes her feel. It's as if the little boy he once was has come to the surface to complain that this wasn't what he'd imagined. It hurts her that she's never had kids, sends her mind rushing back to the question: Is she too old? Medical technology, what they can do nowadays. No. Forty-five. Surely too old? She looks at his slightly troubled face. Girlish eyelashes. His lips are parted and a pinkish bubble of saliva has formed between them. She can only think in understatements: Such a shame. Such a terrible shame. What was it? To come here all alone. That was the thing, the aloneness of it. She imagines him after he made the cuts, still with the time to change his mind. He'd have looked around before his eyes closed, taking in the humble details – taps, tiles, plug – thinking how strange that these should be the last things you see, the last things to say goodbye to. It's the aloneness of it that gets her, somewhere in the solar plexus. She knows it's partly herself she's sorry for, because it's not so hard to see how you get here. Some nights on her way back from the loo in the small hours she feels her own house feeling sorry for her. Poor thing. On her own.

'Yeah, I need an ambulance right now. Thirty-two Roseberry Road, Exeter. There's someone slashed his wrists . . . What? I don't fucking know! I think he's dead . . .'

The pink bubble swells and bursts with a distinct *pup*. Surprised at herself, she puts her fingers next to his lips. Feels it, and with it a shocking surge of adrenalin because she knows now that every second will count.

'He's not dead,' she says. 'Tell them to hurry.'

Luke

'When I was little,' Luke said to Gina, 'Grampy told me suicide was a mortal sin and if you killed yourself your punishment would be seeing the grief of all your loved ones and not being able to do anything about it. There was this story. Someone's shown visions of Hell – he must have got this from Dante, mustn't he? Anyway, there's this guy who's killed himself and he's following his family around going, I'm sorry, I'm sorry, please forgive me, and it's agony because they can't see him, and nothing he says or does can make them feel better. That was his Hell, Grampy said, for ever.'

'Yeah, they don't fuck about, those Catholics,' Gina said. 'That's the appeal, presumably.'

The two of them were in the study, Gina in the battered fireside chair with her legs stretched out, Luke on the hearth rug, knees up under his chin, watching the flames. Drunk themselves sober. It was dusk. Outside was a cool evening, the sky ink and lilac. Lynn and Jake had gone home. Cheryl was in the kitchen, standing at the sink and looking out into the garden. The Lloyd woman had had some sort of turn and had to be sat down for a few minutes. Still trembling when she left, Cheryl said. Adrian was in the office on his own with a bottle of Scotch. Frank had fallen asleep on the couch. The funeral was over.

'That priest was wrong,' Luke said. 'About suicide coming from despair.' He'd listened in church. He'd wanted to know what they were going to say about it. Catholicism fascinated him, the contortions it put itself through to make ends meet. Father Murray had kept returning to the word 'despair'. There'd been a little (bizarre, Luke thought) linguistic diversion into Latin. *Desperare*, formed by the *de* prefix, signifying the removal of or from, and *sperare*, meaning to hope. The removal of hope. That was despair. The reasoning being that you couldn't live without hope. What Murray hadn't said (but what, along with the story of the suicide ghost, Luke remembered from childhood) was that despair was classified as a sin against the Holy Spirit. That was the perverse beauty of the religion: that your daughter could be raped and murdered and yourself still condemned for giving up hope. It was the sort of glacial and inhuman God Luke was inclined to believe in since Lois's death.

'Priests are wrong by definition,' Gina said. She surprised herself with these pronouncements. They came out of her mouth (more often mouth than pen, more often drunk than sober) and nailed down some nebulous part of her thinking or feeling that had been a pain to her for ages without her until that moment having really been aware of it. 'How do I know what I think till I see what I've written?' Cheryl used to quote. Gina had her own version: How do I know what I think till I've got pissed and blurted it out?

260

'Yeah,' Luke said. 'But what I mean is you can live without hope as long as you've got curiosity.'

The word 'curiosity' made them look at each other. Nathan felt them realise simultaneously there could be something between them. It went through Gina like fresh alcohol on top of what was already there. Her scalp tingled. She could handle it. It was an extension of the business with radiators and spoons and trees, the business of things suddenly showing you all the other ways they could be. Something big had to happen to see it. Death. Birth. War. Terror.

Luke felt it as the shifting out of his way of something that had been obstructing his vision. Or as having at last got the message he'd been sending himself for years. Not just that he could go to bed with his sister, found her desirable, but that the previous girls – the handful there had been – had all had elements of her in them. A lot of the half-finished equations down the years were actually this equation, now solved. Amazing.

Both of them felt it, took it in, knew they'd do nothing about it. Not yet, anyway. It was something in their life. Maybe to be made use of in the future. All of which might as well have been a conversation, Nathan thought, though they said nothing.

Gina was trying to think of something to say that would get them away from each other. There was, immediately following the mutual recognition, dizzying embarrassment. Luke was thinking of how many siblings must have this, battened down, unarticulated. It nearly made him laugh. There was no end to things.

'I think he lost his curiosity,' he said. 'Even about Mum. Even about us.' Even about *you*, he'd been going to say, because he didn't put himself in the same league as Gina or for that matter Lois. They'd always preferred the girls. Not that an observer would have known. It would have looked as if he was treated the same. He *was* treated the same. He was loved. None the less he'd known for years they were somehow more . . . excited by his sisters. Was that it? Whatever it was, it was something; he hadn't imagined it. There'd been a big book when he was seven or eight, *The Giant Book of Knowledge.* One page showed the different types of clouds. Cirrus, cumulus, strati, cumulonimbus. All the clouds were drawn on a blue sky. The picture used to hurt his heart and comfort him at the same time. He used to go to it for refuge if he got shouted at. It promised something, a time or place where . . . What? He didn't know. It made everything easier to bear, confirmed his loneliness and salved it. Offered something beyond his mum and dad and having broken the glass door of the front-room cabinet.

Gina yawned, so widely that her eyes filled with water. 'I think he just decided to go and look for Lois,' she said.

Luke thought of that night, himself running, all the city's spaces a conspiracy. He'd had the feeling rounding every corner that Lois had been standing there a second before – only to be whisked away just as he appeared. 'Yeah, maybe,' he said. 'It's a better thought, anyway.'

He watched the fire for a few moments. Funny how quickly they'd assimilated what they'd just seen in each other. Now it accented everything else. Her bare foot was near his shin and the little space separating them was clamorous. He got up, went to the desk, came back with the wooden box. Gina looked up.

'Stole this,' he said.

'What?'

'I stole it. From a shop. I've been nicking things for a while.'

Gina merely blinked. 'Oh?' she said.

Not bothered by the illegality, Nathan saw. She had Cheryl's quiet belief in herself and those she loved as being above the law.

'About a year, on and off,' Luke said. 'Then I read about it.'

'What d'you mean?'

'It's a symptom,' he said. 'It's what people do, apparently.' He laughed, grimly. 'Classic, really. I was at the fucking dentist's, in the waiting room. There was an article about it in a magazine. You want to punish yourself for not having died, so you nick things or whatever in the hope you'll get caught.'

Gina said nothing. Understood. She'd seen something similar in a film. Jeff Bridges?

Very casually, Luke threw the little box on the fire. The gesture made Gina jump. In silence, they watched the flames begin to take it.

'There are loads of cases,' Luke said. 'What people do if someone's died.' He paused. 'And if something like what happened to Lois. That's another thing I read about. I started reading.'

It was no good, he thought, he wasn't going to be able to explain. The disgust because he'd found out it was . . . What? Predictable? The sort of boredom of it? He couldn't get it into words. He wanted to say it had made him feel small. But then it had also nearly made him laugh. He thought of the picture inside the box. When he'd found it in his pigeonhole it was as if someone had known, although if you'd asked him *what* they'd known he wouldn't have been able to answer.

He'd opened the envelope and there'd been that feeling of . . . He still didn't know what. Gentle invitation? For a moment (the box spat out a little shower of sparks with a snap), he thought the essence of the feeling had been relief.

'It's deflating,' he said. 'To find out there's nothing new about it. The way you react to something.'

'Everything's films, now,' Gina said. 'You've seen it.'

'Yeah, it's annoying.'

Luke, it's Mum. He'd been standing in his Halls corridor when she'd phoned to tell him his dad was dead. Among all the other thoughts there'd been the one reserved for the picture in the envelope, tucked into the back of his wardrobe. He'd put it there and not told anyone about it, but now it was as if a time-lock had been sprung, even after all the reading, as if the gentle invitation had been saving this card till the very end. He'd come home not knowing what his future would be. He didn't know even now, he supposed, except that whatever power the gentle invitation had had was gone. *That* future . . . It revolted him that predictability extended to such things. There was a temptation to think of himself as outraged: I'll be *damned* if I'm going to conform to their prediction! But it wasn't that, really. It was more him shucking off a massive weight of boredom.

Gina's mobile rang. Matt. She gave Luke a look – we didn't imagine it, but wait – then got up and walked away, talking quietly into the phone.

For a while after she'd gone Nathan stayed with Luke. The boy's mind wandered, went up dead ends, circled, sent out thoughts that tapered then faded into nothing. Now and again went up to the brink of disgust or horror, but came back. The way he'd been since Lois's death was a weight and he didn't want it any more. He just didn't want it any more. And there was Gina. Maybe that was predictable, too. If that wasn't the future, what was? This was the challenge the dead left you, he thought, to avoid being predictable.

Turning onto his side, he curled up and closed his eyes, letting his face take the warmth of the fire.

Adrian

Adrian was drinking robotically in the office. He wasn't going to get any more drunk except to become unconscious. In Nathan's mental picture Adrian was still in his early twenties, the long-boned face framed by fair, close-cropped curls. (You know your hair makes you look homosexual, don't you? Don't ever wear a cravat, okay? As a friend, you know, I'm telling you. And steer clear of velvet jackets. Adrian always nodded the same bored, tight-mouthed but ultimately contented acknowledgement. Some women, they both knew, thought him extraordinarily beautiful. Cheryl thought him – and had said so in his hearing – almost *angelically* beautiful, but actually half ugly. In a very good way, she'd added, which had been enough for Adrian. Your bird fancies me. Yeah, Nathan had said. My bird fancies *Harpo Marx*. Which was true, Cheryl having a thing for silent comedians.) Meeting him after time apart Nathan was always surprised: the amount of grey, the skin's history of fluorescents and deadlines, the soaked-up worry, the managed stress. Christ, he'd said to him at Paddington the last time he'd gone up for a weekend, what a truly wizened old bastard you are. I'm not surprised you're still single. To which Adrian had replied: Here's a fact. Last week I had sex with a twenty-eight-year-old woman. From behind. Now that's just a fact, you know. I mention it only in passing.

Rightly or wrongly it almost made Nathan laugh. Phantomly. He'd put off going near Adrian all this time. Now there seemed no point. In any case, he missed him. Thirty-five years. They'd been so close it was a miracle the friendship had been able to accommodate Cheryl (love, marriage, children, the transfer of loyalties, Adrian's descent down the lifeboat hierarchy) at all. A miracle facilitated by the admission that Adrian loved her, too, that there was something in potentia there. Had to be. Something they all tacitly agreed to live with. It suited Adrian, Nathan had always thought, gave him a romantic rationale for slipping through one affair after another, committing to none. You're like Lancelot, you are, Nathan had said, once. With the clap, Adrian had added, honestly.

It didn't matter to Nathan, now. Did it? He nearly laughed again. Apparently it was all right. He loved both of them, so what, really, was the problem? He felt sad that it hadn't been any good for either of them. Especially he felt sad for Cheryl, for what her sexual self had become, for what all of her had become. She'd been so wealthily alive. Now it struck him as criminal that she hadn't had more affairs, more lovers, found outlets for whatever elements of herself had fallen dead on him. There must have been some; there always were. What a shame she hadn't had an affair with Adrian sooner, when the two of them were at their best. But then what if she'd left him, Nathan, for Adrian or someone else?

Hard to imagine, given the kids. Not because they called up duty, but because he and Cheryl were so much in cahoots bringing them up. The children were the source of their collusion, something they in spite of what they thought of as their own juvenility were pulling off, getting away with. Hard to imagine Cheryl trading that in for anything. It was their life and she loved it.

Had loved it.

Adrian swallowed what was left in the tumbler then groggily poured himself another, annoyed by the way sooner or later you were like someone doing a bad impersonation of someone completely drunk. Annoyed by everything and sickened to his guts by some things. Science Morgan going on the other week in the pub about how it had been discovered (accidentally, believe it or not) that by passing an electric current through various bits of the brain you could make people miss out the number seven, or feel terribly depressed, or start pissing themselves laughing. Morgan, who was in Adrian's opinion a rotten bastard to the core, had told it pissing him*self* laughing. Adrian, thinking of Cheryl, Lois, Nathan (in that order), had nearly smacked him in the mouth. Pointless. But he couldn't help it. Certain things brought up disgust. Or brought down depression. The pub conversation had expanded from Morgan's electrocuted brains to the material and deterministically mechanical universe in general. Someone had said it didn't mean we weren't free, and Adrian had nearly smacked him in the mouth, too. He'd been Uncle Adrian to the kids, *Poor* Uncle Adrian (a Nathan amendment) as they got older. He'd had glimpses of it, what the household had, the way the kids smelled after their baths, the reflexive ease of shared flesh and blood, the love and sex at the heart of the marriage like a furnace heating the whole place. He'd seen it, oscillated between envy (there were intimations of mortality in the small hours, nightmares, moments of crippling aloneness with some stranger in his bed) and self-congratulation for having avoided it, the stink of emotional routine, responsibility, the heap of fucking laundry that came with domesticated love.

Someone had put a shotgun hole in it.

Adrian swallowed and poured again. He couldn't get the image of Morgan laughing out of his mind. Doesn't mean we're not free. Cheryl had been miles away. Like an alien sent down to impersonate a human, to find out what human experience was like. Ah, Christ, Nate, I'm sorry. I'm sorry . . .

Nathan went close, not knowing whether it would do any good. It's all right. It's really all right. It doesn't matter.

It didn't, as far as he could tell, do any good. Adrian laid his head down on the desk and closed his eyes.

Gina, with a sweater over her shoulders, went past the door. Nathan turned and followed her out of the house.

Gina

Matt wasn't drunk, and so drove. His mum's Mondeo, wan-
gled, Nathan supposed, to take tragic Gina for a soothing
drive after the horror-day of her killed-himself dad's funeral.
They'd let him take the car, but Nathan picked up from
Matt what Matt had picked up from them: that they were
pretty sure he ought not to get any further entangled with
what was (understandably) a barking-mad family under some
sort of death curse.

Not a bad driver, Nathan observed with relief. Passed his
test a month ago, first time. Drove responsibly. Did everything responsibly, played guitar and took drugs responsibly.
He'd go through life managing his indulgences, Nathan
thought.

They went to Haldon, parked and walked up to the site of
the dig. A full moon hung above the hill. Gina'd put her
sweater on over her blouse, but had to take it off again by the
time they reached the top. Warm nights in England courtesy

of fucked weather. Sensuous pleasure and intellectual unease. All the things her generation couldn't enjoy cleanly, thanks to all the generations before. Thanks to my generation, Nathan thought.

The place was deserted. Half a dozen trenches five or six feet deep intersected each other. Urquhart had given them nothing except a grid reference and a plan of the lines to be excavated. Insane. On the other hand (forget the Holy Grail) Exeter was a Roman city, so always worth sticking a spade in. Admitted or not, all of them had dreamed of finding something big. None of them had found anything.

Matt had brought the blanket from the car. He spread it out and lay down on it, hands behind his head. Gina stood for a moment looking down towards the city's lights, then joined him.

'You must be feeling surreal,' he said.

'Yeah, pretty.'

'Sorry I wasn't much use.'

'Don't fish. You were use.'

'How's your mum?'

'I don't want to talk about it. I've been in it all day.'

'Okay, sorry.'

'D'you mind if we don't talk?'

'No, no, fine. Whatever you want.'

She turned to him and he put his arm round her. She rested her head on his chest.

Even on the periphery Nathan could pick up a lot of what there was. Matt was worried. First, that they'd get gang-assaulted (and naturally in Gina's case gang-raped). Three months ago it had happened to a couple just outside Dawlish. Completely unprovoked. The guy had been kicked nearly to death. He'd survived, identified one of the attackers from a line-up, and eventually the whole gang had been arrested and charged with rape and attempted murder. And this was *Devon*. The English Riviera, as the signs outside Torquay proclaimed.

Second, he was worried about whether, if they were going to fuck (and there were signs, God help him), he'd be able to do it. He'd had sex with two other girls before and both had been near disastrous. The condom. You had to stay hard. *Had* to. With the first girl he'd gone emphatically soft, softer it seemed to him than he'd ever been before in his life, as if his cock was trying to make a protest statement. Luckily for him she was experienced. She sucked him, got him hard again, then put the condom on *for* him. Success. Post-coitally, he'd swaggered, and assumed they had something going between them. No, she told him, it was just a one-night thing. The next girl had been as inexperienced as him. He'd gone soft again and got angry. Said something horrible to her, made her cry – and discovered serendipitously cruelty's restorative powers. Hard again, he'd got the condom on and fucked her, *fucked the shit out of her*, as he put it to himself, later.

None of which would work with Gina. He was already afraid of her. She was, simply, bigger than him. Knew more, understood more, felt more. It was all over her and inside her and pouring out of her whenever they were alone together. If he stayed with her much longer the discrepancy between them would become intolerable to her and she'd get rid of him. Therefore the thing to do was get out before she did. Problem was he couldn't. The fact was (Christ, was it?) he was hooked. She looked at him when she sucked him and it was like nothing he'd ever felt before. He wanked about her *all the time*, that look, as if she was absolutely disinterestedly examining his experience of her doing it to him. He had to look away to make it last because looking back at her made him come, instantly. He didn't think he'd survive going soft with her. And the hate approach wouldn't work because he'd never get round her superiority. He'd just hate himself more.

Third, he was worried about the ethics of fucking a girl (assuming they weren't ganged, assuming he stayed hard) on the day they put her old man in the ground. Couldn't she be said to be not in her right mind? And that's not even taking into account what happened to her sister. Ought you to fuck any girl whose sister had been . . . Was any girl whose sister that had happened to ever in her right mind again? But the way she looked at him, she seemed in her right mind, terrifyingly. (There was, too, the question of what it meant to *him*, what had happened to her sister. Was that – oh dear God he sincerely hoped not – part of the appeal? Could it be? Was he already that fucked-up?)

Fourth, he was worried about the blanket. It looked like the sort of thing you'd have to get dry cleaned.

Nathan felt peaceful and tired, lightly attached to the world. There was always more to people than you allowed. The boy's worries recommended him. Better to admit the thoughts than not, even the speculations about Lois. The only alternative was to pretend you didn't think them. The always and for ever unacceptable alternative. Cheryl knew it intuitively, lived it, even now lived it. Matt was ordinary, alive, not bad. About a fifth as good as Gina. Most men wouldn't be even a fifth.

Gina got up on one elbow and leaned over him. 'Kiss me,' she said.

The surge of propriety Nathan was expecting didn't

come. For a while he kept telling himself he was waiting for it. Then realised he wasn't, that it didn't matter. He felt the way in which it would have mattered separate from him and fall away like a veil taken by the wind.

Gina wasn't thinking of Luke, but he was somewhere at the back of her consciousness, adding another layer to what she was doing. Like Nathan she waited for the feeling that she oughtn't to be doing this. Like Nathan, she realised it didn't matter. Further (as she unbuttoned Matt's jeans and took his thickening cock in her hand), that 'oughtn't' was there half the time out of fear. There was – had been perhaps for ever – a collective agreement against . . . she didn't know quite what. Freedom? Truth? Neither word got it. Against the relativity of everything. Against the possibility of losing your virginity on the day of your dad's funeral. (It took something of it away when she realised they'd have written about it, whoever they were, psychoanalysts. There'd be a theory, a PhD thesis, statistics provided by American girls who'd got over the horror and decided in the American way to make it a cause for self-congratulation: yes I did. Yes I did and it felt absolutely *fine*. Not wrong *at all*. In the weirdest way it was like an act of *love* for my dad.) She almost laughed. Stopped herself not because it would have been ungenuine but because she knew Matt was precariously erect and she didn't want to freak him out. It didn't feel to her like an act of love for her dad. Certainly not for Matt.

'Wait,' Matt said. 'I've got to put something on.'

'Don't,' Gina said.

'What?'

'I'm on the pill.'

'Yeah, but—Are you? Fucking hell.'

Gina, astride him, still holding his cock, lifted then lowered herself so that the tip of him was just touching.

'Gina—'

'Shshsh.'

'Oh God.'

'Gently,' she said – to herself, since she was on top. She could see Matt's eyes wide and wet in the moonlight. She looked up, and there, with absurd appropriateness, was the moon, fat and yellowish this low in the sky. Later, she thought, it would look flat, thin, icy; the air around it cold blue.

He'd been thinking of Aids, but only on principle. He knew *he* was safe, so unless she wasn't the virgin she'd claimed to be . . .

Gina was aware of all this, and that he was wondering whether she was lying about being on the pill. She was lying, but knew he'd reassure himself she wouldn't be, couldn't be. In any case, now he was an inch in and she could see from his face that this would stop only if she stopped it. Potential pregnancy (remote: she'd just had her period) and potential death. She let the two things send their shadowy charges through her. She let them, but stood fast, not caring. Ridiculous or not, there was at this moment a limit to her fear of either of them. Could have a child, could die. What was there to say except that it felt right that those two should be there on either side of her like standing stones?

Which brought Lois, the cist, you're *dead* – the reflexive guilt, but again the second feeling growing fine-branched and stubborn around it that her curiosity about herself was more than a match for it. She'd always be more curious about the effect of the guilt than she'd be guilty. A simple ratio she'd have for the rest of her life. She thought of her mother.

As did Nathan. There'd been a conversation one night, some months after Lois's death. They'd been lying in bed, side by side, awake. Nathan hadn't slept. Cheryl had spent the night downstairs, moving quietly from one room to another, standing, sitting, staring out into the back garden or the front street. She'd come upstairs when it started to get light.

'I want to tell you something,' she said.

He turned onto his side to look at her. She'd lost weight. There were new accents around her eyes and mouth. The eyes themselves looked hyperalive, an effect at odds with the dead voice. She remained lying on her back, staring up at the ceiling, or whatever she was seeing instead of it.

'Hermes wasn't just the god of travellers.'

'Cheryl—'

'He was also the god of luck, music, eloquence, commerce, young men, cheats and thieves.'

There was nothing to give her. He put his hand on her midriff.

'He was also the conductor of souls to Hades, the world of the dead.'

'That's the same as saying we should never have taught her to swim.'

'No, because being able to swim might have saved her life one day.'

Best not to say anything. Especially since whether he liked it or not there was a locked-up part of himself waiting for release so that it could blame her, as she wanted to be blamed. You and your fucking stories, your fucking *writing life*. There was this locked-up part, hammering, screaming, but he doubted he'd ever let it out. It would fade soon enough, become ghostly. It was trivial next to love, anyway. He thought of her that morning in the delivery room, the ugliness and agony she'd gone through so Lois could be born.

'That wasn't what I wanted to tell you,' she said.

He waited. Now felt his hand on her as an insult. The patronising assumptions of habit.

'What I wanted to tell you was the first thought that went through my head, the first thing I knew for certain when they told us they'd found her.'

Nathan stilled, the way he might have watching someone on the scaffold, noosed, waiting for the trapdoor to drop.

'The first thing I knew was that I was going to survive,' Cheryl said.

Nathan said nothing.

'I wanted to tell you because I'm guessing you'd never think it. You should know. I've wanted everyone to know. I'd have taken out an ad in the paper if it wasn't for what it'd do to the kids.'

After she'd got up and gone downstairs, Nathan had thought back to the moment when Fowler told them they'd found the body. Cheryl had dropped first onto her knees then onto all fours. Her face had seemed to implode, to discover a new version of itself which inverted its values, a kind of anti-Cheryl. Was she saying that even then, even *then* . . .? He wondered if she was making it up, a new myth to punish herself: You could stand it. You could stand it, you curious, unnatural, disgusting bitch.

Gina had what Cheryl had. What he didn't have. Courage. Nathan felt a last surge of love for his daughter, almost beyond bearing (like the panic of earlier it threatened to close round and destroy him), then it let him go, became something gentler. He had a bizarre intimation of himself as something so big that even his love for his daughter, even *love*, in all its shapes, occupied only a small part of him, of the room he had.

Matt had pushed Gina's skirt up and freed her breasts from the funeral blouse. Gina, astride him (feeling, past the first painful thrusts and the modicum of pleasure that followed, a new animal membership of the species – this was what we *did* – but also how open it was to hijack, by bathos, cruelty, sadness, slapstick; that the world must ache with how rarely we did this right, how little tenderness . . .) had opened his shirt and the bare flesh was pale in the moonlight. She looked down at his face and up at the moon, alternated between these two. She liked him enough. It was all right. She liked him enough for this.

'Touch me here,' she said, guiding his hand. It was an awkward angle. She felt sorry for him, because whatever else was true he did want her to enjoy this, he was, actually, excited by her pleasure, ready to do whatever she asked. 'It's all right,' she said. 'I'll do it.'

It was a while before it got good for either of them. Matt was some distance away from sensation; this new intimacy defied belief, and it was as if he had to get himself mentally far enough away to consider whether it was really taking place. It helped him stay hard. Coming was inconceivable. He was grateful to whatever was making it possible. He couldn't get the inner pornographic voice – bitch move suck spread wiggle – off the ground. There was some weird, neutral mental flailing in its place. He had, too, a feeling of waiting for something, a less trivial version of himself. He was, he discovered, more innocent than he thought. Life was . . . What? Huge? Something like space and history. Jesus.

But eventually they found it, made the switch. They looked at each other in surprise. Gina'd been making herself come for years. This was different. It kept astonishing her that they were outdoors, nothing between themselves and the air, that there really was such a thing as moonlight, so bright you could see the expressions on someone's face. To the left of the hill dark pinewoods ran down into the valley. It was absurd that all this was still available, that the old presences were still in the world, hardly ever attended to. They were like sad old gods wandering around, at a loss. She thought of her Grampy, the way he so often just smiled and raised his eyebrows, sadly, resigned not to having the faintest idea what they were talking about. And for more or less the first time that day she thought of her dad, the reality of his death. All the shapes, contours, details and quantities of her world were altered by the unique and unmeasurable difference of him not being there. Luke the man of the family now. (These archaisms. But something big happened and they stepped forward, knowing they'd be needed.) There was only her stopping her brother cutting himself loose from them altogether.

And herself? Her dad was *dead*.

She thought: It's a relief because he was never right since Lois. All those times she'd found him sitting crying, or staring, or simply standing in the middle of something, yet the rest of the time carrying on as if nothing terrible had happened and everything was fine. He'd had two modes: distress and denial. You needed more than that. If he'd turned his life into a quest to hunt down Lois's killer he'd have lived to be a hundred. Why didn't he do that?

Because I didn't have the strength, Nathan thought. Sorry, angel. I wasn't strong enough.

Matt came. He didn't know what brought him to it, except that the reality of what they were doing seemed suddenly without warning to double in intensity. He didn't know what it was but it was filled with the absolutely astonishing fact of her in this state, her, Gina, the . . . he couldn't, it was as if he loved her or something. Oh dear God. Fuck. Jesus.

She came a few seconds after him; made herself because she knew she'd have to if she was going to come at all: there was the difference of being filled – the dumb incontrovertible satisfaction – where? In the guts? Heart? Soul? Where? – but coming was clitoral. Maybe not if you found the right man. The belief was out there that you might. She doubted it. All these thoughts before the very last stage, in which she sank or rose (which was it?) into a state where the boundaries between herself and her experience burned almost but not completely away. Not completely because there remained the thought that this was profane, dishonourable. Not completely because there remained the counter-thought that nothing was profane in itself, that yesterday's blasphemy was today's joyous Mass. Not completely, finally, because what had been done to Lois *was* blasphemy, and would remain so no matter what, no matter what came from it, no matter what. She'd reject any world which found another way of seeing it.

Shuddering, she leaned forward and put her hands and mouth on him. It all so snugly fitted. Fuck the moon and the stars, the transcendent impulse, the temptation she'd had to go out into whatever was out there; here was skin and bone and muscle and blood and the humble fitting together, ludicrous and too often desperate, but still, at its best, a shout of optimism. This was the flesh's gift and suffering was the flesh's curse. A terrible trade-off. Lois again. Dad.

She didn't bother looking up for a while, just kept close to his body. The moon and scatter of stars, the pinewoods' dark line to the left, even the city lights twinkling below, had joined with what she was doing in that way the world had of suggesting meaning, something *going on* that she was part of. It never specified (although presumably if you were a Christian it specified that this was the journey through Christ's mercy towards God, or if you were a Buddhist that this was a moment in the flux of coming into being and passing away); it never specified to her beyond the hint that here was a clue to the mystery that would ultimately, beyond death, perhaps, be revealed. There *was* something, these *were* clues, the world *wasn't* accidental or chaotic. Her mother had brought her up with this faith.

She'd moved beyond it. Couldn't put her finger on how, exactly. You had to be cunning. You had to simultaneously hold onto the clues and be ready to let them go. It was a sort of dirty game; you had to half-cheat, be two things at once. You had to hold derision of yourself in reserve. Or laughter at least. The world did.

The last of her childhood passed away like the end of a firework, a soft crackle and sparks in the dark, then nothing. It was very sweet for a moment, on top of him, his cock filling her, grass between her fingers and toes and the air cooling her skin. It was still just Matt, and he wouldn't do, in the long run, but they'd had this together and it had been good. She felt friendly towards him. Sad, too, because she'd seen his eyes and behind them the question of love. He'd been ambushed. She thought: He's like that, wide open without knowing it. He'll keep falling in love. Men look for a reason outside themselves to be any good. They're taught to be insufficient to themselves. Dad again. No wonder women feel sorry for them. They could bash you and you'd still feel sorry for them because they were so comprehensively insufficient to themselves. Christ what a fucking mess. Don't think too much. Enjoy this. He's not a bad person and it could have hurt more or been a disaster in so many different ways and actually it was nice, which must put me in a tiny, tiny, tiny minority.

Underneath, there was, too, the pleasant surprise: she'd be able to make men fall in love with her. What would she do with that? She was curious. She crouched there on top of him, very curious about herself, her future, the life she might have.

Cheryl

Nathan moved away. High over the city he spun, slowly, saw the summer constellations, the shadowy hills, the lit roads webbing the darkness. Exeter was a little packet of lights and life. Images flashed: the city smudged and crumpled by bombs, then its buildings going up like backward footage. Normans, Danes, Romans, Celts, the forests. Its time was a crinkle in history, a tiny thing. There were all these convulsions of human activity; things exploded, fell, were rebuilt, busily, with forgetfulness. Families, towns, countries went about with furious urgency, like insects, crimping and creasing history, generally oblivious. Fifteen billion years ago, as Luke had told them, from a dimensionless point of infinite mass and density. Since then, he'd said no, it was something else; but Nathan couldn't remember what.

Along with all the insect activity of explosions and building, like a collective headache, there was the struggle to see past the beginning and past the end, the time before time and the time after. A lousy, perpetual species headache, made worse by certain moments – cloud shadows, a rainbow, the sea at sunset – of coherence.

Beauty, Nathan thought, descending on the new house (he could go where he wanted at will, apparently), wouldn't leave the world, no matter what, but dumbly or aloofly stayed put, insisting on something beyond itself, giving everyone the headache.

Cheryl was in the bathroom, peeing. Her eyes hurt. Every part of her, in fact, hurt. She sat there, consulting regions: knees, ankles, head, face, back. All pain to one degree or another. She didn't know what to do. Here she was, peeing. Her body still did its things, apologetically. Her body had become like a family living under her roof in terror of her. As had her family, she thought. As had. Like. As if. Dear Cheryl *will* keep making connections. When humour left it wasn't the end. You still had irony like a cactus. No beauty, to speak of, but still, life.

She began running a bath. Nathan had always objected to the way she ran baths, which was by running scalding hot first, then adding cold. What if I come in and think, Oh, a nice bath, then step into it before you've put the cold in? Serves you right for taking a bath that doesn't belong to you. Often she didn't actually wash herself but just sat there in hot water going pink, studying her kneecaps or feet or pubes. I'll have that after you, Nathan always said, whether he'd already showered or not, because he couldn't bear to see water go to waste. It's not going to waste, you moron. I'm using it. I'm just not using it to *bath*.

Their marriage had worked because so much of her was strange to him. Adrian would have been too much like her; her identity would have bled into his. Nathan let her get on with the adventure of herself. Adrian would have had to interfere: But what do you *get* from writing? Do you think it's *important?* Nathan never asked. Not because he wasn't interested but because he loved her anyway, writer, ballerina, tea lady. Years ago he and Cheryl had divided the world into Seekers and Expanders. Seekers were, naturally, searching for something as yet unknown as the possible source of enlightenment. Expanders, on the other hand, concentrated on known pleasures. (Seekers and Expanders, they'd said to Adrian. Yes, he'd said. Stockings and Suspenders.) Cheryl was a Seeker, Nathan an Expander. His needs were simple: Cheryl, the kids, Adrian's friendship and enough money not to be stinking poor. Nothing else, in the last analysis, mattered to him.

Which was why he was so easy to live with, Cheryl thought. And why he's dead now. The world can take *those* things away, easy.

And so, monster, we ask: What *can't* the world take away easy?

The bath was full of water too hot to get into with no room to add cold.

Cheryl went round the house, clearing ashtrays, putting things in their place.

People never asked her about Lois, though they were all dying to know, what it felt like, whether it got better, whether you ever forgot for a moment that it had happened. She could have told them if they had asked. It's there in the morning and it's there in the daytime and it's there in the evening and it's there at night. It can get into anything, anywhere, any size or shape. Rain says it. Sun says it. Silence says it. Only certain kinds of noise drown it out for a while, my own voice, talking on the telephone, listening to business's lies and excuses and approximations and costs. Sometimes Gina singing in the bath, some pop song, with satirical soul; she stops if she thinks I'm passing by, listening. She worries that I'll ask her how she can sing, how it isn't there with her in the morning and daytime and evening and night, how it doesn't scream from every cup or pavement. I don't want her to stop, but I can't tell her that. Can't tell her anything. Sartre said all writing's an act of infidelity. So's surviving the dead.

Nathan followed her from room to room. As with Gina, he felt moments not just of love, but of a shift in himself such that even love was only a small object, like a solitary wrapped gift in a cavernous room.

Outside Frank's door she stopped. Frank was standing in the dark, hands in pockets, looking out into the garden. He didn't hear her. She was thinking of a time years before, during Lil's illness, when Frank had been staying with them. For his dad's sake Nathan had got down on his knees and prayed. She'd tiptoed across the landing to listen outside the door. Holy Mary, Mother of God, pray for us sinners, now, and at the hour of our death, Amen. The two men's voices joined had sounded diabolistic. It's all right, son, she'd overheard Frank say when they'd finished, I know you think it's all nonsense, but . . . Then horror, because Frank had broken down in tears and she'd heard Nathan put his arms round him, the rustle of their shirts, Nathan saying, Come on now, Dad, it's all right, it's all right, come on, now . . . This terrible reversal, the son speaking the phrases of comfort learned from the parents in childhood, had tightened her throat with love for both of them, but most fiercely for Nathan, who was doing this – praying to a God he knew wasn't there – simply out of love and respect for his dad. Feeling her own tears welling up, she'd leaned her head against the landing's cool wall and thought, Nathan's a good man. My husband's a good man. Christ, what a selfish, poisonous bitch I am so much of the time. All this goodness and it's not enough. Never enough.

If you loved him, then love his father for his sake. She knew she'd fail. But there was the trying, for his sake. It was what you could do to honour the dead. That was something the dead left you, the challenge of finding a way to honour them.

She found Adrian asleep in the office. The curtains were open. The green-shaded desk lamp was on. He'd curled up on the two-seater, a terrible squeeze. For a while she sat on the edge of the desk, watching him. He opened his eyes.

'Sorry,' he croaked. 'Couldn't move.'

'It's all right,' she said. 'Do you want anything? Water?'

Adrian unfolded himself in what looked like painful increments. 'Christ, I'm old.'

'You should go to bed.'

'Yeah, I will. Cheryl—'

'Don't say anything.'

'I just—'

'No, *really* don't say anything.'

He thought she meant because she didn't want to think or talk about what had happened between them. That wasn't it. It was just that she suddenly felt close to some corner or precipice of herself. Everyone and everything had to keep quiet and still or else she might miss it.

Yes, Nathan thought. That's it. Keep going. Keep *going*.

Adrian shuffled past her, clutching the all-but-empty whisky bottle by its neck. Nathan felt him battening down the impulse to touch her, just for comfort, his own comfort.

He resisted. Made it to the door, closed it behind him, lit a cigarette on the other side, then moved away down the corridor towards the stairs. Poor Uncle Adrian, Nathan thought, phantomly laughing to himself (so the dead could laugh, eventually, depending on the living), and felt, like sunlight, the warmth of their long friendship. Another gift in the room that was one room in a many-mansioned house.

Cheryl switched the desk lamp off. Darkness settled in the office. The window showed the grey garden and black hedge under a starred sky.

Without having done so before (not even when they'd called her from the hospital, not even after she'd seen the body, not even as they lowered the casket into the ground), she found herself imagining the moment Nathan put the blade into his skin.

Alone. To honour Lois. To follow her.

Suddenly, she pitched forward, grabbed the windowsill for support, and vomited in a single sour gout onto the floor. Booze, mainly, since she'd eaten nothing all day. Her eyes streamed, nostrils burned. She leaned, trembling, humbled, sorry for her body. But her body took her back to Nathan's. Vomiting left room for the other sickness that rose because she couldn't bear that he'd hurt himself like that, done that to himself. The hands that had held her, come countless times to her shoulders or hips or waist, sometimes that gesture of the one hand loosely gripping her nape, meaning it's all right, whatever else, you're not alone (they'd never tried that since Fowler brought his news, never since then wanted to put it to the test), those hands had taken the dirty blade and made the dirty slits and then lain in the water with nothing left to do, their history of touch counting for nothing. She thought of their wedding, how in the moment of putting the ring on her finger his hands (and by extension the rest of him) had seemed for a split second completely alien. She'd almost blurted out: Who *are* you? Then she'd looked up at his face and he was Nathan again, the most familiar person in the world. The story passed into family myth: The moment your mother thought she was marrying an alien. At which he'd do an awful face – mouth open, chin shoved back into neck, tongue slack going in and out, eyes blinking and rolling – and go after the kids, and her, and it really despite her being an adult and knowing full well it was a joke used to make her shudder and screw herself up, laughing hysterically with delighted revulsion when he came near her making his retarded-alien noise.

She started to cry. Not just because of the thought of him ending himself like that, alone (she couldn't shake the anger that he'd died alone, *alone*, after all the times they'd said, lying with limbs wrapped round each other, that that would be the worst thing – until Lois, the other kind of alone, the *real* worst thing), not just because of this but because of the wearying thought that sooner or later she'd have to get up and deal with the vomit by the window. What did that mean, except that she wasn't going to kill herself, that nothing had changed, that she'd become further addicted to surviving horror?

She brought her knees up to her chin and wrapped her arms tight round herself. How long since she'd done this? Let herself do this? Two years? Three. Of course three.

Keep going. Keep going, my love.

She had a few moments of peace, when enough of her consciousness shut down for her not really to know anything.

She cried silently, holding herself, since there was no one else to hold her, rocking back and forth the way she had as a girl. All her ages were still there, twelve, six, three, twenty. She went in among them, blurred, let the now slide and curdle, lost herself in the sympathetic crowd.

But eventually had to come back. What else was there, other than eventually having to come back? Her body was still there, waiting like a faithful dog. She felt sorry for it again – and again for Nathan's body, that he'd done that terrible thing to it. She stopped crying. What else was there, other than eventually to stop crying? You have a good cry, lovey, you'll feel better afterwards. You *did* feel better afterwards, but as if you'd conned yourself, fobbed yourself off.

She looked around the room, the dead furniture, the silvery light on the windowsill and desk.

Nathan felt her stopping herself – then she let it through. It'll be easier without him.

For a while, nothing followed. Letting herself think it had brought her to a threshold. But there was no going back.

There was no going back. Even now the thought gave him a faint pain. He started to wonder why, if there was no going back, he'd been allowed this. (Been put through this, he'd have said before.) Was it standard? The right or curse of suicides, granted in proportion to the doubt still remaining when you drew your final breath? But he was exhausted. He had an image of all the ranks of the dead looking on, shaking their heads and laughing. It comforted him, made him laugh with them, the idea of them at any rate.

It amazed him how much room there was around his love

for Cheryl. He was reminded of break-ups in which both parties knew that they might one day be friends, but not until a lot of time had passed.

Aside from all this and equal to the tiredness was a growing curiosity.

Frank

Frank was lying in bed in the dark with the curtains open. There was a yew tree outside his window and he liked to fall asleep watching it. No breeze tonight, nothing. His bones ached. Legs especially. That was the essence of physical age to him, that his fucking *legs* ached. Thigh bones, shin bones, ankles. Body gets worse. They should teach you, drill it into you from your first day of school: your body gets worse. Your body *must* get worse. Use it while you can.

He'd cried a little, on first getting into bed, since getting into bed reminded him either of childhood and how unreasonably close it remained, or of Lil, how he'd loved sharing a bed with her. All right there was the sex and everything they couldn't say about that – but there were all the other things, too. Her feet, icy, and the nightly negotiation about whether she could put them on him to warm them up. In the early days together he used to slide down under the covers and clamp them in his armpit, her giggling in the dark the way people in films did when the lights went out to indicate hanky-panky. He loved doing things for her like that, comforting her body. Whenever he did, it made him ashamed to think how impatient he got with her, how many times he bullied or cut her off. Kissing her shins, her knees, the hem of her nightie, he'd resolve to be kinder to her. Never lasted. She'd misplace the keys or forget the corned beef and there he was, barking at her.

Gone. Her face's threadbare version in the hours between morphine . . . He'd seen her not really recognising him, not really, when it came down to it, caring who he was. It was disgusting, that pain could do that. God should never have allowed pain with the power to do that. What was the point of it, except to shame and disgust everyone? To make a mockery of love? If that was God then fuck God, whether there was a reason for it or not. If there was a reason then fuck the reason. No kind of reason he was interested in any more. What was the point of him, Frank Clark, left alive with his miserable thigh and shin bones aching unspectacularly every night? Him, whose soul had hardly grown since he was a child. He still wanted praise and to be consulted about things. The only difference was he rarely got it and never was. Meanwhile there's Nathan with brains and a family and all, as if they haven't had enough of it with Lois. There was no end to it. No end and no point.

This, Nathan understood, was the old man's nightly routine, more or less. Underneath, fear of not having lived a good enough life. Couldn't quite let go of the faith, but couldn't over Lil's and Lois's dead bodies hold to it, either. No man's land. And now his son. In an access of hatred of God he'd looked suicide up in Lil's old catechism. 'We should not despair of the eternal salvation of persons who have taken their own lives. By ways known to Him alone, God can provide the opportunity for salutary repentance. The Church prays for persons who have taken their own lives.' It was that phrase, 'by ways known to Him alone', which had made Frank grind his teeth, tears falling *putt . . . putt-putt* onto the page. None the less, when it was obvious Cheryl wasn't going to kick up a fuss, he'd said burial, a Catholic service. Funeral Mass. He often fell asleep thinking, You weak bastard. You weak, spineless old man.

Nathan tried to send something out. It's all right, Dad. It doesn't matter. Mum's forgiven you. You're not a bad man. Don't be afraid.

He didn't know if this was true. It didn't seem to matter. There was so little of the old man's life left.

Cheryl

Cheryl lay in the bath, blinking. Pain – the other pain, the
one to which the body and *its* pains was a spectator – kept
coming, in waves, then receding. When it came she shud-
dered silently, each time thinking she couldn't bear it,
couldn't bear it . . . Then it receded, and she was left,
blinking, with a weird feeling, not quite excitement, not
quite fear, like waking up the first morning in a foreign
hotel, not knowing where or when or even who. At these
moments it was as if she was completely free of everything
that had ever happened to her. She looked down the length
of her body – belly, hips, thighs, shins, feet – and couldn't
believe three children had come out of her. The ultrasound
pictures had shown grainy, two-dimensional unlovable aliens,
ghost things. Out of nothing, these creatures had arrived
inside her. Solid, living things where before there hadn't
even been empty space. The dead reversed it, left empty
space where there'd been solid life. The world was littered

with spaces like invisible obelisks. They were everywhere, but you only saw – or bumped into, or tripped over, or cut yourself on – the ones your own dead had left you. The ones that mattered.

She and Nathan used to talk about what would happen if one of them died, whether they'd ever get over it, whether they could imagine being with someone else. The conversations always started in the same mood, a morbid or inverse version of the one behind the conversation about what you'd do if you won a fortune on the lottery. A spirit of perverse daring drove them, as if they knew that talking about it, allowing the possibility of it into the world of words, was tempting fate, was *asking for it*. They started with romantic absolutes – No, I wouldn't want anyone else – then progressed (especially after the children) to realist concessions: you couldn't overestimate the power of loneliness, I'd want you to be happy, etcetera. The difference between them – of which they were both aware – was that it was never much of an effort for Cheryl to imagine not just a different partner, but a different life altogether. For Cheryl, the world had these huge potentialities, like gods who every now and then spoke to her: Come here, let me show you what I could do for you. Nathan heard them, too, but for him they were false gods, and the one true god – love, his wife, his children – would suffer no false gods before it.

It was more or less unmentionable, this difference between them. Which was why each time she'd cheated on him (twice, not counting Adrian) she'd had the feeling he'd known but chosen to say nothing. She'd cheated carefully, men she couldn't possibly have fallen in love with (it wasn't love she was after; insofar as she wanted love she had it with Nathan), somewhat for carnal novelty, yes, but really because carnal novelty was the cheapest metaphor available for all the potentialities love left unfulfilled.

Downstairs, the front door opened and closed. Gina. Keys dropped on the shelf. A cough. Footsteps going towards the kitchen. Doors. Then the murmur of voices. Luke.

Slowly, thinking of the way her surviving children must see her, Cheryl began to wash herself. She had a strange image: Nathan and Cheryl standing with their arms round each other, smiling. Then her, the other or new Cheryl, going up to them, grinning, pulling ugly faces. It was as if Nathan and the old Cheryl were her parents, she their bad child.

Now he was gone, the old Cheryl was alone. In the image, the bad child and the mother stood face to face.

Gina sat opposite Luke at the kitchen table.

'Where'd you go?' he said.

'Up to the site. The dig.'

'What's up there?'

'A view. Holes in the ground. The moon.'

They couldn't look at each other. They'd seen it, and at the time it hadn't seemed too much. Things never did in those moments. It was all the time outside those moments. Luke thought of the picture and the little wooden box. He'd watched them go, gnawed away by the flames. He'd felt as if the knots of himself had come loose. Or looser, he supposed. There was still what the fuck was he going to do with his life. There was still the question of whether to let his mother go completely. There was still Gina.

'Give us one of those.' Luke's Marlboro. A silence they hadn't bargained for while he held the flame to the tip of her cigarette. Then the sounds of first drags a relief. Nathan, nearby, felt Gina thinking: We're not ready to talk about it. Never will be. If it ever happens it'll be because we let it roll over us.

'D'you think she'll keep this place?' Gina said.

Luke shrugged. 'I always wanted us to have a house like this,' he said. 'Like Sean Pearson's.' The Pearsons were very well off. Luke had been friends with Sean for the last couple of years at St Catherine's.

'Yeah, well, careful what you wish for and all that,' Gina said, looking away from him again. Her childhood *had* gone. Nathan could feel the space around her where it used to be. It would come back, but for now it must be banished to give the new consciousness all the available room. By the time she was Cheryl's age she'd be more formidable than Cheryl was now. It was a delight to him to know this, to think of all the weapons she'd have at her disposal, how difficult it would be for people to have power over her. He was less sure about Luke. There was an appalling store of passion in the boy which hadn't yet found an outlet. Because he had no creative life it could only go into love or God or distraction. If Cheryl (or George) took him and put him in Fenn Industries, now, before he'd had a proper chance at either love or God, there was every likelihood he'd become a money-making phenomenon. He knew, had almost asked to be given a job there, was still thinking of asking. Hadn't quite asked. Some good instinct had held him back, or possibly just the inchoate potential between him and Gina. Inchoate no longer. He'd been a quiet child, and retreated further into the margins when loud and spectacular Gina came along. He'd grown up ashamed of the store of passion, whereas Gina (and even Lois) had flashed it around like the currency of millionaires.

Men like that, Nathan knew, were dangerous, even if Luke was free of the other danger.

Gina, either through her father's telepathic influence or on her own newly wise account, realised something: if she let it happen with Luke it would ruin him. It could only ever be a temporary indulgence, a finite quota of sin; he'd know this, deep down, but he'd resist it. She'd come through it superficially muddied, mangled, but underneath usefully enlarged. But he'd keep going back to it. She mustn't let it happen – although, selfishly, she thought how good it would be. All the blood they'd bring to it. Even doing it with Matt had plotted that graph.

Frank, in pyjamas, dressing gown and slippers, shuffled in, hair sticking up all wrong.

'Hi, Grampy,' Gina said.

'Can't sleep,' the old man said.

Gina knew he wanted to talk about her dad. And Lois. There'd be crying if he did. She didn't want it. For herself she felt she might never cry another tear for the rest of her life. She was sick of thinking about everything that had happened to them. She wondered if she'd gone completely hard inside. She didn't feel it. In fact, she felt full of energy.

'D'you want anything? Cup of tea?'

Frank shook his head, flap-flapped in his slippers over to the sink and poured himself a glass of water. They watched him drink it, the old Adam's apple flecked with silver bristles slightly mesmerising. He drank it all, washed the glass, turned it upside down on the draining board. One of the washers-up had left an *Express & Echo* on the counter. He picked it up, brought it to the kitchen table and sat down.

Cheryl came in in her bathrobe, hair still wet, make-up off. She looked tired. Each of them looked up at her and looked away. That was what you did. Gina stubbed her cigarette out.

Cheryl drank water, then came and sat down.

'Listen,' she said. 'I've been thinking.'

Luke and Gina looked at each other. This wasn't the idiom. Them included in her thinking. Three years since she'd opened with something like that. They looked at her. They couldn't help it. Her face looked different.

'I'm sorry,' she said.

It's all right. It's really all right. Don't be afraid. Keep going.

'Ma?' Gina said.

Cheryl had thought she was empty and calm, but Gina hadn't called her that for a long time. She didn't want to cry. She didn't want to frighten them. But there was all her daughter's forgiveness in a single syllable. It had been there all this time. All she'd had to do was ask for it.

'Sorry,' Cheryl said, getting to her feet, chair scraping.

Gina watched her mother turn away, get halfway to the door, stop, cover her face with her hands.

For a moment astonishment froze them. Then Gina got up and went to her.

'Ma? What is it?'

There was a last second in which Cheryl's fear held on. Then Gina touched her elbow.

Luke watched, incredulous, as his mother put her arms around Gina and wept, uglily, saying Sorry, sorry, sorry. Gina looked at him over her mother's shoulder, eyes bright, excited. He looked at Frank. Frank was observing everything with his mouth slightly open and his hands still clutching the newspaper.

Dreamily, Luke got to his feet and moved across the room. If he didn't reach her now he never would. He was tempted (as at the edge of a cliff he'd be tempted to jump) to walk past her, go up to the study, lie down and go to sleep. If he did that his life would be a certain way. That was the appeal, the certainty of something. There was no certainty the other way. She might change again. He had more to lose than Gina. On the other hand, he was wide awake, curious.

He put his hand very lightly on her shoulder, just as Gina eased away. Like a smooth relay-baton change. Cheryl put her arms round him. If she looked him in the eye, he thought, he might not be able to stand it.

Cheryl, perhaps sensing it despite everything, extricated herself after a few moments without quite looking at him, squeezed his hand, then let go of it and sat down on the step in the kitchen doorway. She leaned her head against the doorframe. Luke went to the sink and poured himself a glass of water.

Gina went to the fridge and opened it. There was a lot of food left, cling-filmed, foil-wrapped. She reached in and took a cold chicken drumstick in her fingers.

'I'm starving,' she said. 'Does anyone else want anything?'

Nathan

Nathan had drifted out of the kitchen once they'd started eating. He'd had the thought of taking a look at Adrian but, now that it came to it, he thought he'd go into the study instead, where it was dark and quiet, where Luke had made the little burning.

Something had happened. The spaces around the people in the kitchen had got bigger. He *was* the space, it was inside him. When he concentrated on them, Cheryl, Gina, Luke, Frank, the particularity of each of them was a thing of beauty. They were like beautiful, living enamel brooches. But there was so much steadily increasing room in him that he couldn't escape the feeling that they were getting smaller and smaller. He realised the whole world had been full of these perfect, unique particulars, and he'd wasted such a lot of his time perceiving it in a fog of generality. Now it was too late, but even that didn't seem to matter much. As he moved away from the kitchen, through the lounge, into the hall, up the stairs, he kept thinking, I'll go back and see them tomorrow. Maybe go back now, though. Dad . . .

But he kept going. It was hard to hold onto these thoughts.

The study door was closed. Looking forward to the darkness, the embers, the window's sweep of stars, he passed through.

Exactly like before, he began – then stopped, because it wasn't exactly like before.

Certainly the bed was there, starchy corner turned back, virgin pillow, snowy blankets and the promise of peerless sleep. Certainly the frosted light, pale walls and floor. Certainly, as before, the white door with its brass knob.

The difference wasn't in the room, it was in him. He felt . . . He struggled to represent it to himself . . . He felt *okay*. The dread was missing.

On the other hand, the opposing desires still locked horns, albeit with a somnambulistic lack of urgency. The bed was no less inviting, the door no less intriguing. Buriden's ass, apparently, was still confined to his appalling dilemma, just without the nausea. There was one question he thought he might ask to take him one way or the other, but it was an effort to remember it, or frame it in the right way.

An effort to stay awake, too. Without realising, he'd moved closer to the bed. The desire to get in was all but overwhelming. Each moment he didn't astonished him. Then he remembered the question.

If I go through the door, will Lois be there?

There was a long silence.

At the end of it, the realisation that there was no point in asking the question if there was no one available to answer.

There was one last pull, the thought that he should go back downstairs, find a way of saying goodbye properly, something. Then it passed.

Still fighting off sleep, and wondering how, exactly, he was expected to get it open, Nathan moved towards the door.